A Far Cry From Ordinary

A Far Cry From Ordinary

Ella Kennedy

Dedication

To the memory of Kay Holland, who was known by many as our hometown's librarian – and to me as my grandmother. Through her reading hours, book recommendations, and engaging and quirky personality, she taught me to love characters and the transportive nature of stories.

Chapter 1

"We're going to have to reschedule my return flight, Kels. The bastard is apparently calling in a big dog from D.C. What a shit!" Kat Anderson was tired, hot, and uncharacteristically frazzled.

"Namaste, my friend," Kelsey laughed. "Relax and breathe. You want to talk about shits? You should be in the office today."

"Fair enough," Kat replied. "But that doesn't make me any less pissy."

"Christian Christopher is obviously trying to overcompensate for some shortcoming here. How big are his hands?" Kelsey asked.

Kat laughed. "Thanks for making me smile, Kels. Try to get me a ticket for Friday evening. If something bizarre happens and I'm done early tomorrow, I'll call you. Oh, and email me anything you can find on the Teamsters' General Executive Board or anyone at that level. When Christian was threatening and namedropping today, I thought I heard him mention it. Perhaps that's the big dog's pack. If you see any connection between Christian and any one of them, please let me know."

"Will do. You hang in there. Take a walk. Grab a bite to eat." Kelsey paused. "Are you sleeping?"

Kelsey Harig had always been a fabulous administrative assistant, confidante, and friend. But lately, she had been hyper-vigilant – always checking in and suggesting healthy eating, exercise, and sleep tips. With uncharacteristic persistence, Kelsey inquired about weekend activities (of which there were few) and how and with whom Kat was spending her time. Her concern was both endearing and a little annoying.

"I'm fine, Kels. Just venting a bit. I need to stop letting this guy get under my skin. I've got this. And, yes, I'm taking care of myself." Kat was about to hang up, but thought to add, "No worries."

"No worries," Kelsey echoed. "Just let me know if there's anything else you need tonight. I'm going to collect the girls soon and head home, but you can always text me. I'll do that research as soon as they go to bed. You'll know whatever I do by the time you meet the big dog. Good thing you're a wild Kat, boss."

Kat grinned. "Oh, and Kels, what is that damn password again?"

Kelsey uttered an audible and exasperated sigh. "You are impossible!" she exclaimed. "It's Drew1021!" Kat grabbed the hotel pad and wrote it down.

"Could I make it any easier for you, Kat – your kid, his birthday? I'm out of ideas here."

"Thanks, Kels. Go home now. Have a good night."

Kat clicked off the phone and stared at the screen. Five thirty. Plenty of time to take a shower and settle in for a few hours of review and planning. She stood and stretched. "Enough of these for one day," she groaned, as she kicked her heels under a green, faux leather hotel chair.

The room smelled a bit musty. It was, after all, April in Memphis. It had been an unusually warm week, and the air conditioning unit was whirring and spitting. *"Oh, the luxury of business travel,"* Kat thought, as she eased out of her clothes and headed for the shower. *"At least the sheets are clean."*

The water washed over her head, her face. She stood there for several minutes, inside the warm, penetrating spray, as her shoulders fell and her breathing quieted. It had been a long day, a day of constructive suggestions and irrational responses. Volleys and slams. Entreaties and rejections. Kat was a patient negotiator, but this was her third visit to Memphis in as many weeks. It wasn't a huge bargaining unit. The site didn't have a history of labor unrest. In fact, there had been no more than a half dozen grievances in the last year. But this guy, Christian, was hell-bent on something. She wished she could put her finger on it.

The Company's bargaining committee had offered increases to base pay, had not insisted on additional contributions to healthcare, and was willing to make other concessions. She could never say it out loud, of course, but the Company was not keen on taking a strike at this location. Production was excellent, and demand for the new supplement produced at this site was unusually high. No matter what she did, however, she could not get this guy to budge. And, while she did not consider herself to be overly sensitive, she could not help but think that Christian Christopher, in all of his boisterous, barrel-chested, bald-headed glory, could not find his way to compromise with a woman.

Kat turned to face the spray, breathing in the steamy warmth, as it pulsated sharply against her forehead, eyelids, lips. The nagging pain behind her eyes began to ease as the steam blanketed her and filled her lungs.

Kat never dwelled much on gender. She had started practicing law almost 25 years earlier, when there were very few women at the firm, and they were required to wear skirts, hose, and closed-toed. A pantsuit? Out of the question. But, oddly, Kat had never felt restricted. She thrived on the work, loved the challenge. And her stature was a plus. Nearly six feet tall and certainly

2

not "dainty," Kat either towered over her legal adversaries, or she could look them in the eye. Unlike many of her female colleagues of the time, Kat was never mistaken for a law clerk or administrative assistant. Her presence was generally effective – some might have even said intimidating.

Kat had done well at the law firm, working her way from associate to partner, and she'd likely still be there, if she'd not picked up a headhunter call at a particularly vulnerable moment. Kat was steady. She was loyal. She was not what some might call a "risk taker." Then again, this opportunity had not been much of a risk. It was, after all, with one of the world's largest beverage companies. It was a European company looking for a strong leader to head their industrial and employee-relations team in the U.S.

That was five years earlier, and the role was as interesting and challenging as she had hoped. *"And, oh, so glamorous,"* she reflected, with a grin. That was, after all, how she found herself here, now, at this hotel in Memphis, Tennessee, trying to avoid touching a well-used shower curtain with her naked body and planning to spend the evening adjusting the air conditioner and attempting to read by the greenish glow of a 1980s desk lamp.

Kat stood before the mirror. She toweled her hair and let it hang loosely around her face, curling in long ringlets that nearly touched her shoulders. She looked a bit tired. Was that surprising? It had been a tough week in an even more difficult year.

Slipping into her pajamas, Kat settled into the desk chair and swiveled to face the pressed-wood desk. She dislodged her notes from a binder of papers and began sifting through, highlighter in hand.

The sounds of Beale Street wafted through the dank air, distracting her. Kat massaged her temples with her thumbs. She closed her eyes and rested her head against the chair. Clarinets and tenor saxophones. Blues and jazz. The world outside her musty, makeshift office.

Kat awoke with a start, as the air conditioner banged and rattled its way through another cycle. It was nearly 8:00, and the sun had set. Her room was dark, but for the eerie iridescence of the desk lamp. Kat's neck was kinked. Her stomach growled. When was the last time she'd eaten? Breakfast – the hotel breakfast of make-your-own waffle and coffee by the pool landing?

Kat sighed and reached for the hotel directory. "Room service available Thursday through Sunday," it read. *"Damn it."* The glossy insert suggested that "delicious tavern food" was available downstairs in the "Hideaway Lounge."

Kat cracked open a complimentary bottled water and took a few sips. But her empty stomach was having none of it. Knowing that she was unlikely to sleep if she didn't eat something, Kat begrudgingly pulled on some leggings, refastened her bra, and took an oversized, cotton blouse from her bag. She ran a brush through her hair. Air-drying and humidity were not her friends, Kat thought. In fact, she looked slightly like a Chia Pet. Kat secured her hair with a tie and applied a couple touches of concealer below her eyes. She grabbed the Hideaway Lounge 25%-off coupon from her hotel check-in trifold before heading out the door and down the stairs.

The Hideaway Lounge was just to the right of the concierge desk, or what appeared to be a concierge desk. No concierge was present. It didn't appear that anyone was present at the check-in desk either. The lobby was quiet. Kat approached the big, wooden saloon doors and peeked inside. The place was empty, but for an older gentleman seated at the bar who appeared to be three sheets to the wind. Kat avoided eye contact with him as she walked past to the furthermost booth. Close enough to the bartender to be noticed. Far enough away not to be bothered. And certainly far enough away to not be drawn into a conversation with the drunk guy.

The bartender, a woman who looked to be about Kat's age, but perhaps even more tired, rose from a stool behind the bar and placed her open book, face down, alongside the cash register. "Whatcha drinking, Hon?" she crooned, as she motioned in Kat's direction.

Kat briefly surveyed the bottles behind the bar. From the recesses of her mind, she recalled that quinine has some medicinal quality. "Do you have tonic water?"

"I have a little fresh in the back."

"Then I'll have a G&T." Pausing for a moment, Kat added, "Actually, make it a double.

"Is the kitchen still open?"

"For another hour or so. I'll bring you a menu."

The bartender fished around under the bar and promptly appeared at Kat's booth with a laminated card. As she handed it to Kat, the bartender picked at what appeared to be a spot of dried pizza sauce. "Special today is beer-battered cod and fries."

The bartender's curly black hair protruded from her head as if it was running away from her face. Her lips were fire truck red, and she wore a yellow blouse, which pulled tautly across her chest. The buttons started just below her bra line, and the area between her neck and her prominent cleavage was covered with brightly colored beads. Her nametag read, "Linda." There was a space between the bottom of her shirt and the top of her jeans, where just a bit of her creamy bronzed midriff protruded. Linda was obviously comfortable in her own skin.

"Thank you, Linda," Kat responded, as she glanced at the meager menu. "I'm not much of a fish gal, so I'll go with the appetizer quesadilla with salsa and sour cream."

"We're out of sour cream, but we have refried beans."

"Then refried beans it is," Kat smiled. She returned the laminated card to Linda and wiped her fingers on the paper napkin Linda had placed in front of her.

Linda smiled back, that server's smile that said *thank you for not making a big fuss about the sour cream.* "I'll put in that order and be right back with your drink."

As Linda turned toward the kitchen, she glanced toward the saloon doors and slowed her gait. "Hello, darlin'," she said with a sweet southern drawl the likes of which Kat had not detected earlier. "Haven't seen you in a while. In town for business?"

Chapter 2

Kat glanced in the direction to which Linda had purred. A man stood just inside the swinging doors. A nice looking man. Tall, slender, slightly unshaven, with shoulder length brown hair. He wore a white, long-sleeved t-shirt, with some stitching on the pocket, jeans that fit his body impossibly well, and boots.

Linda sauntered over to the man, glancing his cheek with a quick kiss before heading into the kitchen.

"It's good to see you, too, Lin," the man said, as he took a seat on a stool by the bar. "It's great to be home."

Returning from the kitchen, Linda pulled up a seat across from the man on the other side of the bar, and they began chatting quietly. Linda was animated, gesturing here and there, obviously enjoying his company. Kat watched the two, wondering about their relationship. She was curious about how they met, the secrets they shared, stories they could tell. Kat had always been a student of people – an anthropologist of the simplest sort. It was a bit distracting at times, this keen interest in other people's lives and what was happening in their minds. It was particularly challenging in airports, where Kat created stories in her head about the off-goings and homecomings of strangers – the bedraggled mother of three, herding her brood of tiny ones, all pulling roller boards bedecked with Disney characters and wearing inflatable neck pillows; the man in a borrowed suit, carrying a small bouquet and constantly checking his watch; the elderly woman in a peach calico frock, holding a small dog in a mesh bag and being shuttled by a twenty-something airport support attendant with gauges in his ears.

Kat must have been staring, as she caught Linda's eye. "Oh, my god. I'm so sorry!" Linda called out. "I completely forgot your drink. I'll be right there." Bottles and glasses clanking, Linda set about making Kat's gin and tonic. As she thrust a red plastic spear through a lime and plopped the garnish on what looked to be a very healthy pour, a bell in the kitchen sounded. "Shit!" Linda uttered under her breath (although only *slightly* under her breath).

"Go ahead," laughed the man. "I've got this." Holding his drink in one hand and grabbing the concoction Linda had just finished preparing in the other, he turned toward Kat.

"Very gallant," Kat remarked, as the man placed the glass on a Budweiser coaster on the table in front of her. Glancing up, her eyes alighted on the stitched pocket. "And a fucking Teamster," she groaned.

"Excuse me?"

"Did I say that out loud?" Kat flushed. "Filter, Kat, filter." Her ears warmed, and her cheeks burned. "I am so sorry. It's no excuse, but I've just spent a very long day with a Teamster."

The man laughed, a deep, throaty, comforting laugh. "Not exactly the greeting I was expecting. It's good to be surprised now and again. Keeps one on their toes."

"May I?" he asked, gesturing toward the booth seat opposite Kat.

"If you dare," Kat replied, smiling. "I've obviously been driven to insanity. Nice Minnesota girls don't normally behave this way."

"Minnesota, huh? I was there once. Visited First Avenue with a couple of buddies. That was a lifetime ago."

"Not much has changed, I suspect."

"So what brings you to Memphis, Kat?"

Kat looked inquisitively.

"Remember 'Filter, *Kat*. Filter'?"

"Ah, yes. Kat Anderson. It's nice to meet you . . . ."

"Greg. Greg Bodin."

"It's nice to meet you, Greg."

"I mean, what brings you to Memphis – other than a fucking Teamster?"

Linda set a red plastic basket filled with quesadilla triangles in front of Kat. Shaking a finger vigorously, she chided, "Greg Bodin, you watch your mouth."

"She started it, Sunshine," Greg teased, his smile filling his face and spilling into the room. "How many times have I stirred up trouble in this place?"

"Well . . .," replied Linda, holding up her hand and pretending to count.

"Oh, please, Lin. You're ruining my reputation, and just when I'm getting to know our Minnesota friend here. Linda LaVec, meet Kat Anderson. Kat, meet Linda. Linda is a fixture in this town, a long-time purveyor of drinks and advice, everyone's favorite gal. And a voracious reader. The bar may not always be clean, but Linda will never fail on a good book recommendation."

Linda smacked Greg's arm playfully with the back of her hand. "It's clean enough here for the likes of you," she said. Then, turning to Kat, "It's nice to meet you, Kat. Please let me know if you need anything more." Linda returned to the bar and, with significant flourish, ran a rag over the counter, grabbed her book, and settled back into her chair beneath the brightest light in the otherwise dimly lit room.

Kat took a sip of her drink. She shuttered slightly.

"A triple?" Greg asked, his eyes twinkling with a hint of mischievous humor.

"So that's why the water glass? I was expecting a high ball. I actually ordered a double."

"It was obviously a double kind of day?" Greg asked, settling into his seat and resting his arm across the back, as if he had all the time in the world to listen. He was disarmingly attractive. His full, flowing hair rested on his shoulders and framed his face. His eyes were bright and almost an unnatural color. Was it aqua? He had dark lashes and brows and just the hint of a beard under his prominent cheekbones. In some silly romance novel, Greg Bodin might be described as "chiseled." He was, in fact, extraordinarily good looking. And he was sitting directly across from Kat.

Kat took another sip, enjoying the feel of the gin warming her throat. She paused a moment. "Yes, in fact, it was a double kind of day," she replied.

"Tell me this," she continued. "You're a union man. Presumably, you've negotiated a few collective bargaining agreements in your time."

"A few."

"Well, let's get a little philosophical here. Let's say that big unions were not big business. Let's just imagine that for a moment. And let's say that unions were still focused on doing those things that they set out to do in the '20s and '30s – like, say, protecting workers' rights and representing their interests."

"Yes, I'm still with you," Greg nodded.

"Well, if we can build that tidy little hypothetical, then let's imagine that it's present day, and there are plenty of really great corporations out there that share the same goals, the same values, the same desire to do right by their employees. And let's just imagine that one of those corporate citizens puts a deal on the table that does just that – improves wages and lessens working hours to ensure that its employees are financially secure, safe, and well-rested. And . . ."

"And . . ."

"And can't get those benefits to the employees – employees she cares about – because some asshole across the table can't – no, *won't* – understand that this is a deal that will benefit workers. It's frustrating, that's all. I've been doing this too long to simply let this thing fall apart, and yet I can't seem to get any traction with this guy. I am sure that my team back at the office is formulating strike plans and lining up replacement workers – and I can't manage to save the employees I have. Employees with families. Employees with mortgages. Employees with lives."

Greg had not broken eye contact with Kat during the entire time she'd been talking. It was a bit unnerving. She glanced down at the table.

"So what's the hold up? What's getting in the way?" he asked.

"That's the thing I keep asking myself. I really don't know. Maybe I have a blind spot. It's definitely possible. But I feel like this is a really good deal for our employees. I can't imagine they could do better with anyone else or with any other company in the area. And yet I can't find a way forward." Kat took another drink of her G&T, letting it rest on her tongue and trickle slowly down the back of her throat.

"I'm good at this, Greg. And do you know why I'm good at this?" she asked.

"Why?"

"Because I care, damn it. I work hard to put meaningful packages on the table. I exercise a ton of influence back at the office to ensure that we do the right thing, in the most cost-effective way possible, of course, for our greatest assets. And I don't mean our physical assets. Our greatest assets are our people."

"Bravo, Kat!" Greg clapped, in a manner that did not reveal whether he was agreeing with her or mocking her. "Excellent performance. With passion like that, I don't know why he's not falling for it."

"Falling for what?" Kat asked, a little hurt. "It's not a line of bullshit, Greg. This is how I feel. This is what I do."

Greg raised an eyebrow and stared at her for a moment. "So, maybe he doesn't understand that you're for real, Kat. I don't mean to defend him, but, speaking for myself, we run into a lot of management types who are trying to do things on the cheap, cut corners. They'd rather engage in labor arbitrage, sending jobs offshore and subjugating foreign workers, than engage in meaningful discussions of industrial relations at home."

Kat took yet another pull from her glass. She considered his comments for a moment before responding. "Actually, I think he's simply a giant prick."

Greg laughed and leaned back in his seat. "Perhaps he is," he replied. "And, perhaps you should eat a little something. Pontification can make one very thirsty. If your welcoming introduction was any indication, I'd hate to hear what you think when you drink on an empty stomach."

"Fair enough," Kat noted, reaching into the plastic basket to retrieve a slice of quesadilla. "Filter, Kat. Filter."

Kat looked for a long moment at the piece of stuffed tortilla she held in her hand. "Do you think this cheese looks fresh?" she asked. "Does it look good to you?"

"Everything in this booth looks good to me," Greg replied, with a flirtatious wink.

"Are you making fun?"

"Absolutely not. I'm simply enjoying getting to know you better."

"Well, you're certainly getting to know *someone*. Unfortunately, I'm not acting much like myself this evening. I have let this guy get to me. What is that saying: 'You can't control what someone does; you can only control your reaction'? I'm obviously not doing a great job with that second part."

"So how will you react tomorrow?"

"I won't punch him in his gut?" Kat quickly responded.

Greg smiled. "That's a good start," he offered, motioning to Linda. "Hey, Lin, can you get me another?"

"I'll be right there," Linda responded. "Two paragraphs left in this chapter."

"Oh, by all means, don't hurry," Greg teased.

"Don't kid yourself. I won't," Linda quipped.

"I've been wondering the last couple of days," Kat went on, "if this guy – his name is Christian – is simply having a difficult time compromising with a woman. I really don't think I'm being overly sensitive. I just can't shake the feeling that if I were a man, we would have had a deal two weeks ago. It's something about the way he looks down his nose at me; the dismissive tone he takes with me; the way he continuously refers to me as 'Mrs. Anderson,' when he knows perfectly well that I don't go by that title."

"So you're married?" Greg asked, in a voice that, while Kat may have imagined it, sounded, well, *disappointed*.

"Widowed," Kat replied.

"I'm sorry," Greg said, leaning forward and patting her hand ever so softly.

"Thank you." Kat took another bite of her quesadilla, chewed it slowly, swallowed. "So enough about me. How about you? What's your story, Greg Bodin?"

At that point, Linda appeared at the table. "Great book," she stated, as she showed Kat the cover. "Ever read it?"

"I have, in fact," said Kat. "I loved the main character's blog posts. So authentic and raw."

"I agree," said Linda in an almost familial way. "I like you already." Plopping a glass down in front of Greg, she made a face. "And here's your drink, sir – Sprite, straight up, with a twist of lime."

"Thank you, my dear."

Turning back toward the bar, Linda remarked under her breath, "My dear, my ass. Good thing for you you've always been so darn cute."

Chapter 3

Greg resettled himself, placing his arm along the top of the booth seat. "So where were we?" he resumed, as he cocked his head and looked at her intently.

"You were just about to tell me the story of Greg Bodin, journeyman and Renaissance guy." Now it was Kat's turn to relax back in her seat and listen.

"There's not much to tell," Greg started. "I grew up in Memphis. Linda and I went to school together. Over 600,000 people live here now, but it's always felt a like a small town to me. My parents both passed away when I was in my early twenties. My sister, Martha, was a bit older. She married and moved out East. I have never been able to break the tie to Memphis. I bought a place adjacent to the Meeman-Shelby Forest State Park, about 20 miles out of town, and wherever I go in the world, I continue to call these parts home. I don't get back here as often as I'd like, and that's too bad. I find incredible respite in and around Memphis. It's like a salve for whatever ails me.

"I joined the Army soon after my parents died.   Special Forces. Reconnaissance." Greg shifted in his seat and crossed his arms loosely across his chest. "I wasted a few years after I returned from that tour of duty and then joined the union and have been working a nice, blue collar life ever since. The end."

"That's the condensed version, no doubt."

"Condensed, maybe, but there's really not that much more to tell. I'm a pretty simple guy, Kat." Greg shook his head slowly, as if gathering his thoughts. "I love nature and art – particularly theater and music. I get away to an opera whenever I can manage it. And I get to the Grand Ole Opry now and again. I enjoy my work, and I spend a lot of time doing it. It requires a significant amount of travel. I never married, and I don't have any children of my own, but I try to see my nieces whenever I'm in the Boston area. Oh, and my friend, Linda, and I share a love of reading. I wasn't kidding when I said that she has great book recommendations."

"So you truly are a Renaissance man," Kat observed.

"I don't know about that," Greg replied thoughtfully. "I'd say I'm simply a bit on the eclectic side."

Kat had tired of the quesadilla and pushed the plastic basket containing the last couple of pieces to the side. "May I?" asked Greg, pointing toward the basket.

"Be my guest," Kat replied. "They're all yours. Have you eaten dinner? Do you want to order something? Oh, look at the time. I'm afraid the kitchen may be closed."

"I likely will order something. It's been a busy travel day, and I haven't eaten anything since breakfast. But I do hate to dine alone. Is there any chance I can get you to continue to keep me company until my food arrives?"

"Seems fair to me – since I sat and ate my quesadilla in front of you."

Kat watched Greg as he slid out of the seat and walked over to the bar. He leaned over the counter and conferred with Linda in a hushed voice. They went back and forth for a bit. Linda became increasingly animated – seemingly agitated. Kat couldn't hear what they were saying, but Linda looked concerned. Linda glanced at Kat, and Kat quickly looked away, not wanting to let on that she'd been watching them. And then, just like that, Greg turned back toward the table, and Linda marched off to the kitchen. The drunken patron slept through the entire exchange, his head resting on his arm, which rested, in turn, on the bar.

"That took a bit longer than I anticipated," Greg offered. "Linda's not keen on reopening the kitchen after it closes."

Kat didn't quite buy that explanation, but Greg Bodin was so earnest. He seemed so . . . authentic. Authentic. That was the word that best described him. She had been searching for it while he spoke. There was something about him that was so open, so engaging, so very real.

Greg slid back into his seat and resumed his position against the cushion. "Okay. It's your turn. Tell me the story of Kat. First, is that your real name? Kat?"

"Yes, that's all of it. My parents weren't big on pretense. 'Kathryn' and 'Kathleen' seemed way too exotic to them. If I was going to be Kathy, Katie, or Kay anyway, I might as well just be 'Kat.'

"You talked about Memphis being a small town? Well, I grew up in Taconite, Minnesota, a small community of about 600 people in Itasca County, near the headwaters of the great Mississippi River. My father worked in road construction. My mother stayed home for most of my childhood. He passed away years ago. She still lives nearby, which is one of the reasons I stayed in Minnesota.

"I went to college in Michigan and then to law school in D.C. I loved D.C. It was a place where I spent some of my most formative years. Have you spent much time there?"

"Yes, I have. It is an interesting city."

"No doubt. I joined a firm there right out of school, which is where I met my husband. We moved back to Minnesota when my father fell ill. We raised our boys there."

"So you have children?"

"Yes. Two sons. Drew is 19. Anthony is 21. They're both in college now. Anthony goes to school in Virginia – UVA. Drew stayed close to me. He's attending the University of Minnesota. They're wonderful young men. Although I'm sure that I'm more than a little biased. This last year has been very tough on them. They were really close to their father."

"How did your husband die?"

"Car accident. He was coming home from his office one night. It appeared from the accident investigation that he ran a red light – right in front of an oncoming semi-trailer tractor. They say he likely didn't see it coming. Wouldn't have been aware of any of it. He died instantaneously. It all happened so fast. One day he left for work, and he never came back."

"That kind of loss is really hard," Greg said, reaching out to touch Kat's hand again. This time, instead of patting it, he held it in his own, his thumbs pressed tightly to her wrists. Her immediate instinct was to pull away, but as her eyes met his again, Kat let herself be comforted by this man she'd just met – this man who filled the space around her with energy and warmth. This stranger with whom she felt an intense and uncommon connection.

A shadow fell over them, as Linda unceremoniously shoved a grilled cheese sandwich on a chipped plate between them. Greg slowly released Kat's hand and reached out for the napkin-wrapped utensils that Linda pushed in his direction. "Do you need anything, Kat? How is your drink holding up?"

Kat looked down at her glass and was surprised at how little of her drink was left. No wonder she was babbling on like this. "I'd love a water, Linda."

"No problem, Kat."

"I'll take one, too," Greg added.

"We'll see about that," she growled. Whatever Greg had said to her earlier, Linda remained unhappy with him.

Greg pretended not to notice and continued to ask questions – about Kat's childhood and interests. They shared stories of places to which they had traveled and places they still hoped to go. Greg talked about his sister and her family and his friend Mitch and his family. He spoke fondly of their children and how he loved being an "uncle" to all of them. By the time they paused for new topics, the bar lights were darkening (as if that were even possible), and Linda was rousting the other, lone patron, to send him shuffling off for the morning.

"It's 1:00?" asked Kat. "I can't believe it. I am going to be such a wreck tomorrow."

"Thank you," Greg responded. He sounded rather melancholy.

"Thank you?"

"Yes. Thank you. Thank you for letting me sit here with you. Thank you for filling my evening with energy. Thank you for making me laugh and lose track of time. I haven't enjoyed a night like this in far too long."

Kat frowned.

"What's wrong?" Greg asked.

"I don't know. I just feel like I need to tell you that I don't do this."

"You don't do what?"

"I don't frequent hotel bars. In fact, unless I'm out with clients or customers, I always take room service when I'm traveling. It's far less awkward than eating or drinking alone somewhere. And I generally don't share my life story with complete strangers."

"We're hardly strangers, Kat," Greg replied. "We met nearly five hours ago, and I feel as if I've known you for much longer than that." He stood and took her hands, helping her to her feet. "Let me see you to your room."

Kat hesitated.

"I won't go any farther than the ice machine. I promise. I simply want to ensure you get back to your room safely," he said.

"Thank you."

"Well, I wouldn't sleep tonight if I didn't know you were securely there."

"No," Kat smiled. "I mean thank you for all of the things you said before – for letting me sit here with you; for filling my evening with energy; for making me laugh and lose track of time."

Greg put his arm around Kat's shoulders and gently pulled her close. "It was my sincere pleasure, Kat Anderson. Truly."

Greg placed two bills on the register and leaned over the bar toward Linda. "We'll talk soon," he said. "Take care, my friend."

Linda raised an eyebrow at him. "You take care, Kat. It was really nice to meet you. Thanks for coming in tonight, and please be sure to stop by if you're still in the hotel tomorrow night."

"I will. Good night, Linda."

15

True to his word, Greg walked Kat up the steps, through the heavy fire door, and down the hallway, stopping at the small enclave that seems to house every hotel ice machine. Drawing her into the enclave, he took Kat's chin in his hand and tilted her head up. Without her heels, Kat was only slightly shorter than Greg was, but the difference was just enough that she now gazed up into his eyes. He bent and brushed his lips against hers. It wasn't so much a kiss as a soft glance, a whisper.

"I want to see you again," he said, with a hint of sadness in his quiet voice, "if you'll let me." He handed her a scrap of napkin on which he had written his cell phone number. "I will wait for you to call me, and I really hope you do. Someday, I'd like to think you'll understand how much this evening has meant to me."

This felt like a code – and one that Kat didn't understand. Sure, she hadn't dated for nearly 25 years, but this seemed odd and rather passive even for that time, let alone present day.

"When are you planning to return to Minneapolis?" he asked.

"Right now, I'm planning on heading back on Friday night, unless things go very differently tomorrow than I anticipate they will. If we settle the contract, which I assume is highly unlikely, my assistant will get me on tomorrow night's flight."

"I really hope you stay until Friday. And I really hope you call." Greg leaned in and gave Kat a real kiss this time. A warm, soulful kiss. She put her arms around the back of his neck, relaxing into him. A tear formed in the corner of her eye.

"Good night," she whispered, as she turned and hurried down the hall and into her room. As she closed her door, she heard the clanking sound of the fire door closing. She rested against the wall and caught her breath.

Chapter 4

"What just happened?" Kat wondered aloud, as she moved from the door to the mirror to the bed. Sitting on the mattress, she pulled her legs up to her chest and rested her head on her knees. For the first time all night, she remembered that she was wearing leggings and looked a bit a mess. Hair that had escaped the band hung across her eyes. She touched her lips on which Greg's kiss was still present. She stayed that way for minutes, not lost in thought, but only lost.

Squeezing her knees together, Kat inhaled deeply and tried to clear her head. She gazed at the papers askew on the desk. "Tomorrow will be an impromptu performance," she muttered, as she reached for her laptop. At this point, sleep was more important – that was, if she could manage it.

Mechanical chimes sounded, as the glow of the computer lit up the pillows. Kat leaned back. One quick check in, and she'd be off.

Kelsey had been busy. Kat had three emails from her within the last two hours. Kat popped the first open. Kels was researching Teamsters leadership and was reviewing their bios. Would revert later. Kat popped open the second one. Several members of leadership worked out of or frequented D.C. Kels was narrowing her search. Propping herself up on her pillow, Kat popped open the third. Kels had found two likely suspects. The first was a gentleman named Mitch Thorton. Kels had included a bio and photograph. The second was a guy named Greg Bodin.

Kat stopped breathing. She didn't need to tap the enclosure to know that the face that would emerge was the one she'd been staring at all evening – the chiseled, lovely, earnest, and authentic face over which she'd so childishly swooned. The face of the man who had been called in as the hired gun to bend her to his will during the next day's negotiations.

Kat ran to the bathroom. Her stomach lurched and contracted. She gagged.

How could she have been so stupid? What did she tell him? Kat lowered herself to the cool tile floor and went through each detail of their conversation in her head. Did he know who she was? Of course, he did. She'd even offered that her nemesis's name was "Christian." *"Damn it, Christian! If you hadn't been such a bastard, I never would have breached confidentiality like that."*

Had Greg known where to find her? Had he sought her out? Stopped by the hotel where he knew she'd be in the hopes that she was as stupid as Christian had described her to be?

And what was she going to tell her CEO? That she'd spilled her guts to the union and the plant would now have to go on strike, suspending production, and costing the organization millions?

How could she have let this happen? Kat pounded her fists against the floor tiles. She bit her lip until the tangy taste of copper and salt met her tongue.

She reached for her phone and dialed.

Chapter 5

Greg's phone vibrated in his pocket. He pulled his motorcycle over to the side of the dark road. He removed the phone from his coat and looked at the screen. He didn't recognize the number, but he knew who it would be.

"Hello," he answered.

"Hello, Brother Bodin." Her voice caught, crackled, and was filled with anger and emotion.

"Hello, Kat. I didn't expect to hear from you quite so soon."

"How long into our conversation were we before you realized who I was?" she demanded, steady in her questioning.

"Honestly?"

"Yes. I think honesty would be a nice change of pace at this point, don't you?"

"Honestly, we were probably 1-2 minutes in before I knew that you were the wild and infamous Kat Anderson I'd heard so much about."

"So why didn't you stop me? How could you let me go on like that? Share my strategy?"

"Wait a minute," Greg interjected. "You didn't share any strategy with me."

"I told you that my team was creating strike plans and thinking about replacement workers."

"As I would expect any team to do in a situation like this one. There's nothing unique about that. You didn't share anything with me, Kat, that I didn't already know. If you had started to do so – which I trust you wouldn't have, given your professionalism and integrity – I would have stopped you."

"Oh, yes, I would trust that you would have. *Trust.* Do you want me to explain that word to you?" Kat choked back a sob.

"Kat, I'm sorry that I didn't tell you who I was. I can hear that that hurt you." He paused. "But, to be fair, you never asked."

"What?" Kat was incredulous. "You have got to be f'ing kidding me, Greg! I didn't ask? Really?"

"You never asked. You were so overtaken with your passion for your position that you launched into a lecture on fairness, equity, and the right of the common man before I even had a chance to introduce myself."

"Oh, well then. The fact that you think I'm a self-righteous bitch definitely makes me feel better. I'm really sorry, Greg," Kat continued, sardonically, "It's all my fault."

"I didn't say that, Kat. I appreciate your passion and your conviction. I found them refreshing and, well, rather wonderful." Greg paused. He could hear Kat's uneven breaths. "I should have told you, Kat. I know that now. Linda insisted that I tell you, and I should have heeded her advice."

"So that is why she was so pissed off at you?"

"Yes. She thought I was being dishonest by continuing to talk with you after I realized that I'd been sent to Memphis to, well, to *meet with you*."

"Did you know where I was staying? Did you know where to find me?"

"I did not. That's the truth, Kat. I try to stop in to see Linda whenever I'm in town. I was completely surprised when I realized that the beautiful, thoughtful woman whom I had approached in the bar was the hideous creature of Christian Christopher's fiction.

"And, Kat?"

"Yes."

"I know this may mean nothing to you – and it's not offered as an excuse for me not telling you who I was – but I didn't say anything because, frankly, even two minutes into our conversation, I couldn't bear the thought of ending my time with you. I was quite certain that if I told you who I was before you got to know me, you would have stopped our conversation. Rightly or wrongly, I wanted to learn more about you. I wanted to talk with you. I wanted to kiss you. And, at the end of the evening, it pained me to leave you in the hallway."

Kat sniffled, but said nothing.

Greg went on, "I didn't ask for your number because I knew I wasn't going to call you."

"Another day maker, Greg. No wonder you've never married."

"I wasn't going to call you because I knew that when you discovered who I was – which was bound to happen in the morning, if not before – you would likely feel shocked and betrayed. I don't have the right to expect you to feel differently. And I don't have the right to pursue a relationship with you.

"But, Kat," he continued, "I think you felt like I did tonight. I believe you sensed a connection. And I so want to see you again. Please give me a chance to show you that I was well intentioned, albeit misguided. That I'm telling you the truth when I say that I haven't felt like this – like I don't want to say good night – for the longest time. I haven't felt this sort of mental and physical attraction to someone in years, decades even. I can't explain it. I know it sounds crazy. I can only tell you what I'm experiencing."

Kat wasn't about to give him the satisfaction of sharing that she, too, had felt an incredible connection. What good would that do? He had betrayed her trust, and she was not sure that such a breach could ever be bridged. This felt to her like the Grand Canyon of breaches, and she was not about to start down that treacherous embankment.

"What were you planning to say to me in the morning, Greg? 'Surprise!'"

"I was working through that on the way home. I am not sure that I will end up going to tomorrow's session."

"What? And miss all of the fun? Christian will laugh his ass off when he hears this one. Imagine how smug he will feel."

"I don't give a damn about what Christian may or may not think right now, Kat."

Silence.

"I can tell I'm not making my case any stronger tonight. I'll see you in the morning. Good night, Kat."

"Good night, Brother Bodin."

Chapter 6

Steve Halter met Kat outside the library where the parties had rented meeting rooms. Steve was the facility superintendent and Kat's lead bargaining committee member.

"You look like hell, Kat," Steve astutely observed, as she approached. "Didn't get much sleep?"

"I'm afraid not," Kat replied with a sigh. "So what's the word of the morning?"

"The union met early – maybe 7:00. They are still in their session. They said they'd let us know when they're ready to start."

"Great."

"And, Kat?"

"Yes, Steve."

"They've got a new guy with them. A tall, built guy, in a tailored suit. They say the International sent him from D.C." Steve seemed either nervous or impressed. Either way, Kat was annoyed.

"Then it's a good thing I'm suited up as well, Steve. I look forward to meeting this gentleman. Bring him on," she remarked, with all of the gusto she could muster. "Bring him on."

Steve handed Kat a coffee he had picked up for her at the coffee shop adjacent to the library. "A little caffeine may help."

Kat smiled. "No help needed, Steve, but thank you. The coffee is much welcomed."

Steve opened the door to the library, and the two went in and headed for their breakout room. The other members of the company's bargaining committee were already in place, arguing over donuts.

"Good morning, gentlemen," Kat quipped. "Are you ready for another day in Paradise?"

"If yesterday's session was Paradise, Kat, I think it's time to raise a little hell," offered Dean O'Reilly, a short, stout man of, perhaps 60 years of age.

"I couldn't agree more, Dean," Kat responded, grabbing a maple-glazed donut from the box. Taking a bite, she addressed the group as she chewed, "It's definitely time to raise a little hell."

Twenty minutes passed before there was a knock on the door.

"It's about fucking time," Dean complained, as he went to open it.

Two men stood just outside. There was Greg Bodin in his tailored suit, with his hair pulled back in a way that made it look short, almost military in style. His face was cleanly shaven, and he looked grim and determined. Next to him stood Christian Christopher. Fat, grotesque, sweaty, Christian, in a suit coat that hung unbuttoned and a white shirt that gapped at his mid-drift. Gone, however, was the smug grin, the condescending smirk to which Kat had become so accustomed. Rather, he looked quite ashen and almost demure. Christian stepped inside and reached his hand out to shake Kat's.

"Good morning, Mrs. Anderson – I mean, Kat," he said. "I would like to introduce you to our International Vice President at Large, Greg Bodin."

Kat took Greg's outreached hand, squeezing it as forcefully as she could manage as she shook it. "It's nice to meet you, Mr. Bodin. I'm sorry that Christian felt it necessary to trouble you with this matter, and I hope that we are able to bring this contract to fruition."

"May we sit?" Greg asked.

"Of course, gentlemen," Kat responded, motioning toward the table.

Nodding in acknowledgment at the gathered men, Greg took a seat at the table and continued, "I had the opportunity to review the Company's last contract offer early this morning, and I have met to discuss it with the union's bargaining committee. Frankly, given the relevant market conditions and competitive forces, I was surprised."

"Really?" remarked Kat, trying to camouflage some of the sarcasm in her voice. "How, exactly, were you *surprised*, Mr. Bodin?"

"Frankly, Ms. Anderson, I was surprised that our bargaining committee had not accepted the Company's last offer. I believe that the offer is thoughtful and fair. I have shared my reaction with the bargaining committee, and they agree."

Now it was time for Kat to be surprised. "So you agree to recommend the contract terms that were offered to the membership yesterday?"

"We do," Greg replied. For the first time of the day, he made eye contact with Kat, as he moved two manila envelopes across the table toward her. "Here are two copies of yesterday's agreement. Both have been signed by Mr. Christopher. One copy is for your bargaining committee's final review and signature. This copy," he remarked, as he moved the envelope in her direction, "this one is for you." Greg stood, and Christian hastily followed his lead. "Please let us know when you are ready to adjourn today's bargaining session," Greg instructed. "We'll be waiting next door."

As Dean closed the door behind Christian and Greg, the room erupted in "'Holy shit!' and 'What just happened'?"

"I don't know how to explain it, but we'll certainly take it," Steve grinned.

"Indeed, we will," Kat stated, as she slid the bargaining committee's copy over to Steve. "You guys do me a favor and double-check this copy against yesterday's original. We're not taking any chance with these guys, especially the slick one from D.C. Before we sign, I want to ensure that no changes have been made."

As the committee set about its task, Kat slipped her copy out of its envelope. A yellow sticky had been affixed to the front. The handwritten message said, simply, "Meet me outside your hotel. 11:00 a.m. Wear jeans and closed-toed shoes. <u>Please</u>." Kat quickly folded the note and stuck it in her bag. She'd worry about that later. For now, she had a contract to finalize.

As soon as the committee was satisfied that everything about the document was as it should be, Steve signed the tentative agreement with a flourish, and Kat brought it to the front desk to have a copy made. Greg was waiting outside the meeting room when she returned.

"You're just full of surprises, aren't you, Mr. Bodin?"

"I thought it was a more than fair offer, Kat. I called Mitch Thorton at International HQ, and he agreed."

"It was a fair offer, Greg."

As Kat handed him the envelope with the union's copy inside, Greg took her elbow and held it. He directed her around the corner to an empty conference room and closed the door behind them.

"Kat, I really want to spend the day with you. Please agree to meet me. I will understand either way, but I hope that you'll give me a chance to show you that you can trust me." Greg kissed her softly on the forehead and left. Kat composed herself and returned to her bargaining committee.

The guys were elated as they left the library. "Is it too early to grab lunch?" Steve asked Kat, as they filed out onto the sidewalk.

"I suspect these guys could eat any time," Kat teased. "You go ahead without me. You were right, Steve. I look like hell, and I'm planning to catch a little nap and to see if Kelsey can get me on an evening flight home. I'll definitely miss you guys, though. And, who knows? The folks on the line could fail to ratify the contract."

"Like hell they will!" Steve erupted.

"Well, if they do," Kat added, "I'll be back. I can't let you guys have all of the fun."

Kat gave each of them a quick hug and headed back toward the hotel. She had an hour to try to grab a power nap before she had to wake up and determine the shape the rest of her day would take.

As Kat collapsed, fully dressed, onto the bed, she set her alarm and thought, once again, that after a little sleep and a shower, she would decide.

Chapter 7

Kat had no idea where she was when she awoke an hour later, a string of drool connecting her hair with the pillow. She shook her head and looked around the room. A wave of excited anxiety washed over her.

"Did I even pack jeans?" she wondered, as she got out of bed and began to dig through her bag. Closed-toed shoes, she had. She never failed to pack her kicks, just in case there was a nice place to walk or hike near her hotel. "Voila!" she exclaimed, as her searching fingers made contact with denim. 10:15. Time to shower, dress, and head downstairs.

Kat readied quickly and then checked her purse – driver's license (check), credit card (check), room key (check), comb, lipstick, and compact (check), cell phone (check). Cell phone? Yes. A quick note to Kelsey, Drew, and Anthony, and she'd be off. But what to say?

> *10:45 a.m. (to Kelsey): "Hey, there. Uncertain day. Let's book for tomorrow night. I'll be back in touch."*

> *10:45 a.m. (to Drew): "Back tomorrow night. Dinner Saturday? Feel free to bring your clothes by. Free washer service with meal. Love you!"*

> *10:46 a.m. (to Anthony): "Memphis is . . . interesting. Home tomorrow. Time to chat this weekend?"*

With the home front covered, Kat reached for the door handle. She stopped abruptly and took a step back. Agreeing to meet with Greg Bodin was likely one of the most reckless and possibly ridiculous decisions she had ever made. It was not too late to change her mind, to call Kelsey and catch the next flight out of this city.

Kat reflected for a moment. She turned and went back to the desk. She picked up the sheet from the hotel pad on which she had scribbled a note the day before and flipped it over. On it, she wrote Greg's name and cell phone number in big, unmistakable print – in the unlikely event there was a search for her body. As she placed the note in a space on the desk that could not be missed, Kat caught sight of her keychain. On it, there was a quote attributed to Maya Angelou: "If you're always trying to be normal, you will never know how amazing you can be." She smiled, took a deep breath, returned to the door, and turned the knob.

Greg was waiting at the curb. He looked relieved when he saw her, and he rushed to meet her.

"Thank you for coming, Kat," he said, as he approached. "I wasn't sure that you would."

"I wasn't sure that I would either, Greg. This just isn't *normal*."

Greg nodded, and stepped back.

"But it could be *amazing*," Kat added.

He smiled in agreement – the same smile that, just the night before, had seemed to spill off his face and fill the entire room.

Kat looked around for some hint of what was going to happen next. Greg reached into a bag beside the curb and extracted a helmet and a jacket. "You ever ride one of these?" he asked, as he pointed toward a Harley-Davidson touring bike parked nearby.

"Ever? Yes. Within the last 20 years? No."

"Fortunately, it's just like riding a bicycle. You never forget. Are you game for this? It's a pleasant 3-hour ride to Nashville."

"'Pleasant' is obviously a subjective term," Kat responded. She looked apprehensive, as she pulled on the jacket and slipped the helmet over her head. "Okay," she nodded. "Let's give this a whirl."

Greg fussed for a minute, testing their communications system and showing Kat how to mount the bike. As soon as he was situated on the seat, it was her turn to get on. She hesitated for a moment. He smiled patiently at her and winked. Carefully – and not too gracefully – Kat threw her leg over the seat and pulled herself up behind him. He put a hand on each of her knees, and squeezed. "Are you ready?" he asked into his microphone.

"Just one question," she asked tentatively.

"Which is?"

"Where do I hang on?"

The sound of Greg's soft laugh echoed through the headset. "The safest course is to hang on tightly to the person in front of you. Very tightly. Oh, and to place your head on his shoulder."

"*Oh, really*. That's the safest course?"

"Absolutely. Of course, in the interest of complete and utter transparency, you also can hang on to the handrails beside you or behind you. But, I'd prefer if you hold onto me."

Kat grabbed the handrails, and they were off. City traffic was a little unnerving for Kat, and she was a bit of a backseat driver, cautioning him about approaching vehicles and wondering aloud whether they might be too close to the truck next to them or too far into a given crosswalk. But as they left the city, she relaxed and began to enjoy the passing scenery, bright blue sky, and cool breeze. She raised her hand and felt the pressure of the wind on her wrist and the pads of her fingers. She leaned forward and encircled Greg's chest with her arms, resting her head briefly on his shoulder.

The drive was beautiful. Spring was in full bloom, and the road was framed with lush trees and other vegetation. The Interstate snaked through a garden maze.

"What do you call that color?" Kat asked.

"What color?"

"That vivid spring green. It only lasts a week or two, and there's nothing like it during the rest of the year, anywhere. I've always struggled with naming it. It's so elusive. It's the color of freshness, of newness, of hope. What do you think? Champagne pear?"

"'Champagne pear.' I think that's a good description. I would have said something like 'golden lime.' Whatever you call it, it is beautiful."

"It's even more marvelous when interspersed with those large expanses of yellow wildflowers and the occasional pop of white and pink dogwoods."

"It is, indeed."

They rode on, in silence, for several miles before Kat piped in, "So with this headset on, you're a captive audience. Am I right?"

"I guess that's right," Greg replied, with feigned concern in his voice.

"And you've promised to be honest with me, no matter what?" Kat continued.

"Yes, Kat, I have."

"Then, let's talk, my friend. I have some questions for you."

"Please, proceed."

"So something you said this morning made me wonder."

"Uh-huh. Go on."

"You mentioned that you had Mitch Thorton review the contract, and he agreed that it was fair."

"He did."

"Greg, I know that you don't need someone's permission to enter into a contract – especially a rather insignificant agreement such as that one. Why did you reach out to Mitch Thorton?"

"Is this a cross examination, Kat, in which you don't ask a question unless you already know the answer? You, of all people, certainly must understand why I sought Mitch's opinion." He paused and looked at her in the mirror. "I wanted to avoid any conflicts of interest – whether real or perceived. It's imprudent to be falling in love with a counterparty while signing onto a contract."

"You're falling in love with me?" Kat responded, pulling back slightly and loosening her embrace.

Greg did not respond immediately.

"I suspect I may be, Kat. I don't know how else to explain the way that I am feeling. I'm sorry if that is too blunt or too soon. To quote a very wise person in my life, 'Filter, Greg. Filter.' But you've asked me to be honest with you, and I will be. I believe I'm falling in love with you, Kat Anderson, and this . . . could be . . . amazing."

About an hour outside of Nashville, they drove through beautiful watersheds and then the Tennessee National Wildlife Refuge. Kat took it all in, trying to commit it to memory. She slipped her phone out of her pocket and snapped a shot of the passing countryside – just in case.

It was only when they spotted Nashville in the distance that it first occurred to Kat to ask why they had driven the three hours to get here. "And what are we planning to do in Nashville?"

"You said you'd never been to Nashville. There's no better place, in my opinion, to listen to music. I thought we'd go down to Broadway for a bit and then catch the show at the Grand Ole Opry. That seemed like a safe enough bet for a first date – unless, of course, you hate country music."

"It sounds just lovely," Kat remarked. "Can we wear what we have on?"

"We could, but we won't. A good friend, Lilly, and her husband, Scott, live downtown. They reside above Lilly's dress shop, which is rather convenient for our needs today, and I always keep extra clothes at their place. I called ahead this morning, just in case, and Lilly has a couple of things for you to try. She is sure she has found the perfect dress. Lilly specializes in perfect dresses."

"I'm a bit overwhelmed. How thoughtful," Kat responded. "But what if I hadn't shown up at the curb?"

"Then, Lilly would have put the dresses back on the rack, and she would have been prepared to extend her shoulder for me to cry on and to listen while I told her how stupid I was. She would have done her best to make me feel better, while all the while thinking, 'Yes, you were stupid.' She knows me all too well. But I would have left there this evening feeling better than when I arrived. You can't help but feel better when Lilly is around. You'll see. Lilly likes nothing better than to be happy and to make other people happy."

Chapter 8

Lilly Vanderlaan was exactly as Greg had described her: happy. She was effervescent and welcoming. She greeted Greg and Kat as they entered her little corner boutique, with a huge hug for each and a big kiss on the cheek for Greg. She was a woman of about 5' 8", with long, silver-blond hair. Her hair was tied back in a scarf, and she wore a matching scarf dress, which she later explained was "enough hippie to be cool; enough retro to be mod."

After a quick conversation, Lilly warmly shooed Greg out the back door and up the steps to dress. When he was safely out of earshot, Lilly gave Kat another exuberant hug. "I don't know what exactly is going on with you two," she exclaimed, "but I like it! I could hear something different in his voice this morning – even when he wasn't sure you'd come here with him."

"What did he tell you?" Kat asked timidly.

"Only that he'd met a woman; he'd been a fool; he was hoping to put things right; and if he convinced you to let him try, the two of you would be here about 2:00. Oh, and could I have a dress ready for a night on the town – something fit for a Nordic goddess?"

"A Nordic goddess?" Kat asked skeptically, raising her eyebrow in disbelief.

"Well, okay. I might have embellished that last part a bit, but not really. That's the vision I had in my mind, as he dreamily described your multi-toned blond hair, with soft hints of gold, brown, and red and your big blue eyes with flecks of silver. He also said you were maybe 3-4" taller than I am – but about the same 'hug span,'" she laughed. "He was pretty damn accurate. Everything here should work. I've included both size 10 and 12, just in case. Holler if you have any questions or need help. Oh, and I've removed all of the tags. Greg has taken care of the bill, and he wants you to choose based on what you feel great in – not on what it costs."

"I don't know about that," Kat began, but Lilly would hear none of it and cheerfully spun Kat toward the fitting room and gave her a playful push.

"It doesn't matter," Lilly said. "Try the green one first."

"So what do you think?" Kat asked tentatively, as she stepped from behind the floral, tasseled curtain. The green dress clung to her body, the neckline resting across the base of her shoulders, the high waist gathering slightly below her bust line and framing her hips as it tapered to just above her knee.

"Stunning!" Lilly clapped. "I knew the emerald one would sparkle. It makes the colors in your eyes pop. And the shape flows. It shows off your long legs. Unless you have any doubts, this dress strikes me as the one – and that still gives us 20 minutes to touch up your makeup and to fix the helmet hair."

"It is pretty flat, isn't it?" Kat responded, running her hands through her thick, but bowled, mane.

"Nothing that a quick blowout, a little curling iron, and a few bobby pins can't fix. Take a seat over there by the mirror, and I'll be right back. Size 9-9 ½ shoe?"

"Yes, that's right."

Kat watched in wonder, as Lilly twirled around the store, checking on other customers, and, despite dedicating herself to Kat, magically leaving everyone else feeling like they, too, were the only one in the store.

She returned with a box under her arm and a makeup bag in her hand. She pulled a blow dryer and curling iron from a cabinet behind the counter and plugged them into a nearby socket.

Lilly slipped a pair of black leather shoes out of the box. "Basic black Mary Jane's," she said, as she loosened the straps and placed them on Kat's feet. "They won't detract from the dress, and the heel is flattering, but not overpowering. With his dress shoes on, you'll still be roughly the same height as Greg."

With Kat's feet appropriately shod, Lilly set off on Kat's face, applying a little concealer here and there, commenting about a slight darkness under Kat's eyes and a way to "spruce up" her "skinny lips." Kat sat captive, and captivated, as Lilly pulled, ironed, and twisted Kat's hair. When Lilly finally swiveled the chair around, so she faced the mirror, Kat was surprised by her image. Kat didn't wear much makeup, but Lilly's artistic endeavor didn't look painted or cheap. Kat looked downright natural, simply brighter somehow – more vibrant – and when she smiled, her candy-colored lips ("Candy Passion," Lilly had recited from the side of the applicator) made her teeth appear sparkling white.

"You look beautiful, Kat!" Lilly proudly proclaimed.

"Indeed, you do, Kat," Greg interrupted. He had come in at some point during the cosmetic applying, hair pulling, hair spraying hubbub, and was standing just behind her. He placed a hand on her bare shoulder, and she shuddered slightly as she looked at his reflection in the mirror. He wore black pants and boots, a sports coat, and a cowboy hat.

"You clean up well yourself," she smiled, rising to face him. He leaned in and kissed her softly on her Candy Passion lips.

"Hey, you," Lilly chided. "Be careful not to wreck the good work we've done."

Chapter 9

A driver arrived to pick them up. Their first stop was a honkytonk bar on Broadway. Greg knew one of the band members, and he and Kat made several requests. The music was great, and she enjoyed a cold beer, while Greg had his typical Spite with lime. When the band went on break, Greg and Kat walked down the street and grabbed a bite to eat at a cute little place just off of Printers Alley.

Then, the driver took them out to the Grand Ole Opry. The theater was full and the lights were coming down, as Kat and Greg took their seats along the rail on the mezzanine level.

"Turn this way, Kat," Greg urged suddenly.

Kat turned toward him and peeked behind them to see if she was, perhaps, blocking someone's line of sight.

"The gentleman down there at the far right end of the second row is a local gossip columnist," Greg whispered. "He published a photo of me and my sister once. Embarrassed the shit out of him when he realized what he had done. Martha thought it was hilarious. He is looking our way right now. Keep your head turned this way, and he'll not be able to put a name and a face together." He paused. "I'd be happy to give him something to write about, however."

"Fair enough," Kat whispered, before kissing Greg for no less than half a minute.

"God bless the paparazzi," Greg moaned quietly, as Kat moved away, placing her finger on his lips.

Greg wrapped his arm around Kat's shoulder and held her close. As she relaxed into him, he stroked her arm. The first band began to play.

Kat looked around. It was a folksy setting – with long, red bench seating. The stage was adorned with barn wood, and when the heavy red curtain rose, the famous wooden circle shone brightly at the center of the stage.

Each act was better than the last, and Kat tapped her foot and swayed with the music. She was surprised by the emotions that one of the songs evoked in her. She did not know the artist. She did not know the title. But the song was about motherhood and how quickly one's babies grow up. Kat was not a particularly emotive person, but there was something about this song – at this time – that caused her reflexively to place her hand on her throat and swallow hard, as tears formed in her eyes. Greg said nothing, but he watched her intently and pulled her even closer.

The moment the performance ended but before any encore, Greg tapped Kat's leg, indicating that it was time to leave. He whisked her down the steps, out the door, and into the waiting car.

"So what did you think?" he asked, as he closed the door and reached for her hand.

"That was so much fun! It has been a really long time since I enjoyed an evening out like I have enjoyed this one," she replied contentedly.

They changed clothes at Lilly and Scott's home, packing Kat's dress carefully in the Touring Pack. Lilly was effusive with her hugs and best wishes. Scott was quietly polite. Obviously, he didn't need to say much.

Greg and Kat were laughing as they got up in the saddle and drove to the southwest. The sky was dark, but for a waning crescent moon. Outside the city, the stars were fresh and bright. The miles passed steadily and quickly, as they talked about everything and nothing and enjoyed the closeness of the ride. Kat lost all track of time.

"Kat?" Greg asked, when they were about 40 miles east of Memphis.

"Uh-huh?" she replied.

"Stay with me tonight?"

Kat did not respond for several moments. "Greg, I have loved this day. It is the most wonderful time I've had in years. But . . . ."

"But?"

"I'm afraid." Kat shifted on the seat, placed her hand on Greg's shoulder and rested her chin on her hand. "Completely honest?" she asked quietly.

"Completely."

"I was married a long time, Greg."

"Yes."

"It may sound prehistoric, but, well, I've had one intimate partner in my entire life. One."

"Damn, Kat, you're nearly a virgin," Greg teased, as he reached around and ran his gloved finger from her knee to the inside of her thigh. "Don't worry. I'm not intending to sleep with you tonight."

"You're not?" Kat asked, not knowing whether to feel relieved or hurt. "Even if I beg?"

"Even if you beg," Greg insisted, with a smile in his voice. "My only intention is to not say 'good night.' I don't think I can bear to leave you at the ice machine. Let me take you to my place."

"To your place of respite?"

"Yes. I'd like to share my place of respite with you."

Kat squeezed Greg's arm and lost herself for a moment in her thoughts. They'd gone another several miles before she responded, "Okay."

Greg slowed the bike and turned onto a two-lane, gravel road. "Do you see that dark mass to the left?" he pointed. "That's part of the Chickasaw Bluffs." Forest seemed to rise out of the land around them. "Oak, American beech, hickory, and sweet gum," he recited.

"It's gorgeous out here."

"Just wait until morning. If you're up for it, I'll take you out to see the sun rise."

Chapter 10

Greg cut the engine near a small barn. "We'll park here. The house is just up the path." Greg held the bike in place as Kat carefully dismounted. She stood by what appeared to be an old well and water pump as he pushed the bike inside. The night was completely quiet, other than the sound of the breeze blowing through the leaves and a lone owl. Kat breathed in the cool, evening air, and pulled her jacket around her. She sighed as Greg emerged from behind and wrapped his arms around her, pulling her to his chest. They stood there for a few moments, taking in the night's quietude. When Greg finally released her and reached for her hand, she had calmed and was ready to follow him up the path between the trees and into a shallow clearing, where she could make out the outline of a cabin-like structure, constructed of hewn logs and adorned with cathedral windows.

Greg opened the door and welcomed her in, moving ahead of her and switching on the lights. The front room opened onto a porch that faced the nature reserve. Beyond the front room, Kat could see a spacious kitchen with a fireplace. To the right of the kitchen was a set of wooden steps that led to a loft. On each wall of the home towered tall, wooden bookshelves, filled with volumes and photos. The walls were covered in paintings and sketches of nature. The place was cozy and unassuming, and Kat felt immediately relaxed.

Greg made his way to the kitchen. "Make yourself at home. Are you hungry?"

"No, I'm fine."

"How about a glass of wine?"

"That would be nice."

Greg poured two glasses and returned to the front room. He handed Kat a glass and proposed a toast. "Here's to a day I'd hoped would never end and to moments I will always remember." He raised his glass. They clinked and sipped.

"Your home is beautiful, Greg. It's easy to understand why you love it here. Did you build it yourself?"

"I didn't build it. It was here long before I was born. But a home like this needs a lot of tenderness and maintenance, so I feel as if I've *rebuilt* every piece of it in some small way or another. It's definitely a labor of love."

Greg set about starting a fire in the fireplace, as Kat looked about the room, pausing to peruse a set of shelves. The titles were eclectic – everything from poetry to WWII non-fiction, classics, and mysteries. The photos were similarly varied and unique. Before too long, Greg was at her side. "That's my mother," he said, pointing to a photo of a girl not more than 17, sporting a big white bow in her hair – a graduation photo. Picking up a small, round frame, he held it out to Kat. "And there I am at 6." The photo was one of a handsome, tow-headed child with a toothless smile. Although a black and white print, his eyes sparkled brightly even then. "And that one," he said, pointing, "that's Martha."

"What a pretty child," Kat observed.

"Yes, Martha's still a beauty. Here's one of her, Rick, and the girls: Lydia and Ali." Greg picked up another frame and handed it to Kat. "That was taken here last year. The girls love to come here during the summer. Frankly, the girls love to come here any time. I'm afraid Martha's not too thrilled that they appear to have a bit of Tennessee in them."

There was a photo near the back of the cabinet, a small photo in a heart-shaped frame. Kat picked it up and drew it closer. In the photo, a man of, maybe 20, held a young woman of roughly the same age. The man was obviously Greg, and the girl was lovely, lanky, and blonde, with hair that flowed to the middle of her back and a gorgeous smile. They were beaming, as the camera captured them lying back in tall grasses atop a picnic blanket. "And this?" Kat asked.

"This is Annie. My first true love."

"And?"

"It's a long story, my dear. I haven't seen Annie in over 20 years."

"And yet you keep her photo on your shelf?"

"I guess one never forgets their first true love," Greg responded, as he gently removed the frame from Kat's hands and placed it back on the shelf.

Greg took Kat's fingers in his and led her to the sofa. He went to stoke the fire, as Kat perched on the edge of the cushion and watched him.

"How often do you get here?"

"I try to get back every few weeks. It's not always possible, with my work and travel schedules. I keep an apartment in D.C. as well. A friend of mine checks in on this place when I'm not here, and the park rangers are also good at walking through the site every once in a while."

Thin flames began to lick the wood that Greg had stacked in the hearth. "While this fire takes hold, might I interest you in taking a soak in the hot tub?" he asked. "Martha keeps a bathing suit and cover in the guest room," he smiled, "unless, of course, you'd rather go in naked."

Kat raised an eyebrow. "Where's the guest room?" she quickly retorted.

Greg pointed her toward a small room behind the kitchen. An antique sleigh bed filled the center of the room, and an armoire rested against the far wall. Kat opened the doors of the armoire. There she found a small collection of women's dresses, casual clothes, and shoes. The bathing suit and cover were tucked inside the top drawer.

Greg was in his trunks and a t-shirt waiting by the door to the deck. He led her out the sliding glass to an expansive deck. Kat had no sense of depth or height, just a weightlessness of being. She lowered herself into the steaming tub, allowing the effervescence to overcome her. She tilted her head back until her hair floated around her ears and the water bubbled over her forehead, caressed her eyes. Greg gently kissed her outstretched neck, as he settled in beside her. He put his hands on Kat's hips and in one smooth motion, turned her around in the buoyant water and lowered her onto his lap. Turning to face him, she rested her forehead against his. "Even if I beg?"

"Even if you beg," he laughed, and then kissed her deeply.

Kat turned around and laid her head between Greg's shoulder and chin. She gazed into the infinite sky. For a long while, neither said a word as the water percolated around them and the steamy air warmed their lungs.

"Did you see the falling star?" Greg finally asked, through the enveloping fog.

"I did."

"Did you make a wish?"

"I did."

"Me, too."

The owl renewed its call. This time another owl returned it, and the two echoed each other with slow, hopeful cries.

Kat yawned.

Greg nudged her and grabbed her shoulder playfully with his teeth. "We should probably get you inside and ready for bed. I'm afraid neither of us got much sleep last night. You must be exhausted." He raised her from his lap, freed himself, and grabbed their towels from the banister.

Once inside, Greg sent Kat back to the guest room to change out of her wet things as he retrieved a long t-shirt and discretely dropped it just inside the bedroom door. Kat toweled off and pulled the t-shirt over her head. It clung to her damp body but hung to a respectable length above her knees. Greg was stoking the fire when she returned. The warmth and light of the emerging flames filled the room with an inviting glow. His back was turned to her. He was wearing cotton pajama pants, and his wet hair curled and rested against his shoulders. His back was bare, but for what appeared to be a tattoo that stretched from just below his shoulder blades to his waist. The light was dim, but as she approached, Kat could see the outline of a dragon-looking beast with a bloody heart in its mouth. It looked to be flying away, but its neck craned back to reveal its piercing, red eyes. Kat recoiled a bit at the sight of it. She drew in a short breath.

Greg heard her approach and turned to face her.

"What is that?" Kat asked. Her voice quivered.

"What is what?"

"On your back."

"It's a tattoo, Kat."

"Yes, I know it is a tattoo, Greg. But *what* is it? What does it mean?"

"It means many things, Kat. But mostly, it is there to remind me that while my demons are behind me, I must always be careful to keep them there – behind me. They are not part of my present or part of my future."

Greg sat down on the couch. He motioned for her to sit next to him and handed her a wine glass.

"I told you that I wasted several years when I returned from the desert. I was messed up, Kat. PTSD was only beginning to be understood then, and there was very little help for veterans who suffered from it. I struggled with depression and addiction. I couldn't keep a relationship or a job.

"I had been engaged before I left for the Middle East."

"To Annie?"

"To Annie. She was the love of my life, but I was so afraid of losing her when I returned that I drove her away. She was afraid of me and what I had become. She mourned for the man she had lost. Frankly, so did I. I didn't recognize myself. I got tangled up in some very messy things. I had some brushes with the law.

"I had been working for a few weeks on a manufacturing line, trying to earn enough money to keep from being evicted, when I met Mitch. He was there on union business. He walked the line and talked to people. He recognized something in me that I could not see in myself. He saw hope. He saw potential. He talked me into becoming active with the Local. Many of the guys there were also veterans. Mitch and a couple of the others understood what I was feeling. They didn't push me to be something that I couldn't quite manage at that time. They didn't expect me to be 'normal.' And Mitch stayed connected with me as I emerged from that overwhelming sense of loss. He set me up with some much-needed medical attention. He encouraged me. Ultimately, he offered me a job with the International. Mitch Thorton saved my life. He helped me defeat my demons."

"I'm so sorry."

"There's nothing to be sorry about, Kat. That period of my life was impactful. It changed me. It shaped me. It created in me a groundswell of gratitude and a desire to be present in my life. I wouldn't be who I am today had I not experienced that deep anger, sadness, and loss."

Kat rested her head on Greg's lap and gazed up at his warm and open face. He returned her gaze, holding her with his eyes. He ran his fingers up her side, from her waste, up her rib cage, beside her breast.

Kat shivered under his touch.

"You're making it really hard for me to keep my promise," he whispered.

"Good," she smiled.

Greg slid out from under Kat, helped her to her feet, and led her up the stairs. As he lowered her to the bed, he settled in behind her, wrapping his arms around her and drawing her near. "Sleep well, sweet Kat," he whispered.

Chapter 11

Kat awoke a few hours later to the comforting smell of coffee. It was still dark, but Greg was rustling around downstairs. She heard his feet on the steps, as he ascended to her. He turned on a small light beside the bed and placed a steaming cup on the side table before crawling back under the covers beside her.

"Can I interest you in a coffee and a hike?" he asked hopefully.

"A hike at this hour?" Kat yawned. "What time is it anyway?"

"It's 5:30. The sun will be coming up soon. It's amazing to watch it rise over the park."

"Is the park even open?"

"That's a minor detail." He winked as he handed her the cup.

Kat sat up and took the warm vessel in her hands. She drank the coffee slowly, savoring the steamy goodness. It tasted amazing, and her senses quickly livened. "Give me five minutes," she said happily, as she got out of bed and headed down to the guest room to dress.

Greg led the way, by the light of his headlamp, down a narrow, trampled path leading from the house to the park. Passing through a makeshift hole in a fence, Greg led Kat across an expanse of forest to a park trail. "This is the Chickasaw Bluffs Trail." The trail widened, so they could walk side-by-side.

There was a hint of light on the pink and orange horizon just at the time when the path opened up to a lake. "Poplar Tree Lake. A perfect place to watch the sunrise," Greg remarked, removing his jacket and placing it beside a tree near the shore. He lowered himself to the ground, drawing Kat down in front of him. Perched between Greg's knees, Kat leaned back and rested against his chest as light, colors, and clouds jostled for position in the sky beyond the lake.

"It's like nature's kaleidoscope," Kat observed, with a sigh.

The trill of birds filled the air, and Greg identified each of them in a rather wistful and poetic way.

"La Conte's Sparrow.

"Cedar Waxwing.

"Red-winged Blackbird."

When the light overtook the horizon, Kat freed herself from Greg's embrace and stood. "Stay right there," she directed, as she slipped her cell phone from her pocket. "Picture of the day," she explained, as she framed Greg with the lake behind him. "I take a photo every day of a place, person, or thing that brings me joy. It's something I started doing shortly after the accident. It was then a bridge back to normalcy and a reminder of my many blessings. It's become a habit. I've kept doing it simply because it reminds me to be grateful and makes me happy."

Greg rose to his feet and shook the pine needles gently from his jacket. "That's a beautiful practice," he responded. "May I?" he asked, motioning for the camera. Kat handed it to him, as he stepped behind her, wrapped his other arm around her and kissed her neck behind her ear. He snapped the photo, just as she tilted her head away from him, exposing her entire neck to his warm caress. Greg smirked, as he examined his work on the screen. "Now that's a joyous picture!"

Greg took Kat's hand and they started walking again. "Are you up for a little experiment?" he asked.

"As if the last 24 hours weren't experiment enough?" Kat responded, smiling.

"It's all part of the adventure, my dear."

"Well, then," Kat laughed. "By all means, proceed."

"Let me take you on a mindfulness hike. I discovered long ago that meditation and being in nature are the two things that, without fail, calm my mind and relax my body. Spending time in nature has healing and restorative powers for me. That healing is enhanced through just a few simple exercises."

Greg turned to face Kat and looked intently into her eyes. "First," he instructed, "we must 'stop before we start.' Take a few moments and simply breathe." Kat drew in a breath, then another. She felt oddly quieter and more energized. "Now," Greg continued, "enjoy a few moments of silence, as you look around and study the nature that surrounds us. Look up; explore the sky, the shape of the clouds and the way they move across the horizon. Notice the shadows, patterns, colors, and textures on the ground. If something catches your attention, study it; gently observe its colors; look for subtle details you may have missed at first glance. Allow yourself to become really curious about the thing or things you see."

Kat turned and faced away from Greg, so she could concentrate. She followed his instructions, and for several quiet minutes, she focused exclusively on the nature around her – the topaz sky filled with what struck her as large, white dandelion seeds being scattered above the earth. The budding leaves – in that beautiful, champagne-pear color – were like pompoms decorating the trees. The sun reflected off the dew that dotted the delicate spring grass. She focused on a decaying leaf and noticed its protruding arteries, small bites an insect had taken from its browning flesh, a patch of dusty decay along its edge. She took in the smoky scent of peat and felt the cool air in her lungs and the warm sun on her hair – the sun that would help transform this leaf into the dirt that would support the next generation of vegetation that was coming up everywhere around her, vibrant and hopeful. She smiled.

"This really works," Kat whispered.

Greg stepped closer behind her and put his lips next to her ear. "Yes, it does," he whispered back. "Come on." He led her along the path, pointing out various objects. Occasionally, he'd hand her one – a mossy stick, a smooth stone, a spiny seed, a honeysuckle flower – and have her explore it with her hands, smell it, describe it. After perhaps twenty minutes of this, Greg suggested that they walk quietly for a while, explaining that there was "something wonderful about shared silence."

There was, indeed, something wonderful about the shared silence. In addition to her surroundings, Kat took in everything about Greg as they walked – his gait, the shape of his face, the way that his hair blew back in the breeze, the slight glistening of perspiration on his forehead that reflected the morning sunlight. Her thoughts were filled with peace and gratitude.

After walking this way for a short, but glorious time, Greg stopped and grabbed Kat's hand. "Close your eyes and take three long, deep breaths," he suggested quietly. Kat stood facing him and closed her eyes. She breathed in and out, focusing on the way her chest expanded and contracted with each breath. "Now," Greg continued, "open your eyes and kiss me."

Kat opened her eyes. Greg was looking at her and smiling – that amazing smile that filled his face and spilled into the forest around him. She placed her arms around his neck and kissed him. As she had done earlier in the morning, she explored his mouth with her tongue, taking his lip between her teeth, breathing in his scent and committing everything to her memory. Kat rested her forehead against Greg's shoulder. "I like this form of meditation," she sighed happily.

They spent the rest of the morning walking the trails and talking. He took her down a path that led to a rocky area overlooking the great Mississippi River, and she told him about walking barefoot through the fledgling headwaters of this amazing river in Itasca State Park in Minnesota. As the sun reached high overhead, they went back to the house. They cooked together in the big country kitchen, chatting as they did. They lingered over lunch on the expansive deck overlooking the forest.

As mid-afternoon approached, Kat reluctantly leaned back in her deck chair and pointed sadly to her watch. "I have a 6:00 flight."

"I don't want you to leave, Kat."

"I know."

"When can I see you again?"

"Let's make a plan."

"How about Wednesday."

Kat laughed. "Wednesday?"

"Yes. I have business reasons to travel to Minnesota, although I haven't been there in a while. I am sure that, given a day or so to plan, I could be up there by mid-week. I'd have to be back in D.C. on Friday, but at least we could have dinner together."

"That would be nice."

Chapter 12

"Look what the Kat dragged in!" Linda teased, as the two entered the lobby. She placed her hands on her fulsome hips and smiled broadly. As she sauntered toward them, Linda caught Kat up in a hearty embrace, whispering, "Forgiveness is a glorious thing." Then, she turned to Greg and swatted him on the arm. "And you? You're just a lucky son-of-a bitch."

Greg smiled. "You always say the nicest things. It's what keeps me coming back to this place, Lin."

Back in the hotel room, Greg stretched out on the bed and flipped through a magazine that the house cleaner had left when she tidied the room.

"Give me ten minutes to shower and dress, and I'll be right back," Kat said, grabbing his knee and giving it a squeeze.

As she fastened the last of the buttons on her blouse, Kat emerged from the bathroom and looked for her computer in order to pull up her reservation information. Kat had left her laptop in her briefcase. That was when? Yesterday? The days blurred together in her mind. And she hadn't checked her emails or texts in as many days as well. "Damn it!" she cursed under her breath. As she tapped her Messages app, the screen lit up with texts:

> *2:15 p.m. (from Kelsey): Hey, Kat. Steve Halter sent flowers. The card says, "Congratulations and thanks for everything!" Did you get things wrapped up?*
>
> *4:03 p.m. (from Kelsey): Text me when you get a chance.*
>
> *6:17 p.m. (from Kelsey): Getting worried. Give me a buzz. – Kels*
>
> *9:30 p.m. (from Kelsey): You're really freaking me out here, Kat. Heading to bed soon, but text me when you get this.*
>
> *7:25 a.m. (from Kelsey): I sent the hotel staff up to your room. They say you're not there. Where the hell are you, Kat? Are you okay?*
>
> *11:28 a.m. (from Kelsey): If you're not on that fucking flight, Kat, I'm calling the cops. I am SO worried. Call me!*

Kat looked at the time – 3:15. "Damn it!" she repeated, as her fingers danced across the screen.

Kat was unsure the phone even rang and had to move the phone away from her ear as Kelsey shouted, "Where are you?"

"I'm so sorry, Kels. I didn't mean to frighten you. I should have checked my phone, but I was so exhausted after we settled the contract that I put the thing on Do Not Disturb and fell asleep. I was on a walk when you tried to reach me this morning. It's a beautiful day, so I grabbed my personal phone and have just been wandering around the city, exploring."

"When was the last time you didn't check your work phone for 24 hours?" Kelsey demanded, obviously still angry over the fright Kat had caused.

"It's been too long, Kels. Way too long. Perhaps I just needed a little time away."

Kelsey said nothing.

"But I am really sorry to have caused you to worry. I'm heading to the airport in about 30 minutes. I'll be home tonight. You have a good weekend with the girls, and we can talk on Monday."

"Okay, Kat," Kels responded tentatively. "Are you sure you're alright?"

"I'm better than alright, Kels," Kat replied. Looking at Greg, who was watching her in amusement, she added, "Today, I feel amazing."

"Well, that was a close one," Kat said, as she hung up the call. "Another couple of hours, and Kelsey would have called out the National Guard."

Kat quickly gathered the last of her things and placed them in her bag. She looked for the paper she'd left on the desk, the one on which she'd left Greg's name and telephone number, but that, too, appeared to have been tidied by the room cleaner. *"A lot of good that note would have done me,"* Kat thought to herself, as he grinned at her.

"So we still have 15 minutes?" Greg asked, reaching his hand out to take hers.

"Maybe 20, depending on traffic."

"Then, come here," Greg encouraged, grabbing her wrist and pulling her toward him.

Kat nestled in beside him, resting her head on his chest. He kissed the top of her head.

"What are you thinking, Kat?"

"I'm thinking that I could lay here forever. I'm thinking that I am going to miss you so much. I'm marveling at the fact that I met you only two days ago because I'm having a hard time imagining waking up tomorrow without you.

These things just don't happen, Greg – at least, they don't happen to me." She rolled over and looked at him. "And what are you thinking?"

"We haven't known each other long, but we know each other well."

"Indeed."

They kissed, holding each other in a tight embrace, until the bell tower on the corner chimed 3:30. Kat rolled away, with a sigh.

"I think I am falling in love with you, Kat."

"I know," she smiled.

As the cab left the curb, Kat turned to watch Greg as he stood there waving. She watched until she could no longer see him, as if turning away would break the spell that so mysteriously tied them together.

Her phone lit up with a text.

3:05 p.m. (from Greg): Correction. I <u>am</u> definitely falling in love with you, Kat.

3:06 p.m. (to Greg): ... I know.

Chapter 13

The big house was quiet. It had felt lonely here since Drew moved to campus, but it felt particularly empty now, as Kat opened the front door and fumbled for the light switch in the darkness. She gathered the mail and set it and her keys on the hall table. She threw her jacket over a chair and poured herself a glass of wine.

Kat had not been able to get out of her head during the entire flight – reliving each moment of the last couple of days. She didn't know what to feel. She longed for him. She desired him. She had felt more alive with him than she had felt in the eight months since the accident. Truth be told, she felt more alive with him than she had during the last many years of her marriage. That thought confused her the most. She struggled with feeling overjoyed and completely and utterly guilt ridden.

Kat walked slowly through the house, opening closets and cabinets and examining shelves. Bennett was everywhere. His shoes were in the mudroom, along with sports equipment and old briefcases. His coffee cup sat beside the sink. His clothes still occupied half of her closet, the shirts lined up by color, the pants hung just so. Even his toothbrush – his toothbrush was still in the bathroom. Kat was startled by these discoveries. For months now, she had lived in their house as if nothing had changed. She'd gone about her days impervious to the specters surrounding her.

Tears cascaded over Kat's cheeks as she placed Bennett's toothbrush in the garbage can. Then, she tied her hair back and began. By the time Drew arrived the next evening, Kat had cleaned the house and taken several loads of clothing and gear to Goodwill. As with the polarity of the night before, Kat felt both emotionally and physically exhausted, yet refreshed and somehow lighter.

"Hey, kiddo," Kat said, as Drew came into the house. "How are you doing?"

Drew looked at her. "The better question is how are *you* doing?" he replied. "You look awful."

"Long week," she responded, rising to hug him.

Drew was a tall, lanky kid. Skinny, really. He had short dark hair that was slightly too long around the ears. The style looked a bit like a bowl cut, the type of cut he'd received as a small child, when he wore knickers and little blue canvas tennis shoes. His glasses were round, like those of the Harry Potter character. He had always been a good kid, but he had a concerned air about him. He was serious, too serious for a young man his age – a good student, reliable friend, conscientious son. But did he have any fun? Had he always been this way? He'd matured a lot in the last year.

"Sit and talk with me as I fix dinner," Kat urged. "Tell me everything about your week."

Kat reveled in the normalcy – the stories of his day-to-day life as a college student. Classes, campus, athletics, friends. After dinner, Drew excused himself to wash clothes and play video games in his room.

Kat turned off the lights and headed up to her bedroom. The starkness of the room surprised her, now that it was clean and had been emptied of much of its familiar contents. She curled up on the bed and covered herself with a blanket. As she reached for a book, her phone rang.

"I've missed you today," he said in a warm and familiar voice that seemed to wrap itself around her.

"I've missed you, too," Kat replied, shifting a bit, unsettled. She looked around pensively. It felt so odd to be talking to her intended lover while resting in the bed she had shared with her husband. She gathered the blanket around herself and walked downstairs.

"I spoke with Mitch and arranged to be in Minneapolis on Wednesday. I'm staying at a hotel downtown. I should be done with work by 5:30 and can meet you somewhere."

"I'm looking forward to seeing you."

"Me, too," Greg said quietly. "Will you stay with me?"

"Wednesday night?"

"Yes." He paused. "For starters."

"I would love to."

"Good," Greg replied, with what sounded like relief in his voice.

"Did you have any doubt that I would?" she asked.

"In fact, yes. I did." Greg paused. "When we parted yesterday, I told you . . ."

"You told me that you are falling in love with me," Kat interrupted. "And I responded, 'I know.' I do know, Greg. I'm sorry that my response was less than committal." Kat paused. "I simply needed to reacquaint myself with me. And now that I have, I can say, with certainty, that I am falling in love with you, too."

"I don't understand."

"That's okay. Just know, please, that I have thought about you all night and day, that I can't wait to see you, and that I will most certainly spend the night with you."

"I'm counting the days."

"As am I."

"Sleep well, sweet Kat."

"You, too, Greg. You, too."

Chapter 14

Kelsey was at her desk when Kat walked into the office on Monday. Kat placed a box of Godiva chocolate in front of her.

"Bribery will get you nowhere, Kat," Kelsey said grimly. "You scared the shit out of me last week. What in the world got into you?"

"I don't know, Kelsey," Kat began. "I guess I just needed some alone time." She paused and looked away. "I moved Bennett's things out of the house this weekend."

Kelsey stopped typing and looked up. She took a sip of coffee, as she pondered. "I hate to say it, Kat, but it's about time. Perhaps a day away was good for you after all."

Kat handed Kelsey the contract from Thursday. "The vote is tomorrow. Hopefully, the bargaining unit will ratify this thing, and we'll be done for another three years."

Kat went into her office and booted up her computer.

8:10 a.m. (to Kelsey): What is that stupid password again?

8:11 a.m. (from Kelsey): Drew1021!

8:11 a.m. (to Kelsey): Of course. LOL. How could I forget?

8:15 a.m. (to Kelsey): Hey, Kels. Can you please get me the number for Karen Greeley in HQ?

8:15 a.m. (from Kelsey): The Company's ethics officer?

8:16 a.m. (to Kelsey): Yes.

Kelsey came into the office, a sticky note with a number on it in her hand. "And, why, Kat, would you be AWOL on Friday and in need of an ethics officer on Monday?"

"I'm not *in need* of an ethics officer, Kelsey. I merely have a question I want to run by a friend."

"Sure you do," Kelsey replied sarcastically, as she passed Kat the sticky note.

Kat dialed the phone, unsure of exactly what she would say.
"Karen Greeley."
"Hi, Karen. It's Kat Anderson."
"Hi, Kat. Are you in Chicago this week?"
"No. I'll be in next week, but I wanted to talk with you before then."
"Okay. What's up?"
"Can I ask you to keep this confidential – so long as there's not an ethical reason that you would need to elevate our conversation?"
Karen hesitated.
Kat continued, "I am more than 99% sure that there is no conflict of interest, Karen, and I feel rather silly calling you, but I wanted to make sure."
"Okay, Kat. Go on."
"Well, I met a man."
"*God, that sounded sophomoric,*" Kat groaned, as she shifted uncomfortably in her seat. "He's not just any man. He's a significant officer with the International Brotherhood of Teamsters. We met during my negotiations in Memphis last week. Well, actually, we met in the hotel bar the night before."
"*This is only getting worse,*" Kat reflected. "*Why am I all tongue-tied and inarticulate?*"
"By the time we were together at the bargaining table, I had started to have feelings for this guy. We settled the contract."
"Did you disclose your relationship with this guy to the bargaining committees?" Karen asked, as Kat knew she would. She should.
"No," Kat admitted, adding, "but the fact is that he came in and the union accepted the offer we had put on the table the day before – no changes. And I hadn't met this guy at the time the offer was made. I didn't feel conflicted or that I needed to disclose that I had met Greg the night before because there really was no negotiation with *him*. He did call his boss, however, and disclosed that he had met me, prior to accepting the proposal."
"Let me think a bit more about this, Kat, but from what you have described, it does not strike me that there was a conflict of interest at play during your negotiations." A moment passed before Karen added, "Are you going to continue to see this guy?"
Kat paused. "Yes. I think so. I mean, I hope so. I plan to." Kat laughed nervously. "I'm sorry, Karen, I'm still trying to process what happened with this

guy. I feel a bit like a star-struck teenager when I'm around him. I'm too old to swoon."

Karen laughed. "So what's your go-forward plan?"

Kat was unsure how to respond.

"For the potential business conflict, Kat," Karen prompted.

"I won't negotiate any Teamsters contracts. I'll ask one of my team members to take over that work, so all Teamsters matters will funnel through her. Unless there's a crisis or strike at a Teamsters facility, it's a docket change I can make fairly easily."

"That sounds like a good approach to take," offered Karen. "Is there anything else?"

Kat thought for a moment. "No, I think that's it."

"Kat, as the Ethics Officer for the Company, I feel as if I must also remind you that there can be no pillow talk about anything going on in this organization."

Kat understood the reasons for the instruction, yet she couldn't help but feel a bit wounded by it. The fact that her integrity and commitment to confidentiality would be questioned was a little jarring for her, and she bristled. "Of course, Karen. I take my obligations to this Company very seriously. I have never shared confidential information, not with my husband with whom I had 'pillow talk,' as you call it, for many years, and I will not start doing so now." Kat didn't mean for that to sound defensive, but it obviously had.

"Kat, I'm not accusing you of anything. I trust you completely. And I'm happy for you that you are dating again."

"I'm not *dating*," Kat interrupted awkwardly.

"Then, how about this: I'm happy that you have found someone that you may care about?"

"Okay."

"But you also have to admit that it's a bit of a strange situation we find ourselves in where a senior executive at a multi-national company with many unionized facilities – an executive who is actually in charge of those union relationships in the U.S. – 'has feelings' for a union leader who has the power to impact our business in a very significant way."

"I am developing feelings for a man named Greg, with whom I don't talk shop, Karen."

"And all I'm saying is that it's best that you keep it that way."

"I will. On the other hand, Karen," Kat began, unsure if Karen would find what she was going to say even remotely funny (but really not caring at this point either way), "it would be pretty hard for the Union to argue that a

54

company has union animus if its senior-most executive responsible for industrial relations is sleeping with their boss."

"Touché, Kat. Touché."

Kat fumbled with the house key, balancing a bag of groceries and her computer bag on one arm and a cold gallon of milk in the other hand. Her phone rang. She stumbled inside, setting everything down on the mudroom floor. "Shit!" she exclaimed, as she ruffled through her purse to find it.

"Hello, sweet Kat. How are you tonight?" asked that now-familiar and wonderfully comforting voice.

"Hello to you," she responded.

"What are you doing?" he asked. "You sound a bit winded."

"I just stumbled in the door."

"I forget about the time difference. Do you want me to call you later?" he asked.

"No, this is fine," she assured him. "I'm happy to talk with you now, later, later yet, or all night long."

"Nice. How was your day?"

"It was okay," Kat responded. "A little odd."

"How so?"

"I reached out to the Company's Ethics Officer today."

"Why?" Greg sounded surprised and a little concerned.

"Because even though I was almost a hundred percent certain that nothing about our negotiations could be construed as a conflict of interest, I really felt that I needed to disclose that I had met you the night before the session. As you acknowledged when we were driving to Nashville, it just wouldn't do to be negotiating a contract with someone I am falling in love with."

Greg didn't say anything for a moment. "And what did your Ethics Officer say?" he asked.

"Well, that is the odd part. She was rather cool and guarded with me about the situation – as if she was suspicious of the relationship. Frankly, I was kind of surprised by that."

"I'm sure she was just doing her job, Kat," Greg noted, in a manner that Kat found was just a little too accommodating. "There is no conflict, Kat."

"I know that, Greg. Let's just be sure to keep it that way."

"Of course," he responded. "Frankly, work is not all that interesting in any event." He cleared his throat. "But speaking of work, Kat."

"Yes?"

"Next weekend, there is a significant in-person meeting in D.C. I will be with my leadership team all day on Friday. There is a dinner with spouses and significant others on Friday night and then a formal dance – the International Ball – on Saturday night. I would really like you to come to both, if you're up for it. I'll be completely tied up all day Friday, until dinner, but we'd have some time together on Saturday, and I'd love to have you with me for the dance. It's always a bit awkward to dance alone."

"I'm guessing, my friend, that you never dance alone. I have done my research, remember? It strikes me that you're likely the belle of the ball. 'One of D.C.'s most eligible bachelors,' as I recall one article stating."

"Well, I don't know about that," he responded coyly, "but I really would like you to join me for those events, if you're willing."

Kat hesitated briefly before asking, "Is Christian Christopher going to be there?"

"Yes. He's a member of my extended leadership team."

"Well, that's likely to be a shit show, don't you think? How is he going to react to me coming to this thing as your 'plus one'?"

"You leave Christian Christopher to me, Kat. It will be fine."

"Hmmm."

"Kat?"

"Do you suppose Lilly would be willing to help me with the weekend attire?"

Greg laughed, "I'm sure she'd be thrilled to do that. Does that mean you'll come?"

"I've just checked my calendar, and it looks as if I'm in Chicago for the first part of the week. I was planning to come back home on Friday, but I'll look at changing my flight to D.C. instead."

"Wonderful!"

"I'm counting the hours until our dinner on Wednesday," Kat added. "I got us a 7:00 reservation at a cute little place downtown. Really nice food. Interesting flavors and a vibrant atmosphere. It's in the North Loop of Minneapolis. It has good energy, and it's a short walk from your hotel if you're up for it. The weather's supposed to be decent."

"Sounds good. Perhaps we can meet up for a drink beforehand? I don't want to waste a minute that I can spend with you. I'll text you when I'm nearly done with the day."

"I'll be ready."

"And, Kat?"

"Yes?"

"You're still planning to stay with me?"

"I am."

"I'm glad. Sleep well, sweet Kat."

"You, too, Greg. Lovely dreams."

"No doubt."

Kat sat on a wooden stool by the counter. She was suddenly exhausted. What was happening here? What was happening to her? She shook her head and brushed her hair out of her face and behind her ear. She forced herself to focus solely on her breathing for several minutes. Then she went to collect her groceries.

Chapter 15

Kat took a break from work on Tuesday morning and closed the door to her office. It was about an hour before the store would open and likely a good time to catch Lilly before her exhilarating day of sparkling customer service began.

"Hello, Hon!" Lilly answered the phone, with a flourish.

"Hi, Lilly. It's Kat Anderson."

"I thought so, Kat, given the 612 area code and all," Lilly said, jovially. "I can't say that I get too many calls from up that way."

"I'm hoping you can help me, Lilly."

"The Ball?"

"You know?"

"Well, yes. I spoke with Greg over the weekend. I couldn't help myself. I needed to hear how the rest of the week had gone. Greg's like a brother to me, and it's been a really long time since he brought a woman over. In fact, come to think of it, I don't believe he's ever had a woman over to our place – well, not since Annie, anyway, and that's been a lifetime ago. Oh, don't get me wrong, Kat, he's dated. On a handful of occasions, he's even had more than a couple dates with the same woman. But this is different. He's different. He's completely vulnerable where you're concerned, Kat. I can tell. He seems so, well, happy. And 'happy' is not a term I'd normally use to describe Greg. Thoughtful. Introspective. Kind. Caring. All of those, yes. But happy? Not *happy*.

"Oh, my. I'm rambling," Lilly continued. "I think the question was actually 'how did I know about the ball?' He said he was going to ask you. That, too, is a big step, Kat. Greg is a very private person. He generally keeps his personal life and his work life completely separated. That's, perhaps, why there's so much speculation about him in those gossip pages. He's quite mysterious to people who don't know him."

"You know him very well, don't you, Lilly?"

"Yes, I do. Like I said, Kat, he's sort of like my older brother. Of course, given Greg's job and the role that he plays with the Union, he has an amazing number of acquaintances. But he has a small number of close friends, and to us, he's family – just as Martha and her kids are family and Mitch and his brood are family. Greg is very attached to the people he loves."

"He is a very special man."

"He is. And, it's obvious to me that he believes you are a very special woman, Kat. He's actually giddy when he talks about you. A little obnoxious really," she teased. "So can I help you with your weekend attire?"

"Would you, Lilly?"

"Of course. I've already selected a few things that I think would work perfectly. Trust me. I'll have them shipped to Greg's place in D.C. You can simply send back the ones that don't work."

3:15 p.m. (to Drew): Hey, kiddo. Just checking in to see how your week is going.

3:36 p.m. (from Drew): Hi, Mom. All good. Just found out I don't have class on Th or F. Night out with the high school guys. Planning to walk home to the house and sleep there. K?

Kat sighed.

3:37 p.m. (to Drew): Tomorrow? Wednesday?

3:37 p.m. (from Drew): Yep!

3:48 p.m. (to Drew): K. I have a dinner meeting downtown. It may go late. Should be home by . . . 11:00.

Kat called Greg as soon as she got home from work. She settled into the couch and pulled a quilt around herself.

"Hi, there," he answered.

"Well, hello, handsome."

Kat stalled for a bit, chattering about her day and asking about his. As the chatter slowed, she took a deep breath. "I have some good news and some bad news," she offered.

"Good news first."

"I cannot wait to have dinner with you tomorrow night and will be en route to downtown long before you finish your day, so just text me when you're done, and I'll meet you somewhere as soon as you can get away."

"Perfect. And the bad news?"

"Drew's coming to the house tomorrow night. It was totally unexpected. I won't be able to stay overnight with you. I'm sorry. I don't know how I'd explain being out all night to my 19-year-old son."

"I'm guessing that at 19, he'd likely understand what we were doing."

"Yes, I'm sure that that is the case. However, I'd rather that his initial introduction to you not be in the context of you defiling his mother."

Greg actually snorted. "Kat, you're hilarious – and a tad dramatic. I totally understand."

"Really?"

"Really. I'd rather be introduced to Drew and to Anthony in a little more traditional way as well, when it's time."

Kat sighed in relief. "Thank you for understanding. I'm really looking forward to dinner, but I'm so disappointed about the rest of the night. It will be exceedingly difficult to have you a dozen miles away and not to be with you."

"Well, you'll be in D.C. the following weekend."

"Indeed, I will. And, Greg?"

"Yes."

"Prepare to be defiled."

He laughed a gentle, sustaining laugh. "I will."

"I'll see you tomorrow."

Chapter 16

Kat was distracted all afternoon. At one point, Kelsey, who had been challenged to keep Kat on task, asked Kat if she understood that it took less time to do things right the first time than to do them over.

"Being snarky isn't going to get the work done, Kels," Kat responded, as she flipped through and attempted to triage a growing cadre of unanswered email.

"That may be true, Kat, but daydreaming isn't going to do it either."

"Fair enough, Kels. I'm just a little lost in thought today." Kat pivoted, "Are all of my travel plans in place for next week's trip to headquarters?"

"They are. Your itinerary is attached to the calendar invite. Do you need me to print anything for you?"

"No. As long as I have it on my phone, I'm fine." Kat twisted her hair nervously around her finger. "Hey, Kelsey, how difficult would it be to change my return flight?"

"I could do that. No problem. What time do you want to return?"

"I'm actually hoping to fly to Washington, D.C., on Friday, rather than coming straight home. I'm thinking about meeting up with friends there for the weekend. Of course, I'll pick up any additional expenses, including any charges or change fees, on my personal account. Do you think you could take a look at potential flights for me, just in case a plan comes together?"

"Sure. Chicago to D.C. National on Friday morning and returning from D.C. National to MSP on Sunday night?"

"Sounds good."

"I'm on it. Do you need a hotel as well?"

Kat smiled wistfully, "No. I'm planning to bunk at their place."

Kat read the document in front of her for what seemed like the fifth time. Nothing was clicking. She simply could not concentrate. She closed down her computer and placed it in her bag. While she would not be opening the laptop again tonight, it would never do to leave it at the office. Kat took her computer home every night; not doing so would definitely be cause for suspicion. Kat stepped out to Kelsey's desk. "I'm going to work remotely for a bit. Maybe I'm coming down with something," she said.

"Maybe," Kelsey responded, seemingly unconvinced. "Have a good evening, Kat. Be sure to get some rest."

Kat hurried to her car. Rush hour would just be starting on I-94. It likely would take her twenty or more minutes to get downtown. Adele blared through the speakers, and Kat sang loudly as she drove, tapping her fingers on the steering wheel.

She parked the car in a lot near the restaurant and strolled toward the city center. She was early, but delightfully so. The walk and the warming spring air mellowed her. It was a beautiful late April evening in Minneapolis. She wandered and thought, taking in all of the sights, sounds, and smells of the city – in through her skin; in through her hair; in through her breath and her entire being. She was remarkably present. Present in the moment; present in her life. And it felt good.

5:02 p.m. (from Greg): Just finished up. Heading to the shower. Meet me at the hotel, and we'll walk from here? Room 215.

5:02 p.m. (to Greg): On my way. 10 minutes or so. See you soon!

No sooner had Kat gotten to the door, than Greg opened it. His hair was wet and tousled. His shirt was partially buttoned, and his feet were bare. Reaching out and grabbing Kat's arms, he drew her into the room, leaned her against the wall, and kissed her. She wrapped her arms around his neck and pulled him closer. They melted into each other's embrace. The energy and passion were palpable. When at long last Kat broke away and leaned her head back, Greg ran his finger slowly and lightly behind her ear, down her neck, and across her chest.

"I've missed you," he whispered. The weight of his body pressed against hers, pinning her gently to the wall.

"I've missed you, too," Kat replied, "more than you know." She lowered her arms from his neck and began buttoning his shirt.

"I guess this means we're still going out?" he asked through a cockeyed grin, as he watched Kat button his shirt.

"I think we should. If we do this much longer, I won't be going home tonight."

"Promises, promises," he replied, sweeping the hair away from her shoulder and brushing her neck with his lips.

Greg took a step back and motioned for Kat to take a seat on the bed, as he dug through his bag for his socks. She watched him rummage, visually tracing his muscles through his shirt. She thought about what it would be like to make love to him – this man whom she'd known for such a short time and yet felt like she knew so well. He sat down on the desk chair and pulled on his shoes. He was nearly dressed. Kat leaned back and took in the entire scene.

"You are breathtakingly gorgeous," she said, surprising herself with her unbridled candor.

He smiled. Then he rose and extended a hand to Kat. As he helped her up, he leaned in, once again, and kissed her deeply, taking her bottom lip in his and tugging it gently as he moved away.

"We'd better go," he whispered.

"We should," she responded with a sigh.

They grabbed a drink at a local pub and then walked along the river, holding hands and catching up. Despite the fact that they had spoken every night since they'd been together in Memphis, there seemed so much to share – big and small details of their days apart, along with observations about the city, the river, the bridges, the skyline, and the waning sunshine. Simply talking was a joy, and it was nearly 7:00 when they first checked the time. Kat called the restaurant to let them know that they were on their way.

The dinner conversation was equally absorbing – so much so that Kat failed to notice a man approaching until he was at the table. Kat looked up to find Bennett's former law partner, Tom McCormick, standing over her.

"Tom!" Kat exclaimed, as she pushed her chair away from the table and stood to hug him. "It's so nice to see you."

"It's really nice to see you, too, Kat," Tom replied, as he leaned in and kissed her cheek. "It's been way too long."

"It has been."

"I don't mean to interrupt you, but I saw you from across the restaurant and wanted to stop by and say hello."

Kat glanced down and met Greg's eyes.

"Tom, I'd like you to meet my," Kat paused awkwardly, "my friend, Greg." Greg rose to his feet and shook Tom's hand.

"Greg is here from D.C., so we met up for dinner," Kat interjected. She felt oddly uncomfortable. Perhaps if she'd seen Tom coming, she would have been better prepared to introduce her dead husband's best friend to her soon-to-be lover in a manner that did not seem so incongruent and odd.

As the three stood there smiling at each other, Tom broke the uncomfortable silence. "Well, as I said, I don't want to interrupt you. You look great, Kat. Please say hi to the boys for me, and let's get together sometime soon. Are you still commuting back and forth to Chicago?"

"I am."

"Well, please let me know the next time you are back in town and have time to grab lunch."

"I will. Take care, Tom."

"You, too, Kat. It was nice to meet you, Greg."

"It was nice to meet you as well," Greg replied, as he resumed his seat. Greg took some time to arrange the napkin on his lap before raising his head and looking at Kat. She was watching Tom as he returned to his table. She sat back down and met Greg's gaze.

"Are you okay, Kat?" he asked, with a tinge of sadness in his voice. "That introduction seemed, well, rather painful for you."

"I'm sorry," she sighed, reaching out to touch his hand. "He surprised me. Of course, it shouldn't have surprised me that I would know someone here. I often run into people I know in venues in and around the Twin Cities. I've lived and worked here most of my life, after all. But there was something about meeting Tom here that caught me off guard. Greg, Tom was Bennett's law partner and one of his closest friends, if not his best friend. I somehow wasn't ready for how I would feel when my old life and my current life intersected."

"I understand, Kat," Greg assured her, squeezing her fingers and stroking her thumb. "I do."

"While we're in D.C., let's make a plan for you to meet the boys." Seeing Tom had been too close a call. "If the boys are going to learn of this relationship, it should be from me, not from some friend or a chance encounter on the street or in a restaurant."

"I would like that, Kat," Greg replied softly. Finishing his wine, Greg motioned for the check. When the server returned with the receipt, Greg asked him to take a photo of him and Kat at the table. "Photo of the day?" he asked Kat.

"Absolutely," she replied. "It's been a wonderful evening, filled with so many things for which to be grateful."

Greg walked Kat to her car, and she drove him back to the hotel. She opened her window as he came around, and he leaned in to give her one last kiss for the evening. "It's like you're leaving me at the ice machine," he smiled.

"I love you, Greg Bodin."

"I know," he replied.

Chapter 17

Drew was waiting up for Kat when she got home. He was curled up on the couch, reading a book.

"Nice time with the guys tonight?" she asked, as she took off her jacket and hung it on a counter stool.

"Ya. There were just a few of us, but it was good to get together," he replied, as he rose from the couch and walked toward the kitchen.

"You're home rather early, aren't you, particularly given that you don't have class tomorrow?"

"We decided to just have dinner and call it a night. That's fine with me. I'm exhausted from the week and looking forward to getting a good night's sleep tonight."

"Well, I'm ready to turn in too." Kat gave Drew a hug. "Sleep well, kiddo," she said, as she turned to head up the stairs.

"Mom?"

"Yes, Drew?"

"When did you clean out your closet?" Drew asked, with a slight tremor in his voice. "I realized I didn't have a clean shirt and went in to borrow one of Dad's."

Kat turned back toward him and looked at his dear face, searching to see what emotions she would find there. "I cleaned it out last weekend, Drew."

"Why?" he asked, in a quiet pitch well above his normal baritone.

Kat put her hand on Drew's shoulder. "It was time, Drew. It was just time. It's been really hard to come to grips with the fact that your dad is gone, but I needed to do that in order to live in the moment and to look toward the future. I can't continue to live in the past. It's not healthy."

Drew shrugged, as tears welled up in his brilliantly blue eyes. "I get it," he said.

"I saved some of the most special things," Kat offered. "I folded them up and put them in a plastic tub for you and Anthony to go through when you have a chance."

"Thanks," Drew said, wiping a tear from his cheek.

Kat reached out, and Drew leaned into her. They held each other tightly, as he cried quietly on her shoulder.

After some time, he whispered, "I guess we all need to move on."

"Yes, my sweet boy, I think we do."

Kat brushed tears from her own cheeks. "Do you want some cake?" she asked.

"Sure," Drew replied. He sat on a stool by the island as Kat fixed them each a plate and set one in front of him.

"Mom?" Drew asked tentatively.

"Yes, babe?" Kat responded, as she opened the refrigerator to grab the milk.

"Who is the man in the photos?"

Kat caught her breath. Her chest hurt. She set the milk on the counter and steadied herself. "What photos, Drew?"

Drew silently poured the milk into two glasses.

"What photos are you talking about, Drew?" Kat pressed.

"The photos of the day," he responded at last. "You and I share a Google account, remember? I set that account up for you when you first started your photo-of-the-day project. From time to time I check it to see how you're doing, what you're thinking, what you are grateful for, whether you're feeling hopeful."

Kat gasped. "Oh, Drew. I am so sorry, kiddo. You don't need to worry about me. You don't need to check in on me. I am okay, Drew. I am coming back to life. I am finding joy again." She placed her forehead against his.

"You don't have to tell me about him if you don't want to," Drew began. "It's really none of my business. I just thought . . ."

"It's absolutely your business, Drew, and I'm happy to talk about him. I'm just not sure what to say or where to start. His name is Greg Bodin. He is a wonderful man. He is kind and thoughtful, caring and patient. He's smart and funny, and he makes me laugh. I met him only a short time ago, when I was in Memphis for work, but I feel like I have known him for much longer. And I hope to continue to get to know him better and to spend time with him."

"Like you did tonight?" Drew asked.

"Yes, like I did tonight, Drew. Greg came to town to work – but mainly to have dinner with me."

"So you really like this guy?" Drew asked quietly.

"I do. I really like this guy, and I'm anxious for you to meet him."

"Why didn't you tell me about him?"

"I was trying to figure it out myself. I haven't so much as looked at another man since your dad died, Drew. I certainly haven't dated. And I wasn't looking to date." Drew nodded his head. "My feelings for Greg took me by complete surprise. I didn't know what hit me. And until I was sure, I didn't think that it was necessarily the best parenting move to get you and Anthony all mixed up in my confusion."

"I understand," Drew nodded again. "I really do. It's just that I didn't think we kept secrets from each other."

"We don't," Kat agreed.

"And, frankly, it just feels weird to know that you care so much about someone I have never met and don't know at all. It's like I'm not part of some significant part of your life."

"Oh, kiddo. I love you so very much. You're not just a part of my life. You and your brother, you *are* my life." Kat paused. "Give me a minute?" she asked.

"Okay."

Kat grabbed her purse, quickly climbed the steps to her bedroom, and closed the door. When she came back downstairs, she had her keys with her. "Do you want to meet him now?" she asked.

"It's 11:30."

"And?"

"And . . . sure. Okay then," Drew replied.

Greg ushered them into his room with that smile that lit up everything around him. "It's so nice to meet you, Drew," he welcomed warmly, directing them to chairs that he'd placed alongside the bed. "I have heard a lot about you. Your mom talks about you all the time." Greg went to the minibar and offered each of them a bottle of water before seating himself on the bed facing them.

"That's nice," Drew replied. "She hasn't said anything about you," he noted, and then caught himself, "until tonight. Now she won't shut up about you as well." Drew looked pained. Kat understood the awkwardness and felt for him. Greg did, too.

"Well that's good to hear, Drew," Greg reassured him, with a little laugh. "Your mom means a lot to me."

Greg was charming and completely comfortable with the young man. He asked Drew questions about his interests, his friend, and his hobbies. Greg told Drew about his work, his home in Memphis, his love of horses and dogs. They spent the next hour talking and getting to know one another. Kat sat, saying very little as she watched her precious child warm to this man who had stolen her heart.

At a little after 1:00 a.m., Kat yawned. Greg reached out and touched her hand. He turned to Drew. "Now I think that it's time for you to get your mom home. She's had a long day, and it's been a bit of an emotional night. I suspect you can both use some sleep."

Drew reached out his hand, and Kat placed the keys on his open palm.

"When are you back in town, Greg?" Drew asked.

"Well, your mom's coming out to see me next weekend, Drew," Greg replied. Kat looked quizzically at him. "Are you okay with that?"

Kat waited.

"Yes. I am," Drew responded.

"I'm really glad about that," said Greg. "I am sure your mom agrees that there are no secrets."

Kat nodded.

Greg went on, "But I'm hoping to come back sometime soon after that. And when you get a break from school, I'd really like to have you and your mom visit me in Memphis. With everything you've said about your love of hiking, fishing, and the like, I think you'd really enjoy the reserve near my home there."

Greg shook Drew's hand. He gave Kat a quick hug and a kiss on the forehead. "Thank you for coming here tonight. I am so happy to have met you, Drew."

2:05 a.m. (to Greg): You are amazing.

2:05 a.m. (from Greg): Tonight was my sincere pleasure. He's a great kid. Sleep well, sweet Kat.

Chapter 18

Drew had dinner waiting for Kat when she got home from work the next day.

"What a nice surprise!" she exclaimed as she walked into the kitchen. "Whatever you've made smells delicious."

After dinner, Kat and Drew FaceTimed Anthony and told him about Greg. Drew shared all of the details of the night before, and Kat promised Anthony that as soon as she and Greg could arrange it, they would visit him at UVA, so Anthony could meet Greg, too.

Kat felt so much more settled, now that the boys were aware of her relationship.

As she and Drew said goodnight to Anthony, she pulled out her cell phone. "Photo of the day with the three of us?" she asked, arranging the iPad on the couch behind them. She smiled as the photo appeared on the screen. "I'm so grateful to be your mother!"

When they'd closed the iPad, Kat looked at Drew. "I know we're all about this 'no secrets thing,' kiddo," she started. "But I've been thinking that I'd really like to have my own photo account. While I'm certainly into transparency, I feel a little weird that you're getting all of my pictures. A mom needs at least a little bit of privacy, don't you think?"

"Give me your phone," he said. As Kat went about cleaning the dinner dishes, Drew went to work on her account. "You have both your work and home accounts on here, right?" he asked.

"Yes, I believe so, but you shouldn't mess with the work part."

"I didn't need to. I've got your photo account all set up. But you're obviously not too technically inclined. It looks like your work account has had several attempts at access. It's a little messed up. You may want to have your IT guys take a look at it."

"You know I'm terrible with passwords," she smiled.

"I'd say you're pretty incompetent with all of it," he replied, handing her back her device.

"Hey! At least I take great photos," she responded triumphantly. "And, if you're really good, I'll send you one once in a while," she smiled.

"At least you'll try," he retorted, with a grin.

The week at headquarters flew by. When Kat was in Chicago, she tended to work whenever she wasn't sleeping, and this week was no exception. She went from one meeting to another, with little or no breaks in between and had dinner meetings that went well into the night. Before Kat knew it, it was Friday, and she was deplaning in D.C.

Kat pulled Greg's address from her contacts and summoned a cab. Greg's apartment was in a stately old building just off of E Street NW, near Ford's Theatre. She presented herself to the doorman inside. He was a stately older gentleman, as distinguished as the building itself. "You must be Kat Anderson," he welcomed, smiling warmly and extending his hand. "Mr. Bodin asked me to escort you to his condo. I've also called for a driver who will bring you to the restaurant this evening. The driver will arrive here at 6:45. Is there anything you need before I take your bag and show you upstairs?"

"No. Thank you," Kat replied. "That's very kind. I appreciate the fact that you've lined up a driver. I was a little unsure where I was going after this."

The doorman showed Kat to the condo and, after opening the door and placing her bag inside, he handed her the key. "Enjoy your afternoon, miss," he said earnestly. "Please do not hesitate to give me a call or to stop by if there is anything you need." He passed her a card with his number on it.

As she closed the door, Kat turned and looked around. This place could not have been more different from Greg's home in Tennessee. The walls were all white, with little adornment. The one bookshelf that stood in the otherwise sterile living room was filled with work texts, philosophy, and history tomes. There were no photos, save for the one of Kat and Greg by the lake. It stood out as the bit of warmth and hominess in an otherwise museum-quality space. Windows bedecked the entire front of the living area. The view of the city was amazing and expansive. Kat could only imagine what it would look like at night – a veritable sea of lights. Greg had left a bottle of Perrier, a large bouquet of tulips, and a card on the kitchen table. Kat opened the envelope and removed the note:

My Dearest Kat,

Welcome to my home away from home. I am so happy you're here. Please make yourself comfortable.

Lilly sent what appears (at least to me) to be an entire shop of dresses. They are hanging in the bedroom closet.

If you're in early enough, you might enjoy a walk around the neighborhood. It's a great way to spend an afternoon. Zach, the kind man at the door, can give you some suggestions.

I cannot wait to see you this evening!

With love and my utmost respect & admiration,

Greg

Kat located a glass in the cupboard and poured herself some water. She sipped it as she explored the rest of the apartment– a quaint formal dining space, an office, a bathroom. A hallway opened into a large master bedroom with ensuite. Similar to the rest of the apartment, the walls of the bedroom were stunningly white. The furniture was oversized and a masculine grey color. The only thing that gave the room away as a place where someone lived or slept or dreamed was a colorful, handmade quilt that adorned the king-sized bed in the middle of the space. Kat hesitantly approached the bed – the bed that she would share with Greg that night. She ran her hand over the quilt, admiring the stitching and the love and work that had gone into the piecing and quilting. She suspected that it was a family heirloom, perhaps crafted by Greg's mother or grandmother.

The bathroom was nothing short of luxurious. Big windows allowed natural light to flood the beautifully tiled space. There was a large steam shower along the wall and a clawfoot bathtub in the corner from which one could relax and enjoy the view out the windows. A small vase filled with tulips rested on the vanity.

Kat set her water glass down by the vase and returned to the bedroom. She opened the closet and removed the dresses, placing them side-by-side on the bed. There were eight in all – 4 dinner dresses and 4 gowns. They were all beautiful. Lilly also had packed an assortment of jewelry that had been carefully selected to compliment the dresses. Kat placed that parcel on the bedside table and slipped off her traveling clothes. She tried on each combination and selected a simple navy blue dress with a sweetheart neckline for dinner – eloquent, yet understated. It would go well with the black patent heels she had packed. The gown she really loved was fire engine red with a plunging back. There was nothing understated about it. *"Is it too bold?"* she wondered. She could decide on that tomorrow.

Kat rehung the dresses and stowed them back in the closet. She put her clothes back on and returned to the living room, where she perched on the edge of the sofa and composed a quick text to Lilly:

1:17 p.m. (to Lilly): The dresses R amazing!

1:20 p.m. (from Lilly): I am so glad you like them! What did you decide?

1:20 p.m. (to Lilly): The navy for this evening.

1:20 p.m. (from Lilly): Very Katherine Hepburn. ☺

1:21 p.m. (to Lilly): Toying with the fire engine red for tomorrow. 2 over the top?

1:22 p.m. (from Lilly): My absolute fav! Not 2 much. Gorgeous!

1:22 p.m. (to Lilly): We'll C. ☺

1:23 p.m. (to Lilly): Thx for everything, Lilly!

1:24 p.m. (from Lilly): U R so welcome! Enjoy your weekend! Hugs & love 2 you and Greg!

Kat spent the afternoon walking. The exercise quieted her and cleared her mind. At 5:00, she returned to Greg's apartment and began to ready herself for the evening.

Chapter 19

"I feel badly for Greg," Susan Thorton whispered to her husband Mitch. "He's like a caged cat. Look how nervous he is."

"He's fine, Sue. He just wants this evening to go well," Mitch responded in a quiet voice. "He really cares about this woman."

"Well, I hope she's worth it," Susan responded, glancing back in Greg's direction. "This is painful to watch."

Mitch smiled and nodded in agreement. He knew his old friend well – perhaps better than anyone else – and Greg was behaving oddly. But why wouldn't he be anxious? Greg had never brought a woman to a work event. Never. And this was not just any work event. The International's leadership was present in this place, and his own leadership team was all seated at this table. Moreover, Mitch completely understood the tension that this woman was likely to engender with Christian Christopher. He recalled the 5:00 a.m. call he had received from Greg a few weeks earlier, when Greg had explained the entire situation – the sudden demand from Christian that Greg join what should have been a routine bargaining session in Memphis; Greg's chance meeting with Kat Anderson at the hotel; his thorough review of the contract terms and bargaining history; and his request that Mitch review and approve the last contract offer to avoid any potential conflict that Greg might have, given that he was "very likely falling in love with the counterparty." For the entire time that Mitch had known Greg, Greg had never "fallen in love" with anyone. Of course, Mitch knew about Annie and the history there, but that was, what, some twenty-odd years earlier? Wow. Was it that long ago already?

Mitch grabbed his old friend firmly by the shoulder. "How are you holding up?" he asked.

"I'm fine," Greg responded and smiled reassuringly. "In fact, I'm better than fine, Mitch. I can't wait for you to meet her."

Greg had planned the evening so that everyone was assembled before Kat arrived. He had thought that it might be quicker, easier, and less disruptive if he only needed to introduce her once to everyone gathered. He also had thought that Christian's reaction might be more subdued with all of his peers around him. He was now questioning both of those assumptions.

Theirs was a rectangular table, covered with white linen. Along a line running down the middle of the table ran a string of tea lights in crystal candleholders and bud vases teeming with flowers and greenery. Greg sat at the head of the table, an empty chair to his right where Kat would sit when she arrived. Next to her, Greg had placed Susan and Mitch as a warm and friendly buffer between Kat and the others. Brandy Christopher and Christian were seated to Greg's left, with Christian seated directly across from Mitch – best positioned for Mitch to keep an eye on him.

Brandy was a sweet woman who rarely spoke. *"She may not be allowed to do so,"* Greg thought, as he glanced in her direction. When Brandy did speak, her voice was a full octave higher than one would have expected, and she had a nervous giggle that made her seem far younger and more immature than her nearly 40 years. From what Greg could tell, Brandy didn't get out of the house much. He'd heard that she spent most of her time watching television and playing video games with her sons.

There was a time, about a year earlier, when the office was in need of an interim office manager. Christian had insisted that Brandy would be a perfect fit for the role. She lasted about a week. She was a complete train wreck as an administrator. Her typing and organizational skills were almost non-existent; her voice grated on everyone who called; and she seemed utterly challenged by email. The only thing she appeared to do well was to serve as a distraction for every man who came into the place. For as long as Greg had known Brandy, her provocative outfits had accentuated her substantial breasts. Tonight was no exception. Her cotton candy pink dress had a scoop neckline that exposed a sizeable amount of cleavage. Her fingernails were painted the same cotton candy color, and she wore a ring on every finger.

The table rounded out with four other couples: Rob and Kayla Danielson, Dan and Melanie Washington, Paul and Sally Holland, and Jim and Terri Sebastian. Greg had given Kat a short briefing on each of them. Rob and Kayla had three daughters, all of whom Kayla homeschooled. Rob was a bit of a gun-toting right-winger, but conversations around the dinner table generally veered away from American politics and Second Amendment rights. Dan and Melanie were the youngest of the group. They didn't yet have children, although Melanie talked about children incessantly. Melanie was finishing her Master's Degree, and Dan was all about the work. Other than Christian, of course, Dan was the most likely dinner companion to be concerned about Kat's employment. And Jim and Terri Sebastian. Jim was an enthusiastic fisherman. Their home was filled with mounted catch. Terri was a soccer mom – totally dedicated to their twin boys, who were juniors in high school this year. They'd all known each other for some years and were chattering amongst themselves.

Kayla motioned to Greg to get his attention. "So I understand you have a date for this event, Greg?" she asked. "Hearts will be breaking across the beltway tonight."

"I'm flattered, Kayla," Greg responded, "but I do think the hearts of D.C. will be absolutely fine," he smiled. "Yes, I do have a date tonight, and I'm really glad she was able to come."

"So she's from out of town?"

"Yes. She flew in this morning. I haven't had a chance to see her since she arrived."

"Tell us about her," Kayla pressed.

"Actually, I believe I just received a text from her." Greg slid his phone out of his jacket pocket. "Yes. She's about 2 minutes out. I'll go ahead and let her introduce herself when she comes in. Pardon me," Greg said, as he placed his napkin on the table in front of him. He quickly excused himself from the table and hurried outside to wait for Kat to arrive.

No sooner had Greg left than the talk of the table turned to this mystery woman with whom Greg was so taken.

"Who is she?"

"How long have they known each other?"

"Where is she from?"

"Is she planning to move here?"

"Was anyone else beginning to think that he didn't like women?"

The questions were primarily directed to Mitch, who simply responded with a smile and a shrug. It seemed a bit ridiculous to him that so much attention could be focused on one little date. But, then again, this wasn't just one little date. This was Greg Bodin's date. And, well, Greg Bodin *didn't date*.

As Kat emerged from the car, Greg grabbed her in both arms, lifting her to the curb and literally spinning her around in an embrace.

"Whoa, cowboy!" Kat exclaimed, laughing.

"I've missed you!" he retorted, happily.

Greg tipped the driver and returned to Kat. "You are stunning," he said, looking her up and down.

"Very Katherine Hepburn," Kat remarked.

"And that, my dear, sounds like a Lilly line." He smiled.

Greg took Kat's elbow and directed her away from the door and the windows to the very edge of the building. He gently placed his behind her neck, under her hair, pulled her close, and kissed her. Kat put her hand on his shoulder and could feel the tension in his muscles dissipate as they stood there.

"I've really missed you," he whispered, releasing the back of her neck and running his hand along the expanse of her sweetheart neckline.

"Nervous?" Kat asked.

"No. You're here now. We're together." He smiled. "Besides," he added, "Christian is inside. And there is a throng of people waiting to dissect our every word and move. Why would I be nervous? What can possibly go wrong?"

Kat poked him in the ribs with her index finger. "Listen here, Brother Bodin," she chided playfully. "Why would we want this to be a 'normal' experience? Stick with me. This could be 'amazing.'"

Greg sighed.

"Okay. Let's do this," he said, as he followed Kat toward the restaurant.

"I've got your back," she said, as she opened the door and stepped confidently into the room.

Chapter 20

Everyone at the table pretended not to watch Kat and Greg as they approached – everyone, that is, except Christian Christopher, who stared, mouth agape, as his color flushed from milky white to pink to blotchy red. The intensity of Christian's glare took Greg by surprise and sent a slight shudder through his shoulders. But Kat ignored it, as she walked briskly toward the assembled group.

Greg motioned Kat toward her open chair. She did not sit. Rather, she placed her clutch on the seat and proceeded to work her way around the table, introducing herself to each person individually, shaking hands, exchanging smiles and greetings, and making small talk about the trip, the weather, the city. She poked a little playful fun at Greg's nervousness, to which others around the table reciprocated with warm quips of their own. When it was her turn to greet Christian, Kat smiled and placed her hand on his arm. "It's good to see you again, Christian. In a different setting, I am hoping we can be friends," she offered. "I know how much you and the others around the table mean to Greg."

"I don't know about friends," Christian responded sharply under his breath, so others could not hear, "but I do suspect we can be coldly civil if necessary."

"Well, then that will have to do," Kat remarked cheerfully, never breaking eye contact with him, refusing to be intimidated by the locking nature of his glare.

Brushing by Christian, Kat took Brandy's hand in hers. "And you must be Brandy?" Kat exclaimed in a warm, familiar way. "I love your dress. It looks absolutely beautiful on you. And how did you get your nails to match so wonderfully?"

Brandy looked down at her hands. "Thank you," she squeaked.

Kat smiled. "Greg tells me that you're a lot of fun to talk with. I hope we have a chance to visit later on this evening."

"That would be nice," Brandy smiled. "Greg is very, very sweet." Christian had sat back down and was now tugging on Brandy's sleeve.

"I'm sorry," said Kat to the table, "I'm afraid I'm interrupting the happy hour. I'll take my seat now." But not before approaching Greg, who was still standing at the head of the table, and brushing her lips against his. This small, but very intentional, public display of affection was her coup de grace – a silent statement that she was here with him, intended to be a part of this assembly, and wasn't going anywhere any time soon.

Mitch grinned and gave Susan's knee a quick squeeze. *"Oh, this one is worthy,"* he thought. She could hold her own. He liked her immediately.

Kat ordered a glass of wine, as the others continued their happy hour and resumed their conversation. Greg placed his hand on hers and winked. He was obviously pleased about the first impressions. "We haven't had a chance to talk about the day," he said. "Did you find the place okay? Were you able to get a walk in?"

"No problems," she responded. "Zach was so helpful. Your place is lovely, Greg. It's very different than your home in Tennessee."

"A bit sterile, isn't it? I'm afraid that it still feels like a place I live while I'm working. It doesn't feel like home."

"The view is great. I'll be anxious to see it at night."

"I'm also anxious to get you back there," he said with a smile in his eyes. He squeezed her fingers.

Kayla leaned across the table. "So, Kat, please tell us a bit about yourself," she invited.

"Of course," Kat leaned forward. "I'm afraid there's not a lot to tell. I'm a Minnesota girl, born and raised, although I spent several years out here in D.C. during and right after law school. That was a long time ago, but it felt a little like I was coming home today. I have two wonderful sons, Drew and Anthony, who are both in college now. I travel quite a bit with my work, and I met Greg in Memphis, where, as you all know, he is quite the man about that town."

"So you're divorced," asked wide-eyed Brandy.

"Widowed," Kat responded. "For almost a year."

Brandy recoiled. "I'm so sorry. That was an inappropriate question," she said.

"No, Brandy," Kat reassured. "That wasn't an inappropriate question at all. Bennett and I were married for a long time. He's the father of my children. I'm perfectly comfortable talking about him."

Brandy looked relieved.

"Why don't you tell the folks at the table the kind of work you do?" Christian goaded.

"I am a lawyer by training," Kat offered, without a pause. "I practiced law at a firm for many years, but I am now the head of Industrial & Employee Relations for a multi-national beverage company based out of Europe, with its U.S. headquarters in Chicago," she said, facing Christian. Then, turning to the rest of the table, she continued, "Mr. Christopher and I met during a labor negotiation – actually, during a rather extended and unnecessarily combative labor negotiation – that wrapped up recently. Mr. Christopher has kindly agreed to be, what were your words, Christian? Oh yes, 'coldly civil' this evening, for the benefit of others at the table. Cheers to that, Christian. Nicely done so far," Kat said, raising her glass in a feigned toast.

Dan and Terri laughed. Kayla looked at Rob. Paul looked at Mitch. And Mitch stared intently at Christian. Christian avoided eye contact.

Kat broke the painfully awkward silence. "I look forward to getting to know you better, Christian," she said. "I look forward to getting to know each of you better."

"Now that's something to drink to," said Susan, raising her glass. Everyone, including Christian, did the same. "To friendships – old and new," Susan toasted.

"Cheers!" rang out around the table.

The waiter came around and took the dinner order. As he was finishing up at the other end of the table, Susan turned to Kat. "You and Greg are still planning to come over to the house in the morning?" she enquired warmly.

"I wasn't aware of the plan," said Kat, "but that would be really nice. I have heard so much about you, Mitch, and the kids."

"Yes, Greg is like an uncle to the girls. He's definitely part of our family. He spends quite a bit of time at our place when he's in town. We love to have him around."

"Should we bring anything?" asked Kat.

"Heavens no," Susan replied. "First of all, you're our guests tomorrow. And second, did you happen to peak into any of Greg's cabinets while you were at his place today? The man has almost no cookware in that bachelor pad of his. That kitchen is a food desert."

"Hey, now," Greg interrupted. "I heard that."

"Well, maybe that will change now that you have someone to cook for," Susan responded with a smile.

As Kat picked at her salmon, she took in the conversations around her. Mitch and Greg were talking about some business they had in Canada. Susan was chatting with Kayla about standardized testing and college applications. Dan and Paul were sharing stories about a recent fly-fishing trip to Montana. Brandy and Christian were silent. Kat glanced up. Brandy was moving her food around her plate with her fork, obviously intent on making it appear that she'd eaten more of it than she had. And Christian? He was staring directly at Kat.

She met his eyes. He did not look away. *"Why does he hate me so much?"* she wondered. Try as she might to ignore the intensity of his feelings toward her, it was becoming a bit unsettling. She glanced at Greg, who was still absorbed in conversation with Mitch. She focused on the fish on her plate.

As the waiter was removing the main course dishes and distributing dessert menus, Greg excused himself from the table to use the restroom. Christian did the same. Susan turned to Mitch and whispered something to him. Mitch also excused himself and headed in the direction Greg and Christian had gone.

Greg was the only one in the restroom when Christian entered. "So what do we tell the guys when they ask why you sold them down the river for a skirt?" Christian bellowed. "Is a collective bargaining agreement the price for a whore in Tennessee these days?"

In one reflexive motion, Greg twisted Christian's arm behind his back and slammed his head against the mirror.

"Greg!" Mitch shouted. "Stop it! If you beat the shit out of him, I am going to have to report you. Don't make me do that."

Greg paused. He lowered his fist and released his grip on Christian's neck. Before Christian could catch his breath, Mitch stepped in front of Greg and grabbed Christian's throat. "If you ever say anything so fucking disrespectful again, I will beat you myself. Do you understand?" Mitch demanded.

With the little range of motion Christian had, he nodded. Mitch released him. Christian gasped and folded at the waist.

"Now, take a piss, straighten your suits, and get the hell back out there," Mitch directed the two of them.

Mitch returned to his seat, nodding reassuringly at Susan and Kat.

As Greg sat down, he put his hand on Kat's leg.

"Is everything okay?" Kat asked, worriedly.

"It's fine, Kat," Greg responded quietly. "We can talk about it later."

Christian was the last one to approach the table. He looked pale. He bent down and whispered something in Brandy's ear that caused her to stand immediately and grab her things. Christian walked toward the door as Brandy apologized for having to leave so abruptly. "Christian isn't feeling well," she announced. "He has a migraine coming on. I must get him home," she explained. Turning to Kat, she squeaked, "I'm sorry we didn't get to talk more, Kat. Maybe we can get together for coffee or I can come over to see you when you're next in town?"

"I'd like that, Brandy," Kat responded kindly.

Everyone on the left side of the table moved down two spots, and the conversations continued, cheerfully, over dessert and after-dinner drinks. Greg, Kat, Mitch, and Susan were the last to leave.

"We'll see you in the morning?" Mitch asked Greg. "Eleven o'clock brunch?"

"We'll be there," Greg said, reaching out to give Mitch a quick embrace.

"Thank you, Kat," Mitch said, looking at her and placing his hand on her arm. "You did a beautiful job endearing yourself to a very tough crowd tonight."

"It was my pleasure, Mitch," Kat responded graciously.

Susan gave Kat and Greg quick hugs.

Greg sighed. He took Kat's hand as they headed out into the night. "Let's go home," he said contentedly.

Chapter 21

Kat rode back to the apartment with her head resting against Greg's shoulder and his arm around her. When they arrived, Greg removed his suit coat and poured them each a glass of wine, while Kat slipped off her shoes and let her hair down. She walked over to the big picture windows and gazed upon the lighted cityscape.

Greg handed her a glass and stood behind her. He slipped one arm around her waist and pulled her to his chest, as he sipped his wine with the other hand. They stood like that in silence for several minutes, taking in the view and mutually losing themselves in the closeness and the moment.

Greg took Kat's wine glass and set them both on the window ledge. He carefully moved the hair away from the back of Kat's neck and began kissing the sensitive skin behind her ear and her neck, down to the nape, with sweet, soft, caressing touches. Kat held her breath. She slowly reached her arms behind her neck, unclasping her dress and drawing the zipper down as far as she could reach. Greg finished the task, releasing the zipper to the bottom of Kat's back. He continued to kiss her from the nape of her neck to the midpoint of her spine and then down her spine to where the zipper still held the dress to her body. The energy of his kisses overwhelmed Kat, and she shuddered.

She turned toward him, as the dress slipped over her shoulders, exposing them. He kissed each shoulder, her chest bone, her throat, then down her chest, just above her breasts. She pushed closer to him, and he met her with a passionate kiss, exploring her mouth aggressively with his tongue, as his hands caressed her.

Greg drew back and took Kat's hand, leading her into the bedroom. He lowered her to the bed, and she drew him down on top of her. He fumbled with her strapless bra. Kat laughed, unfastening it with one swift motion, and leaving her breasts exposed to his exploratory kisses. She uttered a small cry when his lips found her nipple and he took it in his mouth. Kat rolled him to the side, where she could face him and unfasten the buttons of his shirt. She did so quickly, and pushed the fabric aside, so she could press her bare chest to his as she kissed him. She ran her hand along his back.

Greg stood and unfastened his pants, letting them fall to the floor. He stepped out of them and helped Kat to her feet, lifting her dress over her head and placing it on the dresser. Greg raised the edge of the quilt and allowed Kat

Ella Kennedy

to crawl between the sheets, nestling in behind her and then positioning himself over her, covering her once again in kisses. Her lips. Her neck. Her chest. Her stomach. The soft part of her pelvis at the top of her underwear. Kat arched her back involuntarily, as Greg continued his journey of kisses, down the inside of her thigh to her ankle and back up the other leg. He kissed her over her panties, running his hand behind her lower back and drawing her hips toward him.

Greg moved up her body again until he was kissing her mouth. Slow, deep, extravagant kisses.

Kat reached her hands down and touched him through his briefs, holding him in her hand and running her fingernail up and down his hardened shaft. She drew the elastic band down his legs, and Greg kicked them off as Kat removed her own. He gently forced her legs apart, so his knees were resting between hers, his body pressing her to the bed. Kat arched her back again, and her breathing became short and irregular. Her whole body twitched with anticipation, as he expertly entered her with his fingers and then slowly positioned himself so he could ease inside her. Slowly. Carefully. Adeptly.

Kat was the first to climax, her body releasing and contracting underneath him. He came shortly after, collapsing onto her and resting his cheek against her chest. He remained inside her as he raised himself on his elbows and looked into her face. "That was amazing, Kat," he whispered.

Kat smiled. "Indeed, it was."

Greg proceeded to kiss Kat's forehead, her eyelids, the curves of her cheekbone, her chin. He slowly shifted to the side and relaxed on the bed next to her, turning her so he rested behind her, his arms around her, the naked curve of her back pressed against his chest. He reached for her hand and caressed her fingers.

They rested there in silence for several minutes, his arms around her, their hands clasped together, his fingers gently running up and down hers.

"Kat?" Greg asked, propping himself on an elbow and looking at her over her shoulder.

"Yes?"

"Did I give you the time and space you needed? Were you ready for this?"

"Did I not seem ready?" she teased.

"It's just that it is important to me that this is what you wanted – what you want."

"It is exactly what I want, Greg."

Kat could feel his renewed hardness pressing against her lower back. She turned toward him, pressing her finger against his lips. "Don't talk," she

84

whispered. "Just let me show you," she said, as she forced him to his back, straddled his hips with her knees, and lowered herself onto him.

Chapter 22

Kat awoke first. It was early, and the tender morning light was starting to come through the windows and filter into the room. Greg had his back to her. He was sleeping soundly, and his slow, steady breaths filled her ears and enveloped her with his warmth.

Kat studied his tattoo, watching it emerge in the growing light. It seemed to come to life before her eyes: its camouflage green body; its dangerous, curved claws; its hideous, gleaming eyes; and the bloody heart between its fangs. She traced its outline in her mind. She wondered what ever could have possessed Greg to brand himself with such a strongly emotive and discomforting image. Kat pressed her lips to it defiantly, willing the demons to never return and praying silently for Greg's health and wellbeing.

Greg responded to her touch and stretched, a slow, morning stretch. Kat wrapped her arms around him and placed her mouth next to his ear. "Good morning, Mr. Bodin," she whispered. "How did you sleep?"

Greg turned to face Kat, his forehead resting against hers. "I slept better than I have in years," he sighed, reaching his hand up and touching her cheek. "How about you?"

"The same. A sweet, blissful, dreamless sleep."

"How long have you been awake?"

"A while. I have so loved waking up with you. I was simply lying here, listening to your restful breathing and watching you."

Greg lowered his head and kissed Kat's neck. "Last night was wonderful."

"It was," Kat smiled. "I thought I'd be nervous."

"If that was nervous, Kat, I'm worried about being with you when you're comfortable," he teased.

"Hey," she responded, swatting his chest with the back of her hand. "Seriously, I didn't know what to expect. I thought I might be concerned about my body and all of its imperfections, but I didn't think about them at all."

"Kat, our bodies are art. They're canvases upon which beauty, life, age, pain, and experiences are drawn. Your body is like a beautiful painting, and I am so grateful that you shared it with me." He paused, then smiled. "Twice."

Kat flushed. "Ya, about that . . ."

"*That*, my dear Kat, was incredible."

Greg ran his hand down Kat's hip and gently navigated it between her legs, awakening all of her senses and filling her with an intense energy. Then he slowly moved himself on top of her, and they made love again, as the morning light penetrated the room and danced off his back.

Greg and Kat arrived at the Thorton's home a little before 11:00. They were met with the exuberant greeting of a large Golden Doodle named Daphne and two young girls. "Uncle Greg!" the two shrieked as they ran across the room and into Greg's waiting arms. He hugged them both and then handed them each a bouquet of flowers that he'd purchased at the farmer's market near the Metro stop. Greg stood and introduced the girls to Kat.

"Kat, I'd like you to meet Ms. Hilary. She's a feisty 8 years of age and one heck of a good soccer player. She also likes to draw and write songs, some of which are rather silly."

Hilary straightened up and twirled her hair with her finger. "It's nice to meet you, Kat," she said, reaching her hand out to shake Kat's.

"And this, Kat, is Ms. Holly. She is a mature 11 years of age. A scientist who will solve all of the world's problems in her lab someday. In the meantime, she likes to read books, the Harry Potter series is her favorite, and she plays lacrosse."

"It's nice to meet you, Kat," Holly echoed, also reaching out and shaking Kat's hand.

The girls quickly returned to Greg. "Come in! Come in!" they shouted.

"Well, that's a grand entrance if I ever heard one!" Susan exclaimed, as she emerged from the kitchen. "Welcome to our quiet home, Kat" she greeted, as she shooed the girls away to put the flowers in water.

"Thank you so much for inviting us, Susan," Kat replied. "Greg has talked so much about your family. It's really nice to be here."

"Mitch is outside, Greg. We decided to make bacon and buttermilk pancakes on the grill. I'm just cutting up a bit of fruit. Can I get the two of you something to drink?"

"I'd love a coffee if you have one brewed," Greg suggested.

"That sounds great to me," Kat added.

"Come on in the kitchen, and I'll grab you each a cup," Susan instructed as she led them down the hall. "Greg, you know where to find the cream and sugar."

Greg went to the refrigerator, as Susan poured two steaming mugs and set them on the counter in front of Kat.

"Can I help you with the fruit?" Kat offered.

"I'll take you up on that," answered Susan. She turned to Greg, "But you, you can head outside. Kat will be fine with me. Go," she instructed, flicking him with a towel.

Greg grabbed his cup, gave Kat a quick peck on the cheek, and headed out the kitchen door to the patio beyond.

Susan handed Kat a cutting board and a knife and placed a container of strawberries on the counter in front of her. "So what did you think of last night?" she enquired.

Kat flushed and her ears burned hot.

"Oh, my god!" laughed Susan until she had tears forming in her eyes. "Oh, poor Kat. If you're going to hang with this crowd, you must develop a better poker face." Susan smiled a big, bright, toothy smile. "I meant the dinner, of course. What did you think of the *dinner*?"

"Yes, of course, the dinner," Kat choked. "The dinner was . . . *interesting*."

"How thoroughly Minnesotan of you, Kat," Susan smiled. "I had a friend in college who hailed from Duluth. I understand the multiple meanings of a Minnesota 'interesting,' almost none of which are good."

Kat nodded. "Fair enough. Truthfully, it was really nice to meet everyone I hadn't already met."

"And I'm sorry that the one you had already met was such an asshole."

"Christian? I just can't figure him out," Kat mused. "I have wracked my brain and simply cannot understand how I evoke such an intense reaction from that man. I wasn't even a bitch during negotiations. I was actually quite reasonable."

"Christian Christopher is a total pain in the ass," Susan responded. "The guy's not stupid. Surprisingly, in fact, he's a PhD Scientist of some sort or another – highly educated, book and research smart. But he is completely lacking in any social skills or graces. You managed him well, though," Susan chuckled. "It would never work to let him bait you. I assume that was your mom voice you used with him. It's the best way to drive him completely bonkers."

"I suppose that was my mom voice," Kat reflected. "Totally involuntary."

"I wish Greg could learn not to let Christian get under his skin and to develop a mom voice. Did he tell you what happened while they were in the washroom?"

"We didn't have a chance to talk." Kat blushed again.

Susan smiled. "Let's just try to keep those two separated tonight."

"Keep who separated?" asked Greg, as he entered the kitchen and grabbed a serving plate from the cupboard.

"Never you mind," shushed Susan.

Hilary and Holly were already seated at the patio table when Kat brought the fruit out. They were regaling Greg and Mitch with stories about sports, friends, dogs, and books, and they chattered away continuously as Mitch made and Greg served pancakes to everyone. Kat imagined for a moment that the girls were little, spring birds chirping in the yard. It was such a joyous sound.

When everyone had finished, Susan had the girls clear away the dishes, while she topped off the coffees and then headed back into the kitchen. Greg followed her to help clean up.

When they were alone, Mitch leaned forward in his chair, folded his hands on the table in front of him, and looked intently at Kat. "So tell me a little more about what you do, Kat," he prompted.

"Do you mean for work?"

"Yes, for work. How is it that the Industrial Relations leader for a large, multi-national company falls head over heels for a union guy?"

"You sound like my Ethics Officer."

"Why? Is your Ethics Officer concerned about your relationship with Greg?" he asked curiously.

"She's not *concerned*," Kat responded, a little more defensively than she hand intended. "She knows me. She understands that integrity is a value I hold dear and that I would never do anything that would compromise my ethics or put the Company at risk. Why do you ask, Mitch?"

"Don't get me wrong, Kat. I'm not concerned either. But as I was sitting at dinner last night, talking with Greg about an issue in Canada, I couldn't help but think that you were sitting right there with us and that I – *that we all* – might have to be a little more careful about what we say around you."

Kat was taken a bit aback. "I'm not a spy in your midst, Mitch," she retorted. "I'm a woman who is falling in love with your best friend."

Mitch's tone softened. "I didn't mean to offend you, Kat."

"I'm not offended, Mitch. I'm simply telling you that my relationship with Greg is not a business transaction. And I can assure you that we have better things to do than to talk shop when we're together."

"Except on the first night you met," Mitch responded, knowingly.

Kat stared at him. She took a long, slow swallow of her coffee and cupped the warm mug in her hands, holding it close to her face. "Yes. You have me there, Mitch. That night, I shared my frustrations with a complete stranger. I didn't know who Greg was then, and while nothing I said revealed any confidences, I shared far more than was normal or wise. That won't happen again."

"I trust that it won't, Kat," Mitch answered quietly.

They both looked out at the garden in silence.

"You really do care about him, don't you?" Mitch asked, as he finally turned back to her.

Kat looked into his face, trying to decipher any deeper meaning in his question. "I do," she responded. "I really do."

"That's wonderful," he said. "I've known Greg for over 20 years, Kat, and I have never seen him like this. In my humble opinion, the guy is completely taken with you. It's hard to believe you've known each other for such a short period of time, given how hopelessly in love he appears to be. It's really nice to see him happy."

"Mitch, Lilly said that as well. In fact, she said that she would never have described Greg as 'happy.' What are you not telling me?"

Mitch paused. "Greg is a complex guy, Kat. You must know that already. He has his demons, as does everyone. I'm sure he has told you how he and I met. He was using drugs, depressed, likely a threat to himself. He's totally turned things around. He is healthy, successful, respected. But his history still weighs upon him from time to time. He hasn't had a depressive episode in probably a dozen years, but he's always a bit wary – unsure when the next wave is going to hit. Are you prepared for that possibility, Kat?"

Kat reflected on Mitch's words. "I won't really know until it happens, I suppose. But I'm a strong woman, Mitch, and as you may recall, I'm also quite familiar with pain and loss."

Mitch nodded.

And, with that, Holly and Hilary burst into the yard with Greg in tow. Kat watched contentedly as the three kicked the soccer ball all around the yard, running, dodging, laughing.

She smiled at Mitch.

He smiled back.

Chapter 23

"So what should I expect at this event?" Kat asked Greg, as he eased the zipper up the back of her gown.

"More smiling. More greeting. More exchanges of pleasantries. Less-than-appetizing appetizers. Maybe a shrimp or two. Some house wine. Dinner – likely surf and turf. And live music and dancing."

"Sounds benign enough."

"And the place is wall to wall with union folks, politicians, and other supporters of the common man."

"Intriguing."

"And the best part of the evening?"

"Yes?"

"Is when we come back here," he proclaimed, reaching around and tugging her ear lobe with his teeth.

Kat straightened her dress and looked in the mirror. The red definitely made a statement. "Too bold?" she asked rather self-consciously.

"Perfect!" Greg exclaimed. "You're absolutely gorgeous, Kat, and I will be the luckiest man there, with you on my arm."

"And me with you on my arm," she replied, straightening his tie and kissing him softly.

As they waited for the car, Kat enlisted Zach to take their photograph. She texted it to Drew:

7:05 p.m. (To Drew): Photo of the Day. We clean up well, don't U think?

7:06 p.m. (From Drew): Lookin' good! Hv fun & b careful.

7:06 p.m. (To Drew): Love you, kiddo! Have a good night! Talk tomorrow?

7:06 p.m. (From Drew): K.

The hall was a blur of people and activity. Greg and Kat found Mitch and Susan, and the two couples began to work their way around the crowd, shaking hands and making introductions.

Kat caught Brandy Christopher out of the corner of her eye. Brandy was making her way toward Kat, moving in and around the crowd. Brandy was wearing a red dress as well – red lace, actually, piled atop what appeared to be a black, silky undergarment. The dress had a lacy bustier that forced her breasts up and together. Brandy smiled as she neared Kat. "Twinsies!" she exclaimed. "I love your red dress!"

"What a coincidence that we both wore red," Kat said accommodatingly. "How fun is that?"

"I had such a nice time talking with you last night, Kat."

"Same, Brandy," Kat replied, feeling rather sorry for this obviously lonesome woman child.

"It must be so hard."

"What must be so hard, Brandy?"

"Well, being a widow and all," she said, with a look of sadness in her eyes.

"It has been challenging, Brandy," Kat replied. "I really appreciate your kind words."

"How did it happen?"

"*Does this woman have no boundaries*," wondered Kat, but she continued, as if explaining the situation to one of the Thorton's daughters. "He had a car accident, Brandy."

"I knew it would be something like that," Brandy replied, staring off to where Kat could see Christian standing, engaged in an animated conversation with a man in military dress. "Christian said the death was likely self inflicted or murder."

"Oh, he did, did he?" Kat responded, her voice ringing with venomous contempt.

"But I said, 'no,' I'm sure it was an accident, Christian," Brandy replied. "I'm so relieved that I was right."

Kat looked over to where Christian stood. He now seemed to be looking for Brandy, as if he'd misplaced something. Scanning the center of the crowd, he located Brandy, but he scowled when he realized with whom she was talking.

Kat turned and smiled pleasantly at Brandy. "Brandy, please tell Christian that if I had managed to get away with murder by tractor trailer – ruining the life of the driver and his family in the works – then I'm far more duplicitous than he even reckoned. Here. Let me write that down for you." Kat took a pen from her clutch and wrote on Brandy's napkin, "d-u-p-l-i-c-i-t-o-u-s."

Brandy snickered. "You're so funny, Kat."

"Tell Christian he ought to be careful," Kat winked.

"I will," Brandy replied cheerfully, patting Kat's arm.

Kat watched as Brandy navigated back through the crowd and handed Christian the napkin.

Susan, who had been eavesdropping, grabbed Kat's elbow. "You're really evil," she offered with feigned disdain. "I so admire that."

As the music started playing, Greg coaxed Kat out onto the dance floor. He was a wonderful dancer. With his hand placed firmly against Kat's waist, he led her around the room, pulling her near him, spinning her away, dipping her low and kissing her playfully as he lifted her up again. His artistry drew significant attention and some random applause. Kat was captivated. She felt graceful and beautiful in his arms.

An older woman with a lovely, gray updo tapped in, and Kat went to sit with Mitch and Susan at a table near the floor. As Kat had suspected, Greg did not want for dance partners. Kat was mesmerized by his movements and completely charmed by his smile, as he glanced over at her. After several dances, Greg politely nodded to the woman in his arms and joined Kat at the table.

A short time later, Greg leaned over and whispered in Kat's ear, "I want you."

"Here?" Kat teased.

"Let me make a few parting gestures, and we can be on our way."

"Hurry back."

The red gown and other pieces of random clothing littered the floor and hung from the furniture between the front door and the bedroom when Greg went to the kitchen to get them morning coffee. "You're obviously comfortable!" he shouted from the living room.

Chapter 24

Greg's cell phone buzzed at about half past ten. Mitch's voice rang out over the speaker. "Did you see this morning's Social Section?" he asked.

"I haven't been on line yet," Greg responded. "Why? What's wrong?"

"I'm not sure that anything is wrong necessarily, but among the photos from last night's event, there's a great one of you and your date. You'll want to check it out."

"Okay," Greg said, thumbing through his phone to try to find the page.

"Christian tells me that the photo has been sent to that local rumor monger, slash, society columnist in Nashville – you know, the one who was so keen on you and your sister at the Opera. Christian suspects there may be questions and unrest at the Memphis facility when they see you and Kat together, especially looking so frickin' lovesick and all. He told me that he is heading down there tomorrow."

"I'm not sure that's a great idea," Greg quickly countered.

"I'm not sure that it's a great idea either, Greg," Mitch responded, "But I don't think that you're the one to go down and try to explain to the locals how it is that you're literally in bed with the Company."

Greg clicked the phone off speaker and held it to his ear.

"What do you want me to do, boss?" he asked, sedately.

"I'll monitor things from my end," Mitch noted. "If it sounds like we might pull a duty-of-fair-representation claim or other board action, I'll go down there myself and explain that I was the one who ultimately approved that contract, not you."

"Thanks, Mitch," Greg replied. "I'm sorry this is complex."

"It's fine, Greg," Mitch assured him. "Nothing we can't handle."

"Please let me know how I can help."

"You stay put – at least for now. But, Greg?"

"Yes?"

"I think you need to warn Kat. She may want to send someone down as a counterbalance to Christian."

"Shit!" Kat exclaimed. "Shit! Shit! Shit! Shit!"

"But at least it's a really nice photo, Kat," Greg managed, with a smile. He had gone to the corner market and purchased a newspaper, which he now held open in his hands. The photo was one among several from the night before. In it, Greg stood behind Kat, as they watched the dancers on the floor. His head rested on her shoulder, his arms around her waist, her hand on his. Both were beaming.

"It looks like an engagement photo, Greg," Kat whined, as she set her work computer on the kitchen table and attempted to get a remote connection. "This damn thing!" she mumbled, as she made several attempts to get into the network.

11:10 a.m. (to Kelsey): Damn computer says I'm already logged in. Tricks or tips?

11:15 a.m. (from Kelsey): Have you tried logging off and on again?

11:16 a.m. (to Kelsey): Yes. Any other suggestions?

11:17 a.m. (from Kelsey): Do you know how to do a screen shot?

11:17 a.m. (to Kelsey): Affirmative. What shot do u want?

11:18 a.m. (from Kelsey): Send me the error message.

Kat emailed a screen shot and waited.

11:20 a.m. (from Kelsey): You and technology. ☹ Looks like you didn't sign out the last time. Turn everything off and start over.

Kat powered down the entire system and tried again. In the meantime, she texted Kelsey a link to the photograph.

11:25 a.m. (to Kelsey): I'm almost in. Watch for email. Think Lisa will need to travel to Memphis tomorrow. Can you look for flights? I'll call her now.

11:30 a.m. (from Kelsey): Who is the guy, Kat?

11:32 a.m. (to Kelsey): Kels, meet Greg Bodin. Look him up. You'll find him under IBT – and in the research you sent to me while I was in Memphis. Long story. TTYL – 2moro.

11:39 a.m. (from Kelsey): Honestly, Kat?

11:39 a.m. (from Kelsey): We have some catching up to do . . . .

Kat called Lisa Young on her cell phone.

"Hello?" Lisa answered groggily. Kat glanced at her phone. 10:40 a.m. *"It is definitely time to get up, Lisa,"* she thought to herself.

"Hi, Lisa. It's Kat."

"Like my boss, Kat?"

"Yes, like that Kat." Kat rolled her eyes and took a deep breath. "I'm so sorry to be calling you on a Sunday, Lisa, but I think I need you to get down to Memphis tomorrow. Kelsey is looking for flight options." Kat went on to explain the situation.

"Holy shit, Kat!" Lisa exclaimed, then quickly caught herself. "Sorry – I forgot this was a work call."

"At the end of the day, Lisa, there's no 'holy shit' about this. The negotiation was totally on the up and up. There was no conflict. It was a fair deal. And while the timing could have been better, there's no 'there there.' I simply need for you to convince a bunch of bargaining unit members of that fact. Oh, and the union guy, Christian Christopher? A total asshole. Watch yourself with him."

"I've got this, Kat," Lisa declared confidently.

"Perhaps a bit too confidently," Kat contemplated.

"And Kat?" Lisa added, her tone changed.

"Yes, Lisa?"

"The guy in the photo is really hot."

Kat sighed. "Please just go down and smooth this thing over?"

"I've got it!"

Greg and Kat looked at each other over their laptops. "We might as well go for a walk, Kat. There's nothing more we can do here, and it would help to clear our heads."

Kat went to change, and they headed out into the damp, May air.

Things felt a bit more settled when they returned to the apartment after lunch. Kelsey had made Lisa's arrangements. Lisa had prepared a full set of talking points, which she dutifully shared with Kat. And it appeared that Kat's flight back to Minnesota would be on time.

Greg was on the couch, his back resting against the arm, his legs stretched out across its length. He motioned for Kat to join him, and she sidled in between his legs, reclining against his chest.

"I'm sorry that today got away from us," he said. "I am not ready to take you to the airport."

Kat sighed. "And I don't want to go."

"It is a lovely photo," Greg teased.

"It was a great weekend," she replied quietly, nestling closer into his body and drawing his arms around her. "Things won't always be this complicated." She paused contemplatively. "Will they?"

Greg laughed. "I'm not sure why not, Kat. You're rather complex. I'm rather complex. And, in any event, as a wise person once said, if we try too hard to make things 'normal,' we'll never know how amazing they might be."

10:03 p.m. (to Greg): Back at the house. Wish I was there with you instead. You're quite extraordinary, you know.

10:04 p.m. (from Greg): Right back at you. Sleep well, my Kat.

Chapter 25

Kelsey was waiting for Kat at the door when she arrived at the office the next morning. "You have some explaining to do, my friend," she said grumpily, shoving a cup of coffee into Kat's hand and directing her toward an open conference room.

Kat told Kelsey the entire story of meeting Greg and the contract negotiations. She told her about their trip to Nashville, Greg's meeting with Drew, and the fairytale ball. As Kat talked, tears welled up in Kelsey's eyes.

"I'm so happy for you, Kat," she said, her voice filled with relief and emotion. "I'm still a little angry that I learned about this guy through a photo in the newspaper, but I am so happy for you."

Kat caught her breath. "I hadn't thought about that, Kelsey," she said, grabbing her phone from her purse. "Who else is likely to see that photo in the paper? I have to call my mother before she hears about Greg from one of her nosy friends." She grabbed her phone and jumped to her feet.

Kelsey laughed. "You deserve this, Kat. You deserve to be happy again."

Late that afternoon, Kat shut herself in her office and called Greg.

"Hey, there," he answered.

"Can you talk for a few minutes?"

"To you? Of course."

"Lisa tells me that the plant superintendent is livid. He seems much more upset by the situation than any of the bargaining unit members do. She's taking him out for dinner and drinks this evening to try to talk him off the ledge."

"I've heard pretty much the same. Christian is stomping around and saber rattling, but my understanding is that he's not getting much traction with the members. It was a good deal after all. And," he added, "they liked you. I believe Christian will come back to D.C. tomorrow."

"How's Mitch doing?" asked Kat.

"He's fine," Greg responded. "Why do you ask?"

"I don't know. I just got the feeling that, perhaps, he is not particularly happy with my line of work. He looks out for you, Greg, and I'm sure that this situation is a bit unsettling for him."

"Mitch is fine, Kat. He's quite good at separating his work life from his personal one. He'd rip me a new one if he thought I'd done anything wrong. That's not personal; that's business. At the same time, he'd be welcoming me into his home, pulling up a chair, and cracking open a beer."

Chapter 26

The next month was memorable, as Greg and Kat engaged in what they playfully referred to as the "meet the family tour."

The first weekend, they visited Anthony in Charlottesville. Kat wasn't sure why, or whether she was overreacting, but Anthony didn't warm as quickly to Greg as Drew had. He was awkward and reserved during dinner. And he was quite visibly put out when he learned that Kat and Greg were going to share a hotel room.

Greg was characteristically charming, however, and as they rested next to each other that first evening, he gently and unassumingly asked Kat to be patient with Anthony. "He's simply trying to get used to the idea of sharing you," Greg said. "He's protective of you. It's nice to see how much he cares. Give him time to get used to this – to get used to *us*."

The next morning, Kat and Greg picked Anthony up on campus, and the three of them drove to Crabtree Falls, about an hour outside of the city. It was a gorgeous near-summer day, and Greg and Anthony were both strong hikers. At one point, they became caught up in some conversation about fishing or the like, oblivious to Kat. She took the opportunity to intentionally lag back a bit and provide them some distance. She'd catch up eventually. In the meantime, it was nice to allow them a little space to get to know each other better, and it gave Kat a chance to enjoy the quiet and immerse herself in the beautiful surroundings.

It was a good twenty minutes before Kat caught sight of them again. As she approached, she could see Greg slowly remove his arm from Anthony's shoulder. Anthony straightened up and wiped his face with the back of his hand. It appeared that Anthony had been crying. Kat sped up, but Greg shook his head, just slightly, to slow her.

"Hey, guys," she said instead. "So nice of you to wait." She smiled sarcastically. As if choreographed, Greg and Anthony fell into place on either side of Kat, each grabbing a hand, and they marched together to the point where the water fell wildly over the falls.

Later, when they walked Anthony back to his dormitory, he hugged both Kat and Greg. Greg patted him on the back during their embrace. "You've got this," he said assuredly.

"So do you," Anthony replied with a slight grin.

"What exactly happened there?" Kat asked, as they watched Anthony disappear into the building.

"He told me how much he hates me right now."

"What?" Kat exclaimed, horrified.

"And I told him how much I understand. He got quite emotional, Kat, and shared with me how much he misses his dad."

Kat inhaled quietly, as a lump formed in her throat. Greg put his arm around her.

"I told him about losing my own father when I was about his age and how even after all of these years, I still think about my dad almost every day. But I assured Anthony that at some point, those thoughts will not be sad thoughts, but, rather, good memories of life well spent."

A tear made its way down Kat's cheek. Greg leaned over and gently kissed it away.

"I also told him, Kat, that I am not trying to take anyone's place. I explained to him that I know full well that a part of your heart will always be with Bennett. I also let him know that I will never try to father him or Drew, but that I plan to spend as much time as I can with you and that I really would like to be his friend, if he's open to that. He said that he is." Greg paused for a moment. "You have remarkable children, Kat."

"Thank you," she mustered, as tears flowed down her cheeks. "Thank you for everything."

The following weekend, Greg took Kat to visit Martha and her family: Rick, Lydia, and Ali. Martha greeted Kat warmly. As was the case with the Thorton girls, Greg's nieces – whom Martha lovingly referred to as "the teenage tyrants" – were little angels in Greg's presence, and he doted on them completely.

That evening, Martha and Kat sipped wine and talked while Greg and the girls played board games. "I've often thought what a shame it is that Greg never had children," Martha confided. "He's so good with the girls. They think the world of him."

"He's been wonderful with my sons, too," Kat agreed. "They're getting used to the idea of there being a man in my life. It's not necessarily an easy adjustment, but Greg is so patient, kind, and understanding."

"You know, Greg was only a boy really when he was left on his own," Martha said sadly. "Our mother had just passed. I couldn't bear to stay in Memphis any longer, so I insisted that Rick marry me and that we move away from there. Greg couldn't bear to leave, so we left him in Memphis – with no family and no support system. I always have felt at least partially responsible for the pain he suffered after that." Martha appeared sincerely at a loss.

Kat listened, not knowing how to respond.

"But enough about that," Martha said, composing herself. "What's your plan, Kat? Have you and Greg talked about what comes next?"

Kat reflected. "That's a really good question," she responded. "You know, Martha, that we've only known each other for a couple of months. We're really living in the moment right now – still learning about each other, meeting each other's loved ones, putting the pieces together."

"Fair enough," Martha responded.

Greg, Kat, and Martha stayed up long after the girls and Rick went to bed, drinking wine and talking. Martha was as charming as Greg had described, and Kat got lost in their conversation – fully engaged by the tales of their youth. Greg, the wild young outdoorsman. Martha, the darling of Memphis. Their loving, doting parents. School sports. Camping trips. Summer evenings on the front porch. It all seemed quite idyllic. Kat took everything in and began to formulate a more complete sketch of the man with whom she had so suddenly fallen in love.

When at last it was time to go to bed, Martha showed Greg and Kat to the guestroom at the back of the house. "It's quiet back here," she kidded. "Virtually soundproof."

"I don't know what you're hinting at, dear sister," Greg replied.

"Of course not, my little brother. Sleep well."

"I'm not sure I can make love in my sister's house," Greg said to Kat moments later, as he crawled into the four-poster bed with a white lace coverlet beside her.

Kat nodded and smiled understandingly.

"But I'm willing to try," he whispered, as he pulled her close and pressed his lips against her neck.

On the third weekend, Kat and Greg took Drew to Memphis. Drew reveled in the log house adjacent to the woods. He and Greg fished the river, and Drew helped Greg cut and stack firewood. The activity was a great diversion, and before long, Drew and Greg were talking like old friends. Kat spent much of the day on Saturday working from the porch as the two men played and toiled. She could not get enough of hearing them chatter on. When night fell, the three of them sat in the hot tub and counted the stars.

"A guy could get used to living out here," Drew remarked contentedly, as he stared into the star-studded sky.

"This guy did," Greg responded with a smile. "I'm glad you like it here, Drew. You are welcome to come down here and use this place whenever you'd like, even if I'm not here. It's a great place to get away from things – to clear your head."

"Really? Any time I'd like?" Drew responded enthusiastically.

"Of course," Greg replied, then looked tentatively at Kat, "so long as your mom is okay with that."

"I understand why you and Drew are so attracted to this area – to this home," Kat replied. "I would be happy if Drew took respite in it, like you do."

"Then, remind me to give you a key before we leave, Drew," Greg responded, sharing what appeared to be a smile among conspirators with the young man.

"You'd talked about that earlier, hadn't you?" Kat asked, with a shake of her finger, as Greg crawled into bed beside her. Greg looked at her with feigned surprise. "Oh, you know what I'm talking about, Greg Bodin. The whole *mi casa es su casa* thing."

"All day, Kat, he talked about how beautiful the setting is – the woods, the river, the lake. He went on about how relaxed and comfortable he feels here. And, yes, I might have mentioned the idea – in passing - before it came up again in the hot tub."

"I'm actually quite impressed that you worked together to pull this off. Drew obviously trusts you. It was such a joy to watch you today. It's the first time in a long time that I remember Drew seeming so – *so carefree.* As it turns out, you're not just good for my soul. You're good for his."

Chapter 27

Greg, Kat, and Drew spent the last day of their Memphis trip in the city, doing typical touristy things: Graceland, Sun Studios, the National Civil Rights Museum. They had an early dinner on Beale Street. Drew was anxious to get back to the house by the woods and to retire to the hot tub and watch the sun set over the tree-lined horizon.

Greg put together a cheese tray with some crackers, as Kat sat at the kitchen island and Drew searched the bookshelves. Drew had always been an avid reader, and the fulsome collection of books utterly intrigued him. As he perused the shelves, he questioned Greg about particular titles; asked for specific recommendations; and started a small collection of "must reads" in the corner of the cupboard, to which he planned to return.

"I could just sit here for hours and read in the hot tub," Drew sighed contentedly, as he joined Kat and Greg in the kitchen.

Greg dried his hands and walked over to the fireplace. He opened a small wooden box that rested on the mantle. "Before I forget," he said, returning with a silver key, "here you go, Drew. Whenever you can get down this way, you will always have a place to stay, woods to explore, a lake and a river to fish, and books to read."

Greg placed the key in Drew's outstretched hand. The young man carefully closed his fingers around it – this key – this tiny treasure filled with the promise of peace of mind, quietude, independence, and adventure.

Another perfect weekend, Kat later reflected gratefully, as the water bubbled around them and heavy steam blurred the darkening red and orange sky.

Drew closed his eyes. He sat silently for a bit. Then he turned and looked at Greg. "Can I ask you a personal question?" he asked hesitantly. "It's something that's been troubling me a bit, but that may be inappropriate for me to ask," he added shyly.

Kat straightened and looked closely at Drew, as she rose above the mist.

"Of course, Drew," Greg responded earnestly. "What's on your mind?"

"You don't have to answer, of course," Drew continued.

"Understood. Please, go ahead."

"Well, I was just wondering," Drew stammered, "as I was looking at the books on the shelves. . . . well, there is a photo near the back of one of them. It's a photo of you and a woman. And I was just wondering, I guess, who she is."

Greg smiled a small, reassuring smile, at the young man, but he said nothing at first. He scanned the horizon, appearing to gather his thoughts. A muscle in his neck twitched slightly.

Drew interjected nervously, "I'm sorry. It's really none of my business."

"It's okay, Drew. Given how close you and your mom are and how much you care about her, I'm not surprised that you would want to know why I keep a photo of myself with another woman on the same shelf where I have a photo of Kat and me. I applaud your courage, Drew.

"Her name was Annie," Greg continued, lowering his eyes from the horizon.

Kat searched her memory. *"Was Annie?"* she wondered. When Greg had mentioned Annie in the past, Kat was sure he had always done so in the present tense.

Greg turned and looked at Kat as he continued, staring gently into her eyes, seeming to steady himself there.

"Annie was my first true love, Drew. We were very young. I met Annie when I was in high school, in fact, when I lived in Memphis with my family. She lived just down the street from us, in a big white house with a wrap-around porch and pink hydrangeas lining the walk.

"We would sit on that porch after school, most nights, holding hands and talking about our futures." Greg appeared now to be looking right through Kat now, fully present only in the past, as if he no longer was sitting there with them. "Annie wanted to be an artist. She made beautiful paintings, and when we'd explore the wooded areas around Memphis, she'd always bring her charcoal pencils or watercolors and her sketchbook. One of her sketchbooks is on that shelf as well.

"I had dreams, too, about what I wanted to do when I grew up. I wanted to be a forest ranger. I dreamed of getting married – to Annie – and having an entire baseball roster of rowdy, tow-headed children.

"Then my parents died, and I was forced to make some different choices in order to eat and pay the bills. I joined the military and I was trained in Special Operations. I was a perfect candidate for that type of work. I was a young and strong outdoorsman, with a lot of wilderness training and experience. I was smart and dutiful. I was an orphan, with very few family or relational ties. And I was angry – quite angry – at the loss of my family and life as I had known it and as I had dreamed it would be.

"I spent two years on various tours of active duty. I saw things and did things that I would never wish upon anyone, let along a young man of your age, Drew." Greg shook his head slightly and looked at the boy, regaining a connection with the present. He swallowed hard and closed his eyes.

"When I returned from my last tour, I was pretty messed up. I had a hard time adjusting to 'normal life.' I didn't know anything about PTSD at that time. I just thought that I was broken. The slightest things – noises, smells, an unexpected touch – would set me off.

"Annie was in college while I was away. She wrote to me every day. She sent stories about her courses, her classmates, pop culture, her evolving dreams and aspirations. All of these things seemed so distant and foreign to me.

"When I was first back, I fell into her arms and pretended that everything was okay – that nothing had changed. But as I increasingly felt distanced from her and from the rest of her world, I turned to drugs to help me cope, to help me get through my days. I lost myself in addiction. I couldn't keep a job. I fought with Annie and belittled the things she had achieved, believing them trivial, shallow, and meaningless. She tried so hard to 'fix me,' but she increasingly could not relate – and the drug use frightened her. It frightened me, too. I wasn't the person with whom Annie had fallen in love. And as that became increasingly obvious – to both of us – I spiraled into deeper addiction and depression. One night, I slapped her." Greg faltered.

"I could see the fear in her eyes. I am sure it mirrored the fear in my own. We were both sobbing, and she insisted on going back to her parent's home – the white house on our old block – where she would stay while I tried to get my life together. She declared that she would not see me again until I was drug free and was prepared to live 'normally' again." Greg breathed out slowly and opened his eyes.

"I insisted on driving her home. I wanted to spend just those few more minutes with her before I left her on the curb beside the hydrangeas and perhaps never saw her again. I was reeling from the unexpected weight of it all. I was out of my mind with sadness, worry, and regret. I didn't see the light or the car approaching from the right. The next thing I knew, I was in the hospital. I woke to find Martha standing over me. My head throbbed. I couldn't feel my legs. Martha sat beside me and took my hand as tears streamed down her face. I had been asking about Annie – asking and asking and asking through the hazy fog of my injured stupor. It was Martha who told me that Annie was dead. There had been an accident, she explained. She tried so hard to convince me that it wasn't my fault. But in my heart, I was responsible – I have always been responsible. I killed my Annie."

No one moved. No one made a noise. Kat locked eyes with Greg and willed him back to the present. Drew looked away.

Greg swallowed hard again and continued. "That was the lowest point in my life. I couldn't find the strength to live with the guilt and the loss. I became despondent. And I spent a long time in the hospital – being treated for my injuries, my drug withdrawal, and my mental health – or what remained of it.

"In their grief, Annie's family pursued criminal actions against me for vehicular homicide, among other things. I was almost relieved and was convinced that I should spend the rest of my life in prison. Martha would hear none of that. She and Rick found me a criminal defense attorney. As soon as I was well enough to leave the hospital, I was taken into custody, pending trial. Ultimately, the jury acquitted me. I'm not sure how or why. I testified on my own behalf, but I don't recall a word of it. I just told my story as I'm doing now, and they gave me a second chance. That is far more than I ever would have given myself."

Something in Greg's eyes awakened. "It was shortly after that, Kat, that I met Mitch and began the long and painful journey back to life – and self-forgiveness." Greg smiled contemplatively at both of them. "I'm sorry. I need to excuse myself," he said. As he rose to go inside, water droplets ran down his back and over the demon with a bloody heart in its mouth. Kat trembled.

Kat stayed with Drew. They talked about what they had heard. Both were shaken.

"I'm so sorry for asking," Drew said. "Greg was in such pain as he talked," he remarked sadly.

"If he had not shared that story tonight, Drew, he would have told it to me on another occasion. I believe he's tried before, but he has not been able to do it. He felt comfortable enough to share with us tonight. And I think that's a good thing. Greg feels safe and surrounded by love in our presence."

When Drew was settled, they both dried off and went inside. Kat's heart physically hurt. She hugged Drew tightly and held on as she stroked his hair. "We'll talk more in the morning," she said, kissing his forehead. "Try to get some sleep."

"I love you, Mom."

"Oh, Drew. I love you so much," she responded, with a catch in her voice.

"Tell Greg that I'm thinking about him," Drew said as he turned toward the guest room.

"I will, kiddo," she replied, steeling herself as she slowly climbed the steps to the loft.

Chapter 28

Kat found Greg lying in bed with one arm under his head and the other over his eyes. She removed her wet swimsuit in the bathroom. The bedroom was lit only by moonlight. Greg didn't move as Kat settled in next to him. She stared at the ceiling and hoped he would say something, *anything*. She knew that he was awake. His breath was almost nonexistent, unlike when he was contentedly sleeping beside her. She could feel his warmth, but she could not even detect the movement of his chest as he inhaled. His stillness was disquieting.

Unable to endure the silence a moment longer, Kat rolled against him, placing her arm around him and resting her cheek against his.

"I am so sorry, my love," she said quietly, brushing his cheek with her lips. From her current vantage point, Kat could hear Greg's heart beat through the pulse in his neck. "Please stay with me," she pleaded, "please come back to the present," she urged.

Greg remained silent, but slowly moved his arm away from his eyes and placed it over her arm that held him. He stroked her elbow slowly with his thumb.

"I wasn't sure you'd come up here," he said in a quiet voice – almost a whimper.

"There was never a chance that I wouldn't come up here," Kat said assuredly, shifting so that her face was directly above his. "It was an accident, Greg. A horrible, devastating, life-altering, accident. But an accident, nonetheless. You were nothing but a scared and confused young man who had lost his way, lost his anchors to the world. I am so grateful that you found your way back, Greg." As Kat talked, she became increasingly adamant and animated. "Listen to me. You are a wonderful, caring, thoughtful man. You have touched my life and the lives of so many with the amazing person you are. You make a difference, Greg. You make the people around you better simply by being you – your giving nature, your humility, your strength of conviction. There is a reason you survived that accident, Greg. And I, for one, am so very grateful you did."

"Did I frighten Drew?" Greg asked.

"I'm not going to lie to you," Kat continued. "Drew was shaken. It's a story that would leave anyone shaken. And the most difficult part for him – for both of us – was the pain that obviously surged through you as you told it. You were somewhere else, Greg, someplace dark and sad. A place that neither Drew nor I can pretend to know or understand. That was hard.

"But do you know the last thing that Drew said to me before I came up here?" Kat insisted.

Greg did not respond.

"He asked that I tell you that he is thinking about you, Greg. He wasn't suggesting that we should leave or questioning whether he would want to see you again – or whether you and I should continue to be together. Drew wanted me to let you know that you are in his thoughts and that he cares about you."

Greg moaned softly and began to sob. Kat held him and kept talking to him as he emptied his sadness into the pillow. She assured him she was with him. She told him how much he was loved – by her, by Martha, by his nieces and the Thorton girls, by Mitch, Susan, and Lilly. She reminded him of all of the ways in which he positively impacted those around him. And she asked him to stay with her in the moment and to leave the dark place he had entered earlier in the evening.

When Greg had no tears left and his body was completely exhausted, he turned noiselessly away from her. Kat didn't release him. She only held him closer. And as she did, she defiantly placed her lips on the demon tattoo. "You are strong," she chanted under her breath. "You are healthy. You are whole."

"I love you, Greg," Kat whispered, as she finally closed her own eyes and fell into a fitful sleep.

Chapter 29

Kat and Drew's flight was scheduled for mid-morning. Kat awoke at a little after 7:00. Greg was not in bed. Kat pulled on a robe and hurried down the steps. Drew was sitting on the couch, reading a book. "I've made coffee," he said, looking up. "Greg needed a walk. He promised to be back within the hour."

"How did he seem?" Kat asked, hesitantly.

"He still seemed sad, but he gave me a hug, and he thanked me for listening last night. He apologized for burdening me with his troubling past. And he told me how much it meant to him that I asked you to tell him that I was thinking of him."

Kat nodded.

"I totally understand his need to walk and clear his head," Drew added. "I suspect that he'll return a bit less sad," he said, knowingly.

Kat stared at her thoughtful, introspective son. "I am sure that he will," she smiled.

Kat poured herself some coffee and then fixed Drew a couple of eggs and some toast.

As promised, Greg returned within the hour. As he entered the house, he approached Kat and kissed her gently on her forehead. "Did you get any sleep?" he asked.

"A bit," she replied. "And you?"

"Yes. The same."

Kat asked Drew to go to the guestroom and pack his bag. They would need to leave for the airport soon. When Drew was out of earshot, Kat turned to Greg. "Do you want me to stay with you?" she asked.

"No, Kat. I need to head back to D.C."

"Then, I can come to D.C. with you," she countered.

Greg faced Kat, pulling her close to him and pressing his mouth to hers. He kissed her deeply, almost desperately. When he pulled back from the kiss, he smiled sadly. "My dear Kat," he said quietly and earnestly, "I have managed my demons for more than 20 years, and I will continue to do so – sometimes more effectively than others. You do not need to take care of me. I will be fine. I will endure. With your love – which is different from your pity," he added, "I will thrive."

"Call me tonight?" Kat asked, kissing him once again.

"Of course," he replied.

Drew spent the night at the house, rather than returning to school. Classes didn't start until later Monday morning, and he seemed unwilling to leave Kat alone. As soon as he'd come in the door, Drew had taken the key that Greg had given him to his room. Then Kat and Drew made dinner together, talked, and enjoyed each other's company.

At about 9:00, Kat retreated to her bedroom. As she was contemplating whether she would reach out to Greg, rather than waiting any longer, her phone rang.

"I made it back to D.C. just fine, Kat."

"That's good to hear,"" she responded. "But what I really want to know right now is when I'm going to see you again."

Greg didn't respond immediately. Kat persisted. "I was thinking that I could come to D.C. on Friday after work. I would likely fly from there to Chicago sometime on Monday, if that works for you."

Silence.

Kat felt a panicky sensation in her stomach. She waited a moment before continuing. "Say, 'Yes, Kat. I would love that, Kat,' and I will book my tickets," she pleaded. "Please don't shut me out, Greg."

"Yes, Kat. I would love that, Kat," Greg replied.

Kat was relieved that she could hear what she believed was the hint of a smile in his voice.

Chapter 30

Kat's work extension rang – area code 312. She didn't immediately recognize the number, so she let it ring over to Kelsey. Within seconds, Kelsey was at her office door.

"It's Karen Greeley from Corporate Ethics," Kelsey announced. She looked at Kat expectantly and appeared concerned.

"Please go ahead and put her through," Kat replied.

"Hi, Karen," Kat answered, "What can I do for you?"

"Hi, Kat. Hey, I'm wondering if you're planning to be in Chicago this week."

"Wednesday through Friday," Kat responded. "Why? What's up?"

Karen paused for a second. "There's been an ethics line complaint, Kat, based on your handling of the Memphis contract. Alleged conflict of interest."

"Well, that's unfortunate," Kat pondered.

"I know that you called me the week following that negotiation, Kat, but I need you to come in for an interview and to give a statement. As you might imagine, it will be important that I understand the complete timeline for when you made your offers, when you met Mr. Bodin, and how the last day of contract negotiations finished."

"I'm happy to walk you through the entire sequence of events, Karen. Do you want to do that now, or should we find time to talk later in the week, when I'm at Corporate?"

"Let's meet in person. It will just be easier, and I can get you to sign the statement right then. In the meantime, Kat, can you please have Kelsey scan and send me all of your session notes and anything else that you may have to confirm the timing?"

"Of course, Karen. Do you also want to talk with Greg?"

Karen made a sound that sounded somewhat like a snicker. "Oh, Kat, I don't believe that talking with your boyfriend right now is either possible or appropriate. You know as well as I do that the union isn't going to want to turn him over to us voluntarily. They're no doubt concerned about pulling a duty-of-fair-representation claim, and, if there's any blame to be had here, they'll do their damnedest to foist that off on us."

"Well, that's bullshit," Kat responded.

"Bullshit or not, it's not my intent to interview Mr. Bodin or anyone other than you at this time, Kat. And I instruct you to keep the fact of the complaint and this investigation absolutely confidential and not to discuss them with anyone. Do you understand my instruction?"

"Yes, I understand your instruction, Karen. I will not engage in any, what was it you called it the last time we spoke? Pillow talk? I will not engage in any pillow talk or otherwise. We'll get those documents to you as soon as possible today, and I look forward to talking with you on Wednesday."

"Thank you, Kat. I understand that this is uncomfortable for you."

"Actually, it's not uncomfortable at all, Karen," Kat retorted. I've done nothing to be uncomfortable about. We'll talk soon."

Kat hung up the phone. Her hands were shaking. She pushed her desk chair back and stood. She took a deep breath and steadied herself against the tabletop.

Kelsey was at her desk and raised her eyebrows at Kat as she approached. "What was up with that?" she asked.

"It's nothing, Kelsey. Karen simply needs to review all of the notes from my Memphis sessions. Can you please scan and send those to her today? Also, I know that you were working on a number of things relating to that matter while I was away. Can you please scan and enclose your notes as well? If there is anything else that you come across that you believe may be helpful, please let me know."

"Helpful to what, Kat?"

Kat reflected for a moment. "Helpful to creating a complete chronology of events for those negotiations, including offers, counteroffers, compromises, and the final settlement."

"Do you want me to draw up a timeline?" Kelsey asked.

"That would be great, if you think you can pull it all together and get it out to Karen Greeley yet today."

"I'm on it, boss," Kelsey said with an obviously forced smile on her face.

"Everything is fine, Kelsey," Kat reassured her. "Trust me."

During her evening call with Greg, Kat found it much more difficult than she could have imagined not to tell him all about the call with Karen Greeley and to seek his advice and counsel. But she kept the confidence, steering the talk of the day to trivial things such as the weather, the great workout she had gotten in after work, and a documentary that she had playing in the background. Greg was unusually quiet, but that was to be expected, perhaps, given how she had left him on the weekend.

Near the end of their conversation, Kat confirmed her travel plans for Friday. Greg needn't pick her up at the airport. She'd have Zach let her into the building and see Greg when he arrived home.

Then, remembering a commitment she'd made to her mother, Kat interjected, "Oh, and my mom is after me again to get you out here to meet her. I was thinking that, as lovely as it's been, rather than continue the drip, drip, drip of our 'meet the family tour,' perhaps we might host a gathering at the house sometime in early July? I can invite friends and family in one fell swoop? A garden party, maybe, to meet the mystery man who has swept me off my feet and kept me away from my fellow Minnesotans for the last couple of months?"

Greg said nothing. While Kat didn't expect him to be exuberant, she did expect some answer. She was a bit annoyed.

"I'll take care of all of the details, Greg. You'll simply have to show up." She paused. "There are a lot of people who are anxious to meet you, my friend."

"That would be lovely, Kat," Greg said. "Just let me know what weekend works, and I'll make my arrangements. Sleep well, sweet Kat."

Kat longed for more. She wanted to tell him she loved him. She wanted to do something that would take them back to the place they were prior to Saturday night. But, in the end, all she could muster was, "You, too, Greg."

Kat settled into bed with a highlighter and some sticky notes and began to review all of the documents Kelsey had compiled and sent to Karen earlier in the day. "This, too, will pass," she whispered to herself.

Chapter 31

Kat flew to Chicago on Tuesday night, so she'd be sure to get to the office on time. No potentially delayed or missed flights. She slept restlessly, but felt energized in the morning, as she dressed in her finest power suit.

An awkward tension filled the air as Kat entered the area where her team sat. It was clear to her that they had learned that she would be meeting with Karen Greeley this morning – and that Lisa (and likely others) knew why.

"Good morning, everyone!" Kat greeted the waiting throng, with more than a little confidence and gusto in her voice. It may have been forced, but *"What is that saying?"* Kat asked herself. *"Fake it 'til you make it?"*

"Good morning, Kat," rang out from various desks in the space.

The allotted conference room was near the back of the office complex. Karen was waiting there for Kat. Kat took a deep breath as she sat and placed her working file and chronology in front of her. "Let's do this," Kat said calmly, and for the next two hours, Kat walked Karen through every detail of the collective bargaining negotiation, the chance meeting with Greg at the hotel bar, the kiss at the ice machine, the heated conversation after Kat had done her due diligence and discovered who Greg was, the cold reception at the library the next morning, the union's acceptance of the offer she had made the day before, the note that Greg had provided her in which he asked her to meet him at 11:00. She walked Karen quickly through the highlights of the day's events – the trip to Nashville and, in particular, their conversation during the ride there about how Greg had contacted Mitch to ensure that he did not have a conflict of interest. Kat did not mention the fact that they'd spent the night together or any of the amazing times together since. The potential conflict ended, after all, when the tentative agreement was signed. And the contract had been ratified by the union.

When they were finished with the chronology and had gone through the documents that Kat and Kelsey had provided, Kat enquired as to whether she could ask a few questions.

"Of course, Kat," Karen said accommodatingly. "What questions do you have?"

"First," Kat replied, "I know that you probably can't tell me who filed the ethics complaint."

Karen nodded affirmatively. "That's correct."

"But do you have any idea why it has taken them this long to do so? That photo from the gala would have been published in the Memphis paper weeks ago. I know that's when the initial kerfuffle happened at the plant."

"I'm not sure, Kat," Karen noted. "Perhaps it just took some time to sink in. Perhaps the bargaining unit members are having buyers' remorse. Or it could be that the facility isn't doing well financially, and now management is wondering whether they, in fact, got the best labor deal that they could have mustered."

Kat was rather shocked. "The facility isn't doing well financially?" she asked. "That facility has been a poster child for earnings. It's one of the reasons that we had to put a good deal on the table. We couldn't afford to take a strike – not with the new product line and all."

"The information I have is that the facility is off its financial target by a couple of million dollars, and it does not appear that it will meet its fiscal year goals," Karen responded.

"I'm sorry to hear that, Karen," Kat noted. "I haven't kept up. Since I turned this facility over to Lisa on my team, I've really stepped away from it. I wanted to be sure to avoid any appearances of a potential conflict of interest."

"Yes, and I appreciate that, Kat," Karen acknowledged. "It will be best if you continue to leave this facility to Lisa, at least for awhile. Do you have any other questions, Kat?"

"Just one more," Kat responded. "Do you have a sense as to when you will wrap up your inquiry?"

"I intend to collect my notes from our conversation and to follow up with a couple of potential witnesses to ensure that I've corroborated the chronology you've provided. To be clear, it appears to me that I should talk with Steve Halter and Dean O'Reilly from the bargaining committee and that it will also be a good idea for me to try to connect with Linda at the hotel bar. Do you recall Linda's last name, Kat?"

"It was something like LaVec," Kat responded thoughtfully. "I'm not exactly sure how it is spelled. I've only met her twice – the night before the last bargaining session and then on that Friday, before I headed to the airport." Kat hesitated a moment. Linda knew that Kat and Greg had spent the night together. *"What if she told Karen? Would Karen feel as if Kat was trying to hide something?"* she wondered.

"Is that everything, Kat?" Karen asked, as if she was reading Kat's mind or at least sensing her discomfort.

"Yes, I believe so, Karen," Kat responded.

"Then I will be back in touch," said Karen. "It most likely will be next week or the following, based upon when we can talk with the other witnesses and complete the review."

"That's fine. Just let me know when you're finished, please. It's a little awkward with this hanging over our heads."

"I understand," Karen responded, seemingly wincing at Kat's use of the word "our."

Kat went back to the space where her team officed. She couldn't focus on work, so she went from team member to team member, catching up and ensuring that everything was going well. When she got to Lisa, Kat asked about the financial issues in Memphis that Karen had mentioned. Lisa had, in fact, heard that the facility was falling behind on its projections. "Steve and the others are hot under the collar," she said. "They're pulling their hair out trying to figure out how to get this product line back in the black."

When Kat had finished her rounds, she found herself still too distracted to work.

3:22 p.m. (to Kelsey): Hi, Kels. Long day at HQ. I'm thinking of heading back to the hotel soon. Anything of note happening back in MSP?

3:24 p.m. (from Kelsey): All is good here. Get some rest, Kat. It's 5:00 somewhere. I'll hold down your email.

3:25 p.m. (to Kelsey): Thx, Kels! Have a good night!

Kat walked slowly back to her hotel, window shopping and trying to forget the events of the day. She wished she could call Greg and debrief, but that couldn't happen. There was a stationary store on the corner, kitty corner from the hotel. Kat went in. She perused the shelves, considering different options for her upcoming garden party. The distraction was helpful. She went back to her room, slipped into her pajamas, and began to compile a guest list. She ordered room service and a glass of wine and got caught up in event planning. It was nearly 10:00 p.m. when at last she looked up from caterer searches. Greg had not called. He had not texted. Kat closed her laptop and looked at herself in the hotel mirror. Should she call him? How hard should she push? It was 11:00 in D.C. Would he still be awake?

10:03 p.m. (to Greg): Long day at work. Miss U. Looking forward to Friday. Sleep well. Talk tomorrow?

Kat fell asleep as she waited for a reply.

1:19 a.m. (from Greg): Miss you, too. Of course. Tomorrow.

Chapter 32

The rest of the week flew by, and before she knew it, Kat found herself in an Uber heading for Greg's place. It was rush hour, and it would likely take her 45 minutes to an hour to get across town from the airport.

5:33 p.m. (to Greg): In the car. Traffic's tough. See you in 45-60?

5:35 p.m. (from Greg): Running late. Have Zach let you in. I'll be there by 7.

5:35 p.m. (to Greg): K. Love you.

It was almost 6:30 when Kat got to E Street NW. Zach greeted her at the door with a handshake and a smile. He told her how happy he was to see her, adding that he was delighted that she was back. He seemed sincerely to mean it. Kat was sure he had experienced Greg's melancholy during the week as well.

The space was quiet and rather sad. It seemed even more sterile than it had when she had first visited. That had been only a little over a month earlier, but it seemed like so much longer ago. Kat looked around. Nothing had changed; everything was still in its place. She was glad to see that their photo was still on the bookshelf in the white living room. She wandered into the bedroom where they had first made love. She slipped off her shoes and stretched out on the bed, resting her head against the pillows. She was lying there when she heard a key in the lock. She didn't know how many seconds – it felt like minutes – passed before Greg appeared at the bedroom door. "There you are," he said quietly, leaning against the doorframe and looking at her. The backlighting from the living room framed his body. "Are you feeling alright?"

"I'm feeling fine," Kat replied. "I was simply enjoying the quiet and resting for a moment." She patted the bed next to her. Greg stayed where he was but continued to look her way.

Kat rolled onto her back and stared at the ceiling. "Please, Greg," she quietly pleaded. "Please come to me."

Greg slowly entered the room. He loosened his tie. Kat shifted over to provide him with more space on the bed. He eased onto the mattress, supporting himself on one elbow and gazing down at her.

"I've missed you, Greg," Kat said, searching his eyes and trying to read him. When he didn't respond, Kat reached up and placed her arms around his neck, pulling him toward her. She kissed him softly, then more aggressively, overcoming his resistance, until he relaxed against her and met her tongue with his own. Kat reached for his belt buckle, but Greg pulled back.

"I thought we'd go out to dinner tonight," he said, taking her hand and placing it back on the bed. Kat was disappointed, but she nodded her head.

"That would be nice," she said. "Give me a few minutes to change and fix my makeup."

Greg took her to a local pub. It was busy and noisy, but after a short wait, they were able to get seated at a booth in the back. Kat tried hard to engage in upbeat conversation and talked on and on about the party she was planning, the proposed catering menu, and the eclectic guest list.

Greg smiled at her. "You're enjoying this party planning, aren't you?"

"I am," Kat said. "Frankly, it's been an exceptionally good distraction this week – something fun and festive to look forward to."

"This gathering means a lot to you, doesn't it?"

"Yes, it does."

Greg looked at her and raised an eyebrow. "Why, Kat? Why do you want so much to throw this public gathering, this grand reveal, this *party*?"

Kat felt a little hurt, defensive. "It's not about a party, Greg. We don't have to have a party," she added, her voice getting increasingly louder as she continued. "In fact, screw the party!"

"Kat," Greg responded, motioning for her to lower her voice.

"I'm not going to make a scene," Kat replied, quieter this time. "I'm simply trying to explain that I don't need a damn party. All I want, Greg, is to introduce you to the people I care about and for them to get to know you. Believe it or not, I had people in my life prior to you entering it. People who care about me, love me, and are concerned about me. They want to meet you and to understand what in the world has gotten into me – why I've been all but completely absent during the last several months. They worry. They're curious. They want to continue to be a part of my life – of *our lives*."

Kat was on a role. "For my part, I want to share the joy that I have found with them. I want you to get to know other people in my life and to be a full and complete part of that life, Greg. Perhaps that is too much to ask. Damn it, Greg. If you've had a change of heart, please let me know. I can't go on much longer guessing and wondering how you're feeling."

Greg looked as if he may cry. He took her hands in his and met her eyes. "I have not had a change of heart, Kat," he said evenly and resolutely. "I will never have a change of heart. I love you, and I'm sorry I caused you to doubt that."

"Can we please go back to your place?" Kat asked.

"Of course," Greg replied, as he signaled for the check.

Greg opened the door to the apartment, and Kat went in. Greg followed, locking the door behind them. Continuing to hold Greg's hand, Kat slipped out of her shoes and gently led him to the bedroom. There, she stood facing him and did not break eye contact with him, as she slowly unbuttoned his shirt and eased it off his shoulders. She unfastened his belt and loosened his trousers. Kat raised her arms, so Greg could lift her blouse over her head. He reached around and unfastened her skirt, letting it slip to the floor. Then, he took her in his arms, and they climbed into bed. They made love, intensely, until they were both exhausted, collapsing against each other, their legs entwined, their chests expanding and deflating in unison as they caught their respective breath.

"I don't deserve you," Greg whispered.

"You deserve all of my love and, oh, so much more," she responded, defiantly, as she settled against him, resting her cheek against his chest and falling soundly and contentedly asleep in his arms.

Chapter 33

When Kat awoke, Greg was standing over her, holding a breakfast tray – eggs, toast, and a steaming cup of coffee. He handed her a robe, as she sat up and adjusted herself in the bed. He watched her intently, as she secured the robe around herself, tucked her hair behind her ears, and reached out to take the tray. Greg sat down beside her. He picked at the food on her tray and sipped on his own coffee as he read her snippets from the *Washington Post* and the *New York Times*. From time to time, he rose and refilled their cups. They spent most of the morning in bed, reading, discussing current events, and simply enjoying each other's company.

"I thought we might head out to the Shenandoah Valley today," Greg offered. "Take a picnic in the mountains? Perhaps walk through some of the little towns?"

"That sounds lovely," Kat responded.

And it was. They spent the day exploring villages among the foothills, pulling off the road to enjoy scenic overlooks, and stopping at a handful of vineyards. When at last they returned to the apartment, it was dark and well past Kat's dinnertime.

Kat made them each a grilled cheese sandwich. "It's my specialty," she offered, "and, frankly, other than scrambled eggs, one of the few things that I am actually good at making," she laughed. She quartered the sandwiches and arranged them, just so, on a plate, which she set on the coffee table in the living room.

"No doubt best with Chianti?" he asked, uncorking a bottle and pouring it into a glass carafe.

"Why, yes, of course," she replied with a smile, "and only the best vintage pairs with Colby-Jack cheese."

Greg stretched himself out on the couch and motioned for Kat to sit between his legs, as she'd done so many times before. The day had been delightfully easy and familiar. Kat sighed happily as she held the plate of sandwiches, handing Greg quarter pieces over her shoulder. They sat and watched the city lights until they began to dim.

Kat stretched. She collected the plate and the glasses and stood up to take them to the kitchen.

"I'm going to take a shower before bed," she announced, heading toward the bedroom. "It will feel good to rinse away the dust from the day."

Kat headed into the bathroom. She folded her dirty clothes and piled them on the vanity, as she heated the water. She slowly stepped into the steam bath. She closed her eyes as she lathered her hair into a thick, foamy, aromatic suds and then let the water rinse over her, sweeping the bubbles over her face and down her body. She wiped the soap away from her face and opened her eyes with a bit of a start.

"Oh, please don't stop on my account," Greg said. She hadn't heard him open the shower door. As he stepped in beside her, Kat was awestruck by him – by his body and his presence. She emptied a bit of shampoo into his hand and then shifted slightly, so he could lather and rinse. She proceeded to lather and wash his chest, his arms, his back. He pressed himself against her. Her breasts and stomach shone white with bubbles. Greg reached for the soap and rubbed it between his hands, warming it. He ran one soapy hand over her nipples, while he slipped the other between her legs. Kat arched her back and pressed herself into his hands. He lowered his head and kissed her deeply, as the water rinsed over them and the soap twirled around the drain.

He held her close, and they danced to faint music streaming from the living room. Just as he had done on the night of the gala, Greg moved her deftly to the music. Kat felt suspended in air, as he pulled her in close and then spun her slowly out. As he faced Kat away from him, Greg stepped behind her, leveraging her against the tiled wall. Kat caught her breath and extended slightly at the hips, bracing herself against the cool tile, as Greg entered from behind her. She gasped and eased herself against him, as he wrapped his arm around her waist and pulled her down onto him. They pulsated against each other as the steam and water surrounded them and held them there, transfixed, until they climaxed.

Kat untangled herself from Greg and turned to face him. He was smiling at her – that amazing smile that filled his face and spilled into the shower around them. Kat kissed him as he reached around her and turned the faucet. They toweled each other off and climbed, contentedly, into bed.

Greg kissed Kat goodnight and then turned to face away from her, settling into the pillows and pulling her arm around him. She placed her lips on his demon tattoo, paused for a moment, and then slowly nestled in behind him.

"Why do you do that, Kat?" Greg asked quietly.

"Do what?"

"Why do you kiss my tattoo?"

"I didn't kiss your tattoo."

Greg pulled away and turned to face her. He looked intently into her eyes, suddenly quite serious. "Just now," he insisted. "Just now, you kissed my tattoo. It strikes me that you do that virtually every time you find yourself behind me. I'm not imagining it, Kat."

Kat rolled on to her back and pushed her damp hair away from her face. She considered her thoughts for a moment before she began. "It may sound silly," she said contemplatively, "but I believe in the healing power of touch, the remedial energy of a kiss." She paused. "When I place my lips on your scar – which is how I think about your tattoo, *as a scar* – I feel as if I am transferring some of my energy, my optimism, my health and wellness to you."

"I'm not broken, Kat. I don't need to be fixed."

"I know that you're not broken, Greg. But none of us who have had as many life experiences as we have is completely whole. When I press my lips to you, I feel as if I am opening a portal to my soul. And I will the demons to stay away, Greg."

"Oh, Kat."

"It's not pity, Greg. I love you. And this is simply one way that I can feel like I am sharing all that I am – all that I have and all that I am able to give – with you."

"I don't know what to say, Kat."

"Just say 'I love you, Kat,' and go to sleep," she sighed.

"I have never felt so loved in my entire life."

"Then my power of touch is working," Kat smiled.

"I love you, Kat."

"I know."

Chapter 34

Greg gently kissed Kat's eyelids. As she fluttered her lashes, she glimpsed traces of morning sunlight. Greg had his arm under his head and was looking at her.

Kat yawned. "How long have you been watching me like that?" she asked.

"Maybe an hour?"

"An hour? What time is it?"

"It's almost 8:00. You were sleeping really well. You're beautiful when you sleep."

Kat smiled.

Greg looked nervous and a little anxious. His face appeared flushed.

Kat's caught her breath. "What's the matter, Greg? What are you thinking?" she asked, concerned.

"Nothing is the matter, Kat. In fact, everything feels right with the world. I've been thinking about what you said last night. It's all I have been able to think about."

Kat cocked her head. "What did I say?"

"I have been thinking about what you said about your healing power and the portal to your soul. I understand that energy, Kat. I feel it. I am whole when I am with you. I have never felt so complete." He paused. "And so completely and frighteningly happy."

Kat laughed. "Well, I have never known anyone else who finds happiness so frightening, Greg."

"I'm frightened only because I can no longer imagine my life without you."

"We haven't known each other long, but we know each other well," Kat responded, with a smile.

"Kat, I don't want to live weekend to weekend. I want to come home and fix grilled cheese sandwiches together on a Tuesday. I want to make love to you on a Thursday morning before work. I want to meet you for lunch on a Monday and walk along the Mall or the river.

"Will you marry me, Kat?"

"What?" Kat choked.

"I am asking you to marry me," Greg repeated.

Kat stared at him, wide eyed. Her mind raced. She could not focus. She could not formulate a response. She was completely without words. Several moments passed during which neither of them spoke.

"I've surprised you," Greg finally said, warily.

Kat hesitated. "Yes."

"I'm sorry. Take your time."

"Yes."

"Think about it," he added.

"Yes."

"I know you have a lot to consider and that I have caught you off guard."

"Yes, Greg, listen to me. I'm saying 'yes.'"

"Oh my god!" he exclaimed. "You mean you're saying 'yes,' you'll marry me?"

"Yes."

"Woot! Woot!" Greg shouted, grabbing Kat close and rolling with her across the bed. He stopped suddenly and looked at her. "I don't have a ring," he stammered. "Well, I do have a ring. It's my mother's ring. It's at the house in Memphis. But you should have your own ring," he continued.

"I would be so honored to wear your mother's ring, Greg. I can think of no symbol of love any more compelling than that."

Greg smiled. "I wish I had it here. I wasn't planning to ask you this. I was caught completely off guard by this as well. I went to sleep thinking about the portal to your soul, and I woke up convinced that we should wed."

Greg sat up with a start. "We need to call your sons."

"Of course, we do, Greg," Kat smiled, as she placed her hand on his arm. But we had best wait a little while. Neither of them is likely to be awake yet. It's only a little after 7:00 a.m. on a Sunday morning in Minnesota after all."

Greg went to get them coffee, and they sat in bed, scripting their conversations with the boys.

11:00 a.m. (to Anthony & Drew): Talk today? FaceTime together at noon (Eastern) / 11:00 a.m. (Central)?

They waited.

11:23 a.m. (from Anthony): K

11:30 a.m. (from Drew): Works 4 me 2.

Greg and Kat were both uncharacteristically tense as they waited for the appointed time.

"Here we go," Kat said assuredly as she gazed into her iPad. Drew came onto the screen first, then Anthony.

"Hi, kiddos!" Kat exclaimed. Greg waived behind her shoulder.

"Hi, Mom. Hi, Greg," said Drew. "What's up?"

"I don't mean to surprise you or put you on the spot, but Greg and I were just talking, and I want to know what you would think if Greg asked me to marry him."

Several rather painful moments of silence followed. Anthony was the first to speak. "Are you happy, Mom?" he asked simply.

"Very happy, Anthony," Kat replied, smiling.

"Then that's all I need to hear," he responded.

"Congratulations, you two!" Drew chimed in enthusiastically.

"Thank you so much guys," Kat said, as a tear formed in her eyes and rolled down her cheek.

"So when is the big event?" Anthony asked.

Kat looked at Greg and shrugged her shoulders.

"When is the garden party, Kat?" Greg asked.

"July 20," she replied and then smiled knowingly.

"It's July 20," Greg replied.

As they hung up the phone, Kat turned to Greg. "That is just a little over three weeks away, Greg."

"Well, then, we have a wedding to plan," he responded.

Chapter 35

During the following week, Greg flew to Memphis to retrieve the ring. He then joined Kat in Minnesota, so they could apply for their marriage license.

Kat began calling friends and family and made all of the arrangements for the garden party. She was so busy with the planning and preparation that she nearly forgot that she was the subject of an ongoing investigation. She was actually somewhat surprised when Karen called her the following week.

"I wanted to give you a quick update on where we're at in terms of our review, Kat. I've completed almost everything. Unfortunately, though, we haven't been able to reach the bartender, Linda. The hotel manager says that Linda quit her job about a month ago, and the hotel hasn't heard from her since. No one else at the hotel can vouch for you being there that night, Kat."

"Linda just left?" Kat wondered aloud. "Did she say where she was going? What she was going to do?"

"I don't know, Kat," Karen said, sounding somewhat concerned that Kat would seem so invested in a barkeep. "The hotel manager simply said that they didn't have a forwarding address or current telephone number for her."

Later that night, as Greg and Kat talked on the phone, Kat casually asked, "When you were in Memphis to retrieve the ring, did you happen to see Linda?"

"No. I didn't have time to stop by the bar. Why do you ask?"

"Well, I thought that maybe, since she was present when we met, she might be curious to know that we're getting married."

Later that night, Greg called back. "I texted Linda, but she didn't respond," he said, his voice tinged with concern. "I called Lilly, and she hasn't heard from Linda either. Linda's brother says she moved away and didn't tell him where she's gone. I'm worried about her, Kat. I know Linda. Like me, she has Memphis blood running through her veins. I can't imagine that she would just leave like that – and I certainly can't believe that she wouldn't let any of us know where she was going."

"I don't know what to say, Greg. Maybe she met someone? Wanted to get a fresh start?"

"Maybe. But my gut tells me that something isn't right."

"I hope she turns up soon," Kat offered. *"That would be best, not only for Linda,"* she thought, *"but also because Linda is the only one – other than a drunken stranger at the bar – who can corroborate when and how you and I met."*

Chapter 36

On the Thursday before the garden party, Kat met with the Company's CEO, Jerry Atkinson, and the Company's Chief Human Resources Officer, Diane Baker, to provide her quarterly labor relations update. When the meeting was coming to a close, Kat asked if they could stay another ten minutes. "I've also asked someone from Corporate Communications to join us," Kat said. "She'll be right up."

When they were all assembled, Kat began. "This is embarrassing for me," she stammered.

"What's wrong, Kat?" Diane asked.

"Nothing's wrong," Kat continued. "I simply wanted to let you know that I'm getting married the day after tomorrow."

They both looked surprised.

"Congratulations, Kat!" Jerry offered, sincerely. "That's wonderful news."

"I wouldn't normally call you all together to announce my wedding plans," Kat continued, flushing, "but I'm told that, as ridiculous as it may seem, the media may take an interest in my wedding, given that I'm marrying Greg Bodin of the IBT. There's apparently something quite salacious about a leader in the International Brotherhood marrying the head of a multi-national company's union avoidance efforts. And, again, while I think it is absolute nonsense that the media would spend any time thinking about Greg's marriage, I have been surprised by how much time and attention they have focused on his bachelorhood."

The woman from Corporate Communications (Kat could not for the life of her remember her name) looked at Kat with wide eyes. "Do you mean *the* Greg Bodin? Wait," she said in wonder, "you're the woman at the theater and at the gala."

"See what I mean?" Kat asked, looking exasperatingly at Diane.

The woman from Corporate Communications persisted. "Greg Bodin. Most eligible and sought after bachelor inside the Beltway?"

"Yes, that Greg Bodin," Kat replied, a little annoyed. "Although I would disagree strongly with the 'eligible' part."

"Hearts across D.C., Virginia, and Maryland will be breaking on Saturday," the woman continued, undeterred.

"In any event," Kat continued, intentionally facing away from the woman and toward Diane and Jerry, "I wanted to let you know about my relationship before you hear about it from someone else – let alone, god forbid, read about it somewhere.

"Most of all, I want you both to be comfortable that there is no conflict of interest. As you may already know, when Greg and I first started seeing each other earlier this year, I went immediately to Karen Greeley to ask for her opinion. Although I was sure there was no conflict, I wanted to know that she agreed with my assessment. She did. I understand that a concern has since been raised through the ethics line about a potential conflict, and Karen is reviewing that concern, but I don't believe that her position on a conflict has changed. That being said, now that Greg and I are taking our relationship from that of 'dating' to 'marriage,' I wanted to elevate the matter to you. I respect both of you too much not to talk with you directly about this.

"Even though I don't believe that there is a conflict, I have stopped interacting with the IBT and have placed one of my employees, Lisa, between me and the other team members, so if there is any issue with the Teamsters – whether that be a campaign, collective bargaining, contract interpretation, or an unfair labor practice – those issues go directly to her. It's likely an unnecessary step, but it does make me feel better."

Kat noticed first the woman from Corporate Communications and then Diane respectively attend to their computers, and Diane adjusted her screen.

"Did you just send her a photo?" Kat demanded of the woman from Corporate Communications.

Diane laughed. "He really is attractive, Kat. I have to agree with our friend here that hearts may be breaking this weekend."

"The two of you are not making this any less embarrassing for me," Kat smiled uncomfortably.

Diane laughed.

Kat rolled her eyes and continued, "I, too, of course, find him attractive, but he's also smart, thoughtful, caring, creative, funny, adventuresome, a bit mysterious. I could go on and on. I feel very lucky to have him in my life. "

"Good for you, Kat. I wish you only the best," Jerry noted.

"And, if any of you happens to be in my neighborhood in Minnesota on Saturday afternoon, the wedding is planned for 1:00. But please keep it quiet. Other than me, Greg, my two sons, and the justice of the peace, no one else knows that it's a wedding. They simply think they are coming to a backyard gathering to meet Greg. As long as everyone was gathered anyway, we thought 'what the hell, we might as well get married.'"

Kat stopped by Karen's office on the way back from the meeting to share the plans with her. Karen appeared less than happy to hear the news.

Chapter 37

The weather on Saturday was uncharacteristically cool for July and offered a welcome respite from summer's oppressive heat. The sky was a deep turquoise, with tiny wisps of white gathering in what appeared to Kat to be cloud bouquets in the heavens.

Of course, Lilly had helped Kat pick a dress for the party, and, at Greg's coaxing, she and Scott had journeyed to Minnesota for the event, as had Mitch and Susan and Martha and Rick. Kat also had assembled a host of family and friends. Anthony had arrived home on Friday evening, and he and Drew spent the night at the house. The four of them – Greg, Kat, Anthony, and Drew – cooked and ate together, played board games, and talked. Kat had taken all of it in, amazed at the ease and joy of it all.

The caterer was busy preparing the food and setting the tables that were arranged inside two giant tents that decorated the back yard. Kat helped place vases brimming with a mix of flowers from her garden on the tables.

Greg's contribution to the celebration was a three-piece string ensemble.

About an hour before the first guests were set to arrive, Kat went inside to shower and dress. As she passed Greg in the hallway, he hurriedly slid his phone in his pocket and threw his arms around her neck. "Are you nervous?" he asked.

"Not in the least. And you?"

"No," he responded, placing a kiss on her nose. "This is going to be the happiest day of my life."

"Hmmm," Kat responded. "I'd be a little nervous if I were you," she teased.

"And why is that?"

"I can hazard to guess that this is the longest-term contract you've ever negotiated, my dear union brother. It's one that cannot simply be re-opened a year from now, and the management rights clause is totally skewed in my favor."

"At least the benefits are amazing," Greg retorted, grabbing Kat's rear end with both hands.

"I'd say that this contract is mutually beneficial," she smiled, running her hand up his leg and across the front of his pants.

Drew cleared his throat. "I think it's probably time for the two of you to knock it off and get ready already," he interrupted with a smile. He rolled his eyes. His own hair was wet, and he was struggling with the tie around his neck. "I'm so glad it's cooler today."

By the time Kat finished dressing, Drew and Anthony were greeting the first of the guests in the driveway and showing them to the backyard. The ensemble was playing, and the caterer was busy distributing finger sandwiches and mimosas. Lilly had selected a beautiful 1950s-style swing dress for the occasion. It was baby blue polka dotted with a navy sash around the waist and a Sabrina neckline. Kat felt like she had just dropped in from the set of *Mad Men*.

Greg met her at the door in a navy blue suit, and with a baby blue, polka dotted tie. He placed two fingers in his mouth and whistled for the boys, who excused themselves from the early guests and joined Greg and Kat on the steps.

"First, a photo of the day," Greg announced, summoning a caterer's assistant to take a picture of the four of them.

"I absolutely love it," Kat remarked, as she looked at the screen. "I cannot think of anything for which I am more grateful right now than the three of you!" Kat hugged each one in turn.

"We have something for you," Greg noted, eagerly. "While we're trying to be very discrete, we wanted to be sure that you have something old, something new, something borrowed, and something blue for the ceremony. We are a bit superstitious, you know, and don't want to leave anything to chance."

"We were each responsible for one of them," Drew added.

"I have something old," said Greg, reaching into his pants pocket and withdrawing the ring case that held his mother's wedding ring. As he opened the lid, Kat could see that it was non-traditional, adorned with antique opals and rubies.

"It is absolutely gorgeous, Greg!" Kat exclaimed. "It truly is one of the most beautiful pieces of jewelry I have ever seen."

"I'm so glad you like it," Greg replied, closing the lid and handing the box to Anthony for safekeeping.

"I have something new," Drew chimed in, handing her a little satin bag with a yellow ribbon wrapped around it. As Kat untied the ribbon, a small, smooth stone dropped into her hand. "It's a worry stone," said Drew. "I had it engraved with each of our names. You can keep it in your pocket, and if you get nervous or afraid – either today or any day – you can hold it in your hand and know that we are here for you and that you are surrounded by love."

"What a thoughtful gift, Drew," Kat responded, with tears filling her eyes. She reached up and kissed his forehead.

"And I have something borrowed," added Anthony, "because you're already wearing blue." He pulled a hatbox from behind his back. In it, Kat found a lovely pin box hat with a blue satin bow and a pair of white gloves. "I think Grandma Eve was a bit worried about me when I asked if I could borrow these," Anthony grinned. "She looked at me a little funny."

Kat laughed. "These were in her closet when I was a little girl," she said. "They belonged to my grandmother, and my mother would let me look at them. One time she let me try them on, and I danced around the house as if I was a princess at a ball."

"You're a princess today," Greg remarked.

Anthony offered, "I'll set these behind the bar, so you can put them on right before the ceremony."

"That would be wonderful, Anthony," Kat remarked, as she hugged him. "Thank you all for your thoughtfulness! Now, we'd best be off to visit with the guests."

The boys continued to usher friends and family from their cars to the backyard, greeting everyone and introducing themselves to Greg's friends and family. Kat and Greg met the guests as they came around the side of the house into the area where the stone path opened up into the garden. They laughed and talked with everyone and totally immersed themselves in the intersection of their lives.

Martha and Rick were seated by Kat's mother, Eve, and Martha and Eve were sharing stories about young Greg and young Kat. Tom McCormick and his wife Greta visited with Mitch and Sue. Kat's best friend from college, Robin Phillips, sat smiling, as Lilly entertained her with stories of who knows what. And Kelsey was visiting with the boys, catching up on their college happenings and asking questions that resulted in tolerant groans and feigned protests from each. It was a festive atmosphere, and Greg and Kat joyously soaked it all in.

As noon approached, the caterers ushered everyone to tables and began to serve lunch. As the last guests were finishing their meals, Greg stood and raised a glass. "I would like to propose a toast," he offered. "Thank you all so much for coming here today. When Kat first mentioned bringing friends and family together, primarily to meet me, I was a little less than enthusiastic. I felt a little like a Debutante or a Quinceañera."

Several people laughed. Greg continued, "but this has been such a special day – a wonderful blend of friends, old and new, and family – a beautiful collage of our pasts, presents, our futures coming together in this stunning garden on this perfect summer day. So here's a toast to all of you with sincerest appreciation and gratitude. Thank you, particularly, to all of you who love Kat for welcoming me into your lives and tolerating my monopoly of her time over the last several months."

"Cheers!" rang out across the yard.

Kat stood, and Greg slipped his arm around her waist. She raised her glass. "I also want to add my heartfelt thanks to my good friends and family who have come here today – some out of love, some curiosity, others to ensure that I've not completely lost my mind, and all to meet Greg and to welcome him into our lives, into my village. And I want to offer my deepest thanks to Mitch, Susan, Martha, Rick, Lilly, and Scott for coming all of this way. It is so very amazing to have so many people we care about in one place." Kat raised her glass.

"Cheers!"

Kat nodded at Greg to speak again, as she ducked behind the bar to grab the borrowed hat and gloves. He smiled and cleared his throat. "Now we know that it is a summer Saturday and that several of you need to leave sometime soon. For everyone else, please feel free to have seconds, grab dessert, indulge in more wine or mimosas, and stay as long as you're able."

Kat pinned the hat into place and was drawing on the gloves, as Greg continued. "For now, however, we'd ask that all of you remain for at least another 10 minutes, as we would be honored if you would bear witness to our marriage vows." A whispered hush swept over the gathering, as everyone looked around in wonder and disbelief.

Kat broke the awkward silence, "Your Honor? Boys?"

The Wedding Officiant stood and took her place at the front of the garden. Greg joined her. Anthony and Drew each grabbed a handful of flowers from a vase on the back table and wrapped the dripping flowers with a silk ribbon. Anthony handed the makeshift bouquet to Kat, as he and Drew posted on either side of her and walked her over to where the Officiate and Greg were assembled.

Mitch stood and began to clap, and everyone rose to their feet and joined in. Kat and Greg beamed as they looked out over the assembly. As everyone finally quieted and took their seats, Kat turned to face Greg, "We have not known each other long, but we know each other well," she began. "From the moment I met you, I knew that you were special. Within 24 hours, I questioned whether I ever could live without you. Today, I promise you my love and my life – everything I am and everything I have – 'til death parts us. I know what true love is, Greg. I have been so blessed to have found it, not once, but twice in my life." Kat glanced at her former mother-in-law, who was smiling through her tears. "My soul is forever intertwined with yours, as today I vow to love you – always."

The Officiant asked for the ring, and Anthony opened the small box and handed it to Greg. "Do you, Kat Elizabeth Anderson, take this man to be your husband, to have and to hold, to love and to cherish, 'til death parts you?"

"I do," Kat laughed, as Greg placed the ring on her finger.

Now it was Greg's turn. "I have never been one to believe in fairy tales or love at first sight – until April. I knew within minutes of meeting you, Kat, that my life had changed forever. My heart opened, and I wanted nothing more than to hold you within it forever. You complete me in a way that no one ever has. I am whole when I am with you. You fill my life with joy and light, optimism, and a zest for the future. You make me laugh. You see in me the man I long to be, and I am better because of it. I am not a particularly religious man, but I thank God every day for bringing you into my life. I love you, Kat."

The Officiant prompted Drew for the band, and Kat placed it upon Greg's finger, as the Officiant recited, "Do you, Gregory Michael Bodin, take this woman to be your wife, to have and to hold, to love and to cherish, 'til death parts you?"

"I do."

"Then, by the powers vested in me by the State of Minnesota – and with Anthony and Drew and your collective village as your witnesses – I now pronounce you married." Before the Officiant could continue, Greg had wrapped Kat in his arms, dipped her low, and kissed her. The ensemble began to play, and the gathering erupted into applause once again.

The caterers placed individual white cakes at every plate, as the guests approached Kat and Greg, surrounding them with hugs, kisses, and well wishes.

The party went late into the evening. Mitch and Susan were the last to leave. Mitch embraced Greg and said something to him that Kat could not hear. Greg smiled broadly and nodded his head. Mitch grabbed him tenderly by the shoulders.

Greg closed the door and followed Kat to their bedroom – the bedroom she had once shared with Bennett and that she now opened, utterly and completely, to him.

Chapter 38

On Sunday, Greg and Kat had brunch with Mitch, Susan, and the boys and then took Anthony to the airport. On the way back to the house, they stopped off at Minnehaha Falls for a long walk. They returned to the house, happily exhausted and spent the evening looking through old photo albums, as Kat took Greg on a pictorial journey of her life. They fell into bed, slightly overwhelmed by the joy of it all.

On Monday and Tuesday, Kat took Greg to many other beautiful places in and around the Twin Cities. They biked, hiked, kayaked, and indulged in Minnesota's summer splendor. Between exploring nature and each other, their honeymoon was brief but blissful. The next day, they would fly to D.C., where Kat would work remotely for the remainder of the week, and the week after that? That was still up in the air.

"What is our plan, Kat?" Greg asked earnestly, as they had dinner together in the garden on their last night in Minnesota. "You'll work from D.C. this week, but what about next week or the one after that? I don't want to commute every week, if we can help it. I'd really like to spend as much time together as we can. What are your thoughts?"

"I can work from anywhere, but I will still need to be in Chicago at least a couple of weeks a month. You'll be traveling as well. But if you are wondering where we call 'home,' I am completely flexible. Drew is all settled in at school, and I feel like he's in a really solid place. While it might be nice to keep a house in Minnesota where he and Anthony can come 'home,' I'm beginning to think that 'home' is simply where I am – where *we are*. I saw how comfortable Drew was in Memphis, and I think they'd both enjoy coming to spend time with us in D.C. as well."

"I don't think I'm ready to leave Memphis, Kat."

"I wouldn't ask you to do that."

"I know we can't live there full time, but I would like us to build memories together in that place."

"I'd like that." Kat smiled as she placed her hand on Greg's arm.

"In the meantime, should we look for a place near D.C. that would not be mine or yours, but ours?"

"That sounds wonderful," Kat replied. Later, she fell asleep dreaming of a small, Colonial-style home in Northern Virginia that they would share.

Kat worked from Greg's apartment on Wednesday afternoon and Thursday. After work on Thursday evening, they met Mitch and Susan for dinner. "Hello, dear Kat," Mitch greeted her, with a hug and a kiss on the cheek. "How have you enjoyed your first week of marriage?"

Kat blushed.

Susan laughed. "Oh, Kat," she grinned. "It's obviously been wonderful."

"Indeed."

"The two of you definitely surprised us on Saturday," Susan continued. "Not by the fact of the marriage – any fool could see that that was likely inevitable – but by the timing. A little over three months together, is it? What took you so long?" she teased.

Chapter 39

Karen Greeley called Kat on Friday. "Will you be in Chicago next week?"

"Yes," Kat replied. "I'm planning to fly in Sunday night and stay through Thursday."

"Great," Karen responded. "Are you staying at the Intercontinental?"

"I am," Kat responded. "Just a short walk to the office. I should be there by 8:00 a.m. Do you want to meet that morning?"

"Let's play it by ear. I'll be back in touch," Karen rather abruptly wrapped up.

On Sunday morning, Kat awoke with Greg's arms around her. She stayed still, not wanting to wake him. She enjoyed the comfort of his warm embrace. They'd been together every day for ten days now, and the thought of going to Chicago that evening saddened her. Oh, how her life had transformed over the course of the last several months. She'd always been so carefree about her travels and the Chicago commute, but today, the mere thought of it seemed heavy and wilting.

Greg stirred, and Kat rolled over, so she could lay her head on his shoulder. She stroked his chest.

"Penny for your thoughts, Kat."

"I was just reflecting on how frighteningly happy I am."

Greg squeezed her tight. "Happiness should never be frightening, Kat."

"You stole my line," Kat smiled.

"My how things have changed," he responded. "At least you'll only be gone a few days."

"I know. I'll be back Thursday night. But four days seems a lot longer to me now then it ever used to."

Greg ran his fingers down Kat's side, alongside her breast, and then down to her hip. She leaned into him and pressed her full body against his. His energy overwhelmed her, and they made love passionately and with abandon. Afterward, they fell back asleep until late in the morning and then rose and made brunch. They lounged around until it was time to leave for the airport, rejoicing in the ordinary – reading the paper together, sipping coffee, washing and folding clothes, tidying up, taking out the garbage.

Greg refused to let Kat take an Uber or a cab to the airport. He drove her to Reagan National and walked her to the security area. He kissed her gently and watched her walk through security. She waved at him from the other side, blew him a kiss, and turned away, just in time to reach her gate and board.

Bang! Bang! Bang! Kat awoke at the hotel, disoriented, not knowing where she was or registering the noise. "It's the FBI! Please open the door. I repeat, Kat Anderson, please open the door." Kat grabbed a robe from the back of the closet and wrapped it around herself. She proceeded cautiously to the door and looked out the peek hole. She could see three men in black coats with the FBI logo emblazoned on them.

"Just a minute," she shouted, as she fumbled with the lock and the chain. As she opened the door a crack, the first officer pushed it with some force.

"We have to come in ma'am," he sounded off. "Please step back and let us pass."

"What's the meaning of this?" Kat inquired in a frightened voice. "What are you doing here?"

"Do you have a laptop in the room, Ma'am?"

"Yes."

"And a telephone?"

"Yes."

"We'll need you to turn those over to us, Ms. Anderson."

"Do you have a search warrant? How about identification?"

"In fact, we do," the agent replied, removing a folded piece of paper and a badge from his jacket pocket and handing them to her.

"I want to speak with my lawyer," Kat demanded, as the agents dug through her bag and collected her computer and her cell.

"By all means, Ms. Anderson," the first agent responded. "We simply want to take you in for a little questioning."

"And I want to talk with my lawyer first," Kat repeated. "Please hand me my phone."

The agent gave Kat her cell phone and watched as she dialed.

"Hello?"

"Kat, is that you?"

"I need you to represent me, Tom. Can you please come to Chicago?"

"What's going on, Kat?"

"I have no idea, Tom. FBI agents came to my hotel room. They are taking my computer and my phone. They haven't told me why."

"Don't say anything to them, Kat. Wait until I get there. I'll try to catch the first flight out. Let me talk with the agent in charge."

Before Kat handed the phone away, she whispered, "Tom, please call Greg."

The officers allowed Kat to dress and took her to an office complex near the center of the city. There, she was allowed time alone to talk with Tom. He was in a taxi on his way to the airport in Minneapolis.

"What the hell is going on, Tom? Have you learned anything more?"

"Very little, Kat. It's something about potential theft. It sounds as if they believe that embezzlement is happening through your email account."

"What? That's ridiculous, Tom! Embezzlement? Me?"

"I said it's happening through your account, Kat. I didn't say that I thought you were doing it." Tom paused. "I'm bringing one of my white collar crime partners, Kat. Do you remember Brian Needle? He and Bennett worked together for years."

Kat remembered Brian. He'd hit on her at a holiday party once when he was sloshy drunk. She always thought that he was a rather arrogant asshole, but perhaps that's what she needed right now. "Yes, I do remember Brian. Thanks so much to both of you!"

Tom continued, "Don't thank us yet, Kat. We don't know what we're dealing with at this point, but we'll keep digging."

"Were you able to get ahold of Greg?" Kat asked.

"I tried his number, but he didn't pick up."

"Please keep trying," Kat pleaded. "He will be worried when he can't reach me. When will I get to talk with him, Tom?"

"I'll try to get that worked out when I arrive, Kat. In the meantime, hold tight and stay calm. We are catching the first flight to Chicago. It's a short flight, and we'll be there as soon as we can."

"Thank you."

"Kat, who else has access to your devices?"

"My assistant, Kelsey Harig does." It suddenly dawned on Kat why he was asking. "But I am positive that Kelsey had nothing to do with this, Tom. She is one of my closest friends. I trust her with everything. She's a mother, Tom. She has little girls. I'm her youngest child's godmother."

"Does Greg have your password?"

Kat reacted angrily. "No, Tom. Greg does not have my password. What are you suggesting?"

"I'm not suggesting anything, Kat. I'm simply trying to sort out what I need to do here in order to help you get out of this situation.

"Does anyone else have your password, Kat?"

"No, I don't think . . ." She gasped. "Oh, my god, Tom! Drew. I gave Drew my password. He helped me sort out an issue on my phone. Oh, Tom. Don't let them talk with Drew."

"I'll send someone over to his dorm to meet with him now, Kat. I'm sure that someone from the FBI will want to interview him."

Kat uttered a small cry.

"Don't worry, Kat. We'll represent him. We will take care of Bennett Anderson's wife and son."

Chapter 40

Kat sat in a room alone until Tom arrived. An agent brought her coffee and a scone. She felt sick to her stomach, but she picked at the pastry. With the travel and the late arrival into Chicago the night before, it had been a while since she'd eaten.

Tom arrived around 2:00 in the afternoon. Kat threw herself into his arms, and all of the emotions of the day came spilling out in fitful sobs. Brian came in quietly behind Tom and took a chair without saying a word. He looked terribly uncomfortable when, at last, Kat backed away from Tom and wiped her eyes and her running nose on the handkerchief that Tom handed to her. At least streaking mascara had not been a problem. There had been no time for makeup with FBI agents waiting impatiently in her room.

"Hello, Brian," Kat choked, as she fought to compose herself. "Thank you for coming. I really appreciate that you both are here." Brian rose and gave Kat a light embrace.

"It's been a long time, Kat," he said, smiling oddly at her.

Kat diverted her eyes and turned to Tom. "Is someone with Drew?"

"Yes, Kat. We sent another partner over to talk with the boy. He is fine, and it seems unlikely that the FBI will interview him until at least tomorrow."

"What about Greg?" Kat asked, with a catch in her voice.

"It's our understanding that the FBI showed up at Greg's apartment and your home in Minnesota this morning, at exactly the same time that they visited you. Greg was also taken into custody."

"Is he represented by legal counsel? Can you represent him, Tom? I don't want them questioning Greg without an attorney present."

"I don't know if he asked for counsel, Kat. I haven't had a chance yet to look into any of those details. I've been worried about getting here to you."

"When can I talk with him, Tom?"

"I will find out, but I suspect that they won't let you talk with each other until after each of you has been interviewed and you've given fulsome statements."

"What could they possibly want from Greg? If it's embezzlement they're after, he has nothing to do with the Company. He's never used my computer. And he doesn't have my password."

"Don't worry, Kat. We'll get this figured out. I'm having some background searches run now, and I have posed questions to both the agency here and in D.C."

"Background searches? Of whom?"

"Kelsey and Greg, for starters."

Kat's voice reached a screeching pitch, "They are not involved in any criminal embezzlement, Tom!"

"Calm down, Kat. And please let me do my job." Tom placed his hand firmly on Kat's shoulder and faced her. "Trust me."

Kat folded herself into a chair. She wrapped her arms around her knees and drew them up to her chin.

"You were at our home earlier this month, Tom," she quietly reflected. "How do I go from that to this in just over a week?"

"I'm sorry, Kat," Tom replied. "You seemed so happy."

"I *am* happy, Tom. I *am* happy." She closed her eyes. The room was spinning, and her sight began to darken. "I think I'm going to be sick," she uttered, as Tom quickly helped her of the chair and to the wastebasket.

Tom spent over an hour with the agents, while Kat and Brian sat in silence. Brian pecked away at his computer and glanced at Kat periodically. Kat sat with her head resting against the chair back and her eyes closed. So many thoughts chattered in her head. Every so often, she would raise a glass of water to her lips, rinse her parched mouth, and swallow slowly, reflexively.

When Tom returned to the room, Kat opened her eyes. Tom joined Brian at the table. Brian pushed his laptop over to Tom, as he pointed at the screen. Tom sat, reading, seemingly transfixed.

"What is it, Tom?" Kat asked. "What have you learned?"

"The agents want a full interview first thing in the morning. I have convinced them to release you into my custody. We'll get you fed and all head over to the hotel. You will get some rest, so you are fresh in the morning."

Tom paused. He adjusted his glasses to the top of his head and rubbed his eyes.

"What else have you learned?"

Tom swallowed and looked at Kat intently, holding her attention. "The agents believe that Greg may be responsible for this, Kat."

"That's ridiculous!"

"They are gathering evidence. They aren't sharing much yet, but they are increasingly certain that he's not innocent in this thing."

"I don't believe it!" Kat remarked bitterly. "I won't believe it. It isn't true!"

"How well do you know this guy, Kat?"

"He's my husband, Tom."

Brian looked up, surprised. Tom nodded at him. *"Did Tom not tell Brian that Greg and I are married? Did that not seem like an important fact?"* Kat wondered, angrily.

"Yes, Kat, but how well do you really know him? You met him, what, four months ago?"

Kat glared at Tom.

"I know this hurts, Kat, and it's confusing. But, as best I can tell, the embezzlement also began four months ago. Coincidence? Maybe. But we – I – can't be so certain at this point."

Now it was Brian's turn to talk, "And, Kat. We received the background search results on Greg. He was tried for criminal vehicular homicide in 1994."

"I know that, Brian," Kat interjected. "It was an accident. He was distracted. He was hit from the right side. Annie was in the car. Annie died. He was acquitted."

"But not before a lengthy trial, Kat," Brian noted. "There were other claims as well, including theft by swindle. It seems that Greg may have been stealing money from his girlfriend."

Kat grimaced. "Fuck you, Brian. Fuck you." She sat and put her head in her hands, rocking back and forth. She was so weary. She turned to Tom. "Can we go now?"

When they finally arrived at the hotel, Brian and Tom checked in. Tom directed Kat to the elevator. "I got us a suite with two bedrooms."

Kat sighed. "Thank you, Tom. I may have at least a chance of sleeping, if I'm not completely alone with my thoughts."

"Oh, you'll sleep, Kat," Tom said, as they walked to the room. He handed her two capsules and a bottle of water. "I'm not taking any chances that you're a tired mess in the morning." He opened the door and followed her inside.

Kat sat on her bed. She was exhausted. Tom stood just inside her bedroom door for a time.

Kat looked up at him. "Before I take this medication and go to sleep as I've been instructed," she asked, "may I make one call?"

"I can't let you call Greg," Tom said.

Kate looked completely dejected.

"I'm sorry," Tom continued, "but I can't. When they ask you tomorrow whether you have had any contact with him, I need for you to be able to say that you have not."

Kat sighed. "May I call Mitch?" she asked.

"Why Mitch?"

"Mitch is Greg's best friend. I need to know that someone is there for Greg. I will rest easier if I know that Mitch or Martha are by his side."

Tom contemplated for a moment. He sighed. "I have to listen to your conversation, Kat. You can call Mitch, but you must do so on speakerphone, so I can listen in and attest, if necessary, to what is said. And please be smart about it."

Tom sat down on the bed next to Kat and handed her his phone.

"Hello? Mitch Thorton here," said a familiar voice on the other end of the line.

"Mitch, it's Kat."

"Kat! Are you okay? Where are you? We've been so worried about you!"

"I'm fine, Mitch. Tired. Shaken. But fine. What about Greg? How is Greg? Have you been with him? How is he doing? My god, I've been beside myself today with worry about him!"

"He's okay, Kat. He can't talk with you, you know."

"I know."

"I'm so sorry."

"I'm just so glad that you're there, Mitch. And, Mitch, does Greg have legal counsel?"

"We retained someone for him today – Martha and I did. He had already spoken with the agents, though." Mitch paused. "Dear Kat, I must go."

"Tell him that I love him, Mitch? Please?" Kat pleaded. "Tell him that I love him so very much!"

"You're on speakerphone, Kat."

Tom sighed. "Well, I guess that doesn't count as talking with him, given that you didn't know that he was there, and he did not respond," he said. "Remember that when you are asked tomorrow. You did not talk with Greg."

"I did not talk with Greg," Kat repeated.

"Now, be a dear and go brush your teeth and change into the pajamas in your bag," Tom instructed, as he gave her a tired, but reassuring smile. "I'm going to be up working for a while next door, but I'll be quiet. Hopefully, you'll be able to sleep right through."

Kat swallowed the pills with a sip of water and went into the bathroom to change and to prepare for bed. As she crawled under the comforter, she felt overcome with exhaustion. Before she could say goodnight to Tom and to thank him again for his help, she was asleep.

Chapter 41

"Please raise your right hand, ma'am."

Kat obliged.

"Do you swear to tell the truth, the whole truth, and nothing but the truth, so help you God?"

"I do."

"Okay, please have a seat and make yourself comfortable, Ms. Anderson. My name is Agent North. Thank you to you and your legal counsel for coming in voluntarily to talk with us today."

"Well, I wouldn't actually say this is voluntary," Kat said.

Tom shot her a warning glance.

"I mean, if I didn't need to be here, I would rather be someplace else," Kat added, with a smile.

"Then, thank you for feeling the need to be here, Ms. Anderson," the Agent responded in a completely deadpan manner. "We have some very important questions to ask you."

"Then shoot," Kat replied. "I mean, not literally, of course." She laughed, nervously. "I'm sorry. I'm just a bit tired and punchy. Obviously, I'm not at my most articulate."

"That's fine, Ms. Anderson. We'll take this slowly."

"Can you please call me Kat? It's going to be such a long day if you keep referring to me as Ms. Anderson."

"Yes, Kat, if that's what you prefer," Agent North smiled patiently. "Are you ready for me to ask my questions now?"

"Yes, of course."

Agent North took Kat through her educational and work history. He asked her about her role with the Company and her many work responsibilities. He asked about her family, her finances, her mortgage and debts. He asked about Bennett's death and the toll that had taken on her and the boys. He was kind, but thorough, and forced her to go into everything in minute detail. When they were finished with the preliminaries, they took a 10-minute break.

"He is going to ask about Greg next, isn't he?" Kat asked Tom as they grabbed a coffee from the machine in the hallway.

"I suspect that he will." Tom smiled reassuringly at her. "Are you ready?"

"Yes." Kat took three deep breaths and attempted to smile back.

Tom reached for Kat's hand and squeezed it. "You're doing well, Kat. Just keep your cool. They have a job to do. They aren't accusing either of you of anything – yet. Simply listen to his questions and keep your head about you."

As Kat had suspected, as soon as they returned to the interview room, the agent started in on his questioning around Kat's relationship with Greg. He walked her in painstaking detail through their chance meeting at the hotel bar in Memphis. Kat smiled when she talked about how she felt Greg's smile lit up his face and spilled into the room. She explained how they talked until Linda closed the bar and how he kissed her and left her at the ice machine – close enough to ensure she got back to her room safely, but not so close as to make her feel uncomfortable.

She walked him through receiving Kelsey's email about the Teamsters' leadership and how angry she had been when she learned that Greg was the "hired gun from D.C." who had been summoned to manage her during negotiations.

"So you felt that he deceived you?" the agent asked.

"At the time, yes," Kat responded thoughtfully. "However, I came to learn later that he had not actively lied to me, but, rather, he had not disclosed his identity because he was afraid that if he told me who he was, I wouldn't have continued to talk with him, and he wouldn't have had the opportunity to get to know me better."

"Okay. And how was it that you came to believe that?"

"Greg told me that."

"I see," the agent continued, taking a note in his pad.

The agent questioned her about the next morning's negotiations and the unexpected turn-around of the union's position. And then they talked through, detail by detail, the day in Memphis – from the motorcycle ride to Lilly's dresses to the Grand Ole Opry performance and the local gossip columnist. He had her recount everything she could remember about their night together. He had her do the same with respect to the next morning: hiking, watching the sun rise, sitting by the lake, going back to the hotel room before she left.

"You were working during this trip to Memphis?" the agent confirmed.

"Yes. I was negotiating a collective bargaining agreement," Kat responded.

"Did you have your computer with you?"

"Of course. Yes."

"Did you have your computer with you in Nashville?"

149

"No. I left it in my hotel room."

"Was it in the safety box?"

"No. I left it in my bag in the hotel room."

"And was the computer in your bag in the hotel room when you returned to the room to shower on Friday?"

"Yes."

"Your bag, where was it in the room?"

"I'm sorry. What do you mean?"

"I mean, was it in the bathroom, the closet, beside the bed, on the desk?"

"As I recall, my bag, with my computer in it, was on the desk chair. I packed it in my carryon, but that was right before I left for the airport."

"Now, Kat," the agent continued. "We talked with Kelsey yesterday. She told us that you were having some problems with your password while you were in Memphis?"

"Yes. We are forced to change our passwords every couple of months. I had just done so – well, actually, Kelsey had just done so for me," Kat added, hesitantly, "and I called her to remind me of it on Wednesday, so I could get some work done in my room in anticipation of Thursday's meeting."

"Did you record that password in any way? Did you, for example, write it on a legal pad? Put it on a stickie? Type it into your phone? Keep track of it in any other way, so you'd have it and might actually remember it?"

Kat reflected. "I didn't have my computer open during my call with Kelsey. I scribbled the password down on a hotel notepad, you know, the ones they often leave by the phone."

"Okay," the agent said. "And what happened to that paper?"

"What do you mean?"

"I mean, did you leave it on the desk? Did you rip it up and throw it in the trash? Did you stick it in your purse?"

Kat looked apprehensively at Tom. He sat up straighter and nodded for her to continue. "I wrote Greg's full name and cell phone number on the back of the slip of paper and left it in the center of the desk."

No one said anything, so she continued, "I didn't know this guy, and I was planning to spend the day with him. My family didn't know where I was going or with whom. Kelsey didn't know either. No one did. Perhaps I've watched too many crime shows on television, but I thought that it was in my best interest to leave some information about my whereabouts, just in case I went missing."

Tom looked at her quizzically.

The agent continued, "So when you came back to the hotel room, what did you do with the paper with the password and Greg's name and number on it?"

"It was gone," Kat responded. "When I finished showering, I went to pack the stuff I had left on the desk. The note was gone. Maid service must have thought it was trash and thrown it away. I remember laughing to myself a bit, as I thought about how little good that clue would have done me when the cleaning person shit-canned it."

"Had you noticed the note on the desk, Kat, before you went into the shower?"

"No. I didn't think about it until I was getting ready – and at that time, I was like, well, that note is kind of embarrassing. How am I going to explain to the man with whom I am falling in love that I was hedging my bets that, perhaps, he was, in fact, a serial killer?"

"I could see how that could be a little awkward," Agent North agreed.

After another break, the agent asked her about every other encounter with Greg up until the night before she left for Chicago. He didn't go into the same level of detail, but he was persistent nonetheless. When at last he completed his interview nine hours after it had begun, Kat was drained.

"They didn't ask me about Drew," Kat whispered to Tom as they were leaving the interview room.

"My associate persuaded the authorities not to talk with Drew until they have exhausted all other avenues. He's just a kid who helped his tech-challenged mother with an app," Tom smiled. "I don't believe that anyone thinks that he was capable of this," he assured her.

Kat squeezed Tom's arm and took a deep breath. She steadied herself, as relief swept through her and, with it, her last remaining bit of energy.

Tom called a cab, and the three of them headed for the airport. "I've arranged for our flights back to Minnesota," he said. "I'll drop you off at your house. I've asked your mom to spend the night, so you're not alone. I'm instructing you not to talk with Greg tonight or to have any contact with him whatsoever until after we meet tomorrow."

"Can I call Mitch?"

Tom was obviously frustrated. He looked at Kat and shook his head. "Can you just give it a rest, Kat? Honestly. This is very serious business. Greg is a full-grown adult. He's apparently been fine without you for decades. I am sure that he will be fine without you for this one night."

Chapter 42

Tom and Brian were waiting in the conference room when Kat arrived at their office the next morning. *"It is so odd being here, particularly under these circumstances,"* she thought. How many times had she been to this building with Bennett? Law firm functions. A jumping off place for dinner. Keeping him company on Saturday mornings, as he finished up a couple of things at his desk. She hadn't been inside the building for over a year, but everything felt so eerily familiar. She wondered who was in Bennett's office now. She was glad that the conference room was on a different floor, so she didn't have to walk by and see the foreign nameplate, the fresh furnishings.

Tom greeted Kat with a quick hug and a kiss on the cheek. He did not seem as agitated or glum as he had the night before, but he still appeared tired. Kat imagined that he had worked late into the night.

"How did you sleep?" he asked.

"As well as can be expected, I suppose," Kat responded. "I got a few hours."

"Good," Tom replied. "We're likely to have you here for the entire morning, Kat. We want to debrief from yesterday, ask you some follow-up questions, and update you on what we have learned since we last spoke."

Brian motioned for Kat to sit. "From our vantage point, there are some troubling facts."

"Troubling facts, Brian?" Kat responded defensively. She recalled, with only a slight twinge of regret, that the last thing she had said to him was "fuck you." But still, he grated on her nerves.

"What Brian means, Kat," Tom interrupted, "is that it appears that the Government's case against Greg is mounting."

Kat stared at him in disbelief. "How can that be, Tom? Greg has done nothing wrong."

Tom looked rather exasperated. Brian rolled his eyes.

Kat bristled. "I'm sorry, Brian," she began, fiercely, "I know that you are trying to help, and I appreciate the fact that you accompanied Tom to Chicago when I called. I really do. But I must say, honestly, that you are really starting to piss me off. Please quit treating me like a misguided child. I understand the severity of the allegations. I was, after all, the one whose home and hotel room were broken into by FBI agents. I also know that my husband, Greg Bodin, is not involved in any of this. He is a kind, generous, loving man. He would never hurt me intentionally or steal from me or from the Company I work for. You don't know him. You've never even met him. And you have no right to judge him." She paused and caught her breath. "I would be grateful if you would at least give me the benefit of acting as if I have at a modicum of intelligence and common sense."

"Of course, Kat," Brian responded in a subdued tone. "I did not mean to offend you. I have the utmost respect for you." He paused. "I always have." Did Kat imagine that he blushed? Perhaps he, too, remembered the infamous holiday party.

Brian continued, "I'm simply struggling with your seeming inability to get your head around the fact – actually, even the *mere possibility* – that Greg Bodin may not be the person you thought he was. It's dangerous, Kat, this blind devotion, particularly in a situation where you need to be thinking clearly."

Kat sighed. She turned to Tom. "I'm listening to you, Tom," she said in a tone that clearly dismissed Brian.

"I think Brian's concern, which I share, is that you're not out of the woods yet, Kat. Everything points to the fact that the embezzlement occurred through your email account. During your interview with the agents yesterday, you were obviously forthright. You answered all of their questions in a straightforward and non-defensive manner, even those questions about your personal and intimate moments. You were very credible, Kat, and I don't believe you have given the agents any reason at all to believe that you are the criminal here. But a crime has been committed, and it is their duty to figure out who has done it.

"Here are the facts that I believe lead them to suspect Greg." Tom paused and placed his hand on hers. "Now, please just listen quietly and try to consider how these things appear to them – to objective observers who don't know you or Greg."

Kat inhaled and nodded for Tom to continue.

"First, Greg coincidentally appears at a hotel where he could very well know you will be. The union likely knows where you're staying. His friend Linda works at the hotel. He is a man about town in Memphis and is familiar with a number of the locals. He takes to you immediately. Now, don't get me wrong, Kat, you're very attractive and personable." Tom shifted in his chair. "But you're also a fairly recent widow whom the Government will suspect is a bit more vulnerable than the norm. Greg is the one responsible for the union's sudden change of direction and cooperation, which he immediately follows with an invitation to go on a date with him – a date that is choreographed down to the last detail – a perfectly scripted event with an almost story-book quality. He sees you back to your hotel room the next day, and while you are safely in the shower, he is alone with your computer – and a note on which you have written both your password and his name and telephone number."

"We don't know that the note was there, Tom," Kat added half-heartedly.

Tom ignored her comment and continued, "The connection appears to have been made within 48 hours. They also have identified multiple occasions after that during which you had your workbag and computer with you when you visited Greg or he visited you.

Tom looked sympathetically at Kat. "Then there is the matter of the quickie relationship, the unexpected marriage proposal, and accelerated wedding date. Kat, you went to law school. You understand the meaning of a marital privilege. You must know that the Government cannot compel Greg to testify against you – or you to testify against him. That will seem a little too convenient to the authorities, don't you think?"

"And to you, Tom? How does it seem to you?" Kat asked with an edge in her voice.

"It's my job to protect you, Kat, and to advocate for you. That means being willing to consider any possibility, including this one."

"This one being the hypothesis that the last four months of my life have been one big lie to cover up a crime?"

"I know how that may sound to you, Kat, but Brian and I need to be realistic."

"Huh," Kat responded, her jaw clenched tightly.

Tom ticked through a number of other facts that he thought potentially damaging to Greg – the 1994 trial allegations; his history (albeit long since passed) of addiction and lack of financial resources; the fact that many people (including media and social column reporters) described Greg as quiet, introspective, even mysterious.

Kat was completely depleted when Tom and Brian finally announced that they were done for the day. Her body felt drained and unresponsive. It took what seemed like an inordinate effort simply to rise from the chair. And she was having increasing difficulty formulating a thought, let alone articulating one.

"May I have a moment with you, Tom? Alone?"

Brian smiled and nodded at Tom. "That's my cue," he said. "We'll talk again soon, Kat." Brian gathered his things and left the room, quietly closing the door behind him.

When Kat and Tom were alone in the conference room, Kat mustered the strength to turn toward him. Her eyes filled with tears, but she didn't have the energy to cry.

"I've been listening, Tom. I really have." She faltered. "I have."

Tom reached out and took her hand in his.

"But I also know what I've experienced. I know how he looks at me, the sound of his voice, what he says, how he makes me feel. I'm the only one who does. You can't make this up, Tom. No one can fake this."

Silence filled the space between them.

"Can they?" she asked softly.

Tom met Kat's eyes. "I don't want to believe it either, Kat, not for Greg's sake – frankly, I'm still a bit baffled by and distrustful of how quickly everything happened. But I don't want to believe it for your sake."

Tom continued, "I don't remember you ever being this radiant, Kat – this overwhelmingly happy." He paused and took a deep and intentional breath. "Not even when you were married to Bennett."

Kat smiled faintly. "You've known me a long time, Tom," she said.

"Yes, I have."

"And you know that I've never had a good poker face."

"You did pretty well with that yesterday, thank you," Tom smiled.

Kat looked out the window. "I loved Bennett. He's the father of my children. We had a very good life together, and I miss him. I do." Kat paused. "But I have never in my life felt about anyone like I feel about Greg."

Tom squeezed her hand tenderly.

"Please be patient with me," Kat said quietly. "I can't bring myself to believe that I've been played by him – that I've somehow acted the part of a pathetic, vulnerable widow who simply wanted so badly for someone to love her."

Chapter 43

Kat and Eve were settling in after dinner. Kat had protested, but Eve insisted on staying over for at least a few more nights. Eve wanted to ensure Kat ate, slept, and maintained relative normalcy, despite the criminal investigation. They were resting in the living room, and Eve was sorting through Netflix options, when there was a sharp knock at the door.

"Tom!" Kat exclaimed as she rushed to let him in. "What's the matter?"

Tom looked at Eve and then at Kat. "The agents raided Greg's Memphis home today. Kat, they found a yellow blouse on the property that they believe may have belonged to . . ."

"To Linda?" Kat squeaked, her voice failing.

"Yes, to Linda LaVec. As I understand it, her family hasn't seen or heard from her for several weeks now. The authorities are having DNA testing done to confirm the identity of the blouse's owner, Kat. Assuming that the clothing did belong to her . . . "

"Does belong to her, Tom," Kat interrupted, "not *did* belong to her."

"Okay, Kat. Assuming the clothing does belong to Linda LaVec, the investigation will, of course, take a whole new direction."

Kat lowered herself to the floor. She was shaking, and her legs would not hold her upright. Tom and Eve left her sitting there in silence while the tremors mitigated. Then they helped her to the couch.

"May I call Mitch, Tom?"

"What? Are you serious?" Tom was incredulous. He removed his glasses and rubbed his eyes.

"May I call Mitch?"

"I'm worried about you, Kat," Eve began.

"I'm worried about me, too, mom. In the interest of my f'ing sanity – or whatever is left of it – will you please let me call Mitch?" She turned to Tom.

"Here are the rules, Kat," Tom responded sternly and resolutely, as he handed her his phone. "You talk only to Mitch. This time, you ask if you are on speakerphone and insist that he take you off speaker. We only had one chance at plausible deniability on that count, Kat. You will be on speaker on this end, and your mother and I will listen in. Assume that someone else may be listening as well. At this point, *always* assume that someone else is listening. And don't say anything that you'll soon regret. Please." He paused. "Do you understand my instructions?"

"I do."

One ring. Two rings. Three rings.

"Mitch Thorton."

"Mitch, it's Kat. What the hell is happening, Mitch?"

"I likely know less than you do, Kat."

"Mitch, listen to me. I can't be there, but you can. Everything I have is his. I will give you power of attorney over everything other than the college funds. You must be wiling to use anything I have in his defense."

Tom shook his head and reached for the phone.

Kat pulled away and spoke faster and more urgently. "I don't know whom you have hired to represent him, but I want you to retain the very best criminal defense counsel. I have an old law school professor named Shannon Finley. We've remained in touch. Call her. She will know who the best person is.

"I will not testify against Greg. They cannot compel me to do so. Of course, I have nothing to say that could hurt him because he isn't involved in any of this. He can't be. But I won't be used as a pawn against him – not in any way."

Eve was behind Kat. She grabbed the phone out of Kat's hand and tossed it to Tom. As she did so, Kat yelled, "I love you, Greg!"

Tom caught the phone and put it to his ear.

"Mitch. This is Tom McCormick," he said – to Mitch and to anyone else who could be listening. "My client is completely distraught by the news today that, in addition to being a potential thief, her so-called husband may also be somehow involved with the disappearance of Linda LaVec. She just learned this news and is obviously not thinking straight. You currently have no rights to any of my client's assets, and I aim to keep it that way. I would have you kindly forget anything that was just said."

"What the hell were you thinking?" Tom shouted, as he clicked off the call.

Chapter 44

Tom called the next morning. "The FBI needs to talk with you about Linda LaVec."

"I know nothing about Linda LaVec," Kat replied.

"Well, then, it shouldn't be a very long conversation, should it?" Tom answered coolly. He clearly was still angry about Kat's performance the night before. "I told them we could have you to their offices by 10:00 a.m. Meet Brian and I here at 9:00, and we'll walk over together."

Kat had an hour to get ready before she needed to drive downtown. Eve made her some breakfast while Kat showered and dressed.

Tom was alone in his office when Kat arrived. He was seated behind his desk and did not get up when she entered. He motioned her into the room. "I thought we'd have a quick conversation before Brian gets here," he said. "Please, have a seat."

Kat took the chair facing him across his desk.

"I have been thinking about what happened last night," Tom began. "I should have been more vigilant. I have given you a lot of flexibility, Kat, because you're not only a client, you're also a friend, and I care about you a lot. *Too much.* I have allowed our friendship to cloud my professional judgment. I can't afford to do that. Correction. *You* can't afford for me to do that. I will do you a disservice and perhaps even commit malpractice if we continue down this path. So here's the crossroads I find us at. I want to continue to represent you. I truly believe that I am the best lawyer for this job. But I will withdraw if we cannot align around my representation of you."

Kat knew he was serious, and she felt her heart knock uncomfortably against her ribs. She also knew that he was telling the truth when he said that he was the best-qualified lawyer for this task – not just because of his technical skills and abilities, but also because of his loyalty and dedication. He would do his very best work for Bennett Anderson's widow.

"I'm listening, Tom."

"Well, that's a relief." He paused. "Of course, I have heard that before."

Tom looked at her intently for a moment before continuing. "First, you have to do what I ask, Kat. I won't make this any harder than it has to be. I promise. If and when it is safe for you to talk with Mitch – or Greg, for that matter – again, I will make it happen. Until then, you will have no contact. I will connect with them. I will share some of your messages. I may not share all. But you have to trust me. Everything I do is in your best interest."

"But," Kat began.

"But, nothing, Kat," Tom responded, sternly. "Let me finish."

Kat nodded and remained quiet. She bit her lip.

"I know you love him, and I will support that. I will do nothing that intentionally jeopardizes Greg or his legal position. If there is a strategy that benefits you but puts him at any disadvantage, I will talk with you about it first. I am not looking to help the Government make a case against Greg. I hope to God that they are not able to do so."

"Thank you, Tom," Kat whispered.

"With respect to your assets, Kat. I cannot sit by and let you sign over full power of attorney to Mitch Thorton. However, I can work with you to ensure that any proceeds from any assets you wish to liquidate are put toward Greg's defense costs, if that is what you wish. I need to be in control of those processes, however. Fair?"

"Okay."

"Only two more conditions."

"Another two?"

"Yes, another two." Kat thought she detected a slight smile on Tom's face.

"First, you have to continue to take care of yourself. Let Eve stay with you. Get out and get some exercise. Eat well. Sleep when you can."

"And the second?"

"Lay off Brian. He is doing a damn good job with respect to this matter, and both of us need his assistance. He's a little rough around the edges, yes, but his heart is in the right place; he's the best that I have; and he's working his ass off on this."

"Fair enough. But so help me if he rolls his eyes at me."

"Oh, I don't think he'll dare do that again, Kat," Tom laughed.

Chapter 45

"Welcome back, Kat," said Agent North. "Please, be seated, but, before you do, let me swear you under oath again."

"Is that necessary?" asked Tom.

"I believe it is – at least precautionary," Agent North replied. After administering the oath, he asked Kat, again, to tell him when she had met Linda LaVec and everything that Linda had said and done during that first evening in the bar. Kat walked through with him everything she could recall.

"So at some point during the evening, Mr. Bodin had a conversation with Ms. LaVec that upset her. Is that correct?" Agent North asked.

"Yes, that's correct."

"And you did not hear any part of that conversation? You only saw Ms. LaVec's reaction during the conversation and then afterward."

"That is right."

"And it's your understanding that Mr. Bodin talked with Ms. LaVec about the fact that he was deceiving you by not telling you who he was?" the agent asked.

"Not in so many words," Kat responded. "I'm certain he did not tell her that he was 'deceiving' me, as he did not believe he was, in fact, 'deceiving' me. It was error by omission, if you will. However, he did tell her that he was struggling with his decision not to disclose his full identity."

"And what was Ms. LaVec's reaction to whatever Mr. Bodin said?"

"She was clearly upset. She swatted Greg on the arm. When she would come to the table, she'd talk only to me. It was obvious to me that she was shunning him, scolding him, and disapproving of his choice. I could see right away that Greg and Linda have a special relationship. Greg told me that they have known each other since high school and that whenever he is in Memphis, he tries to swing by and see her. She is clearly fond of him. It struck me that they were sort of like siblings with the way they behaved toward one another."

"Interesting," the agent remarked.

"Is it?" Kat enquired, sarcastically. The hairs on the back of her neck were standing up. She tried not to physically react to the thought that the agent would somehow find Greg and Linda's relationship "interesting."

Agent North ignored her reaction. "So when did you see Ms. LaVec again?" he continued.

"We saw her on Friday when we returned to the hotel. She was in the lobby. As I recall, she made some joke like, 'Look what that Kat (k-a-t) dragged in.' She seemed happy to see us together."

"How did you know that?"

"She was smiling and greeted us with an effusive laugh. She wrapped me up in a huge hug. She whispered in my ear, 'Forgiveness is a glorious thing.' She told Greg that he was a 'lucky son-of-a-bitch,' or words to that effect."

"'Forgiveness is a glorious thing'?" the agent asked. "That's what she said?"

"Yes."

"Did Ms. LaVec say, what, in fact, might need to be forgiven?"

"No, but I understood her to mean that she was happy that I had forgiven Greg for not sharing his true identity with me two nights before."

"Did you see Ms. LaVec again that day?"

"No, I did not."

"Did Mr. Bodin see Ms. LaVec again that day?"

"I do not know."

"Okay."

"I took a cab to the airport. I caught it at the curb. Greg stayed there with me until I rode off. I do not know whether he went back into the hotel after I left or headed straight home."

"Did you, yourself, ever talk with Ms. LaVec again?"

"No. I have not seen, talked with, or otherwise communicated with Linda since. My Company's ethics officer, Karen Greeley, told me several weeks later that they had tried to reach out to Linda as part of the investigation I described to you earlier and that they were unable to reach her."

"Did you talk with Mr. Bodin about the fact that Ms. LaVec was missing?"

"Not at first."

"Go on."

"I hadn't told Greg about the internal investigation. Karen asked me to keep it strictly confidential, and I did. The ethics complaint, as you will recall, was about whether I had a conflict of interest because of my relationship with Greg."

"Are there other significant things you haven't shared with Mr. Bodin, Kat?" the agent asked.

Tom shot Kat a warning glance. She straightened up, breathed in through her nose, and responded calmly, "I don't believe so, no. The fact is that I was instructed to keep the investigation confidential by an officer of my

Ella Kennedy

Company, and I took that instruction very seriously." Tom nodded his head, ever so slightly.

"Have you ever talked with Mr. Bodin about the fact that Ms. LaVec is missing?" the agent continued.

"I have."

"Tell me about that."

"I wanted to talk with Greg about Linda. I was worried about her, and I knew that he would be worried as well. I could not talk with him about the investigation or let on that I had information I hadn't shared with him, but I wanted him to know about Linda, so I suggested to him that he reach out to tell her that we were getting married. She was, after all, present on the evening we met, and I figured she would want to know and might even be able to come to the ceremony in Minnesota."

"'The ceremony' was the secret wedding in Minnesota?" the agent prodded.

"The wedding wasn't a *secret*. It was a *surprise*."

"Okay," the agent continued. "And to your knowledge, did Mr. Bodin reach out to Ms. LaVec to invite her to the surprise wedding?"

"Yes, I believe he did, because when I next spoke with him, he was really concerned about her. He said that he had tried to reach her, but she had not gotten back to him, which was very unusual for her. He also said that he had reached out to Linda's brother, I believe, and that he had told Greg that Linda had quit her job at the restaurant and left town. The family had not heard from Linda for some period of time."

"Do you know anything more about Ms. LaVec, Kat?"

"What do you mean?"

"I mean, do you know anything more about her, her history, the nature of her work, the nature of her relationship with Greg?"

"I don't."

"Then I believe we're done for today. Thank you, again, for coming in, Kat. I know that this has not been easy for you." Agent North backed away from the table and reached over to shake Kat's hand.

When Tom, Kat, and Brian were back in the car, Kat asked, "What more is there to know about Linda, gentlemen?"

"From what I've found so far, Kat, it appears to me that Linda is a Madam," Brian said.

"So I've just described to federal authorities that my husband has a 'special relationship' with a prostitute?"

"Yes, it appears that you have."

Chapter 46

On Friday, Kat asked to meet with Tom again. "It's been five days, Tom," she began. "I have been very patient, and I have been the ideal client, following all of your various instructions." She paused thoughtfully. "At least for the last several days," she added. "And I just need to know, Tom, when I can talk with Greg."

"I'm surprised you've waited this long to ask," Tom replied with a slight sigh. He motioned toward a chair. "Sit down."

Kat took a seat across the mahogany desk.

"Truth is, I have been trying for two days to make a connection with Greg."

Kat looked surprised. Tom tilted his head and grinned. "I promised you I would, Kat, and I keep my promises." Tom's eyes were red, and he seemed even more tired than he had been earlier in the week. "I'm sorry, Kat, but Greg won't take my calls, and Mitch says that Greg does not want to talk with anyone."

"Not anyone?"

"No one. He's apparently been in and out of questioning all week, and he's not holding up well. Mitch tells me that Greg is becoming increasingly despondent. It's my understanding that he has suffered with some depression in the past?"

Kat nodded her head.

"I have no doubt that the stress of this situation has been really difficult for him, as it has been for you. He also apparently feels as if he has somehow brought all of this on you and your family – as if he is responsible."

"I need to talk with him, Tom. Can I go to him?"

"You can't leave the state right now."

Kat felt as if her internal organs were being squeezed. Everything hurt inside her. She had a difficult time catching her breath, and her heart pounded wildly, as if trying to escape from her chest. She looked at Tom.

"Perhaps he isn't the person I thought he was," she managed, fitfully.

"He's ill, Kat."

"The Greg I know wouldn't just abandon me at a time like this."

Tom looked so sympathetic – not pityingly, but truly as if he was experiencing her anguish. Kat noticed how his blondish-brown hair framed his face; how his jaw line disappeared behind his ear; how his glasses sat upon his nose and refracted the light behind his grey-green eyes.

Tom put his hand on hers. Kat shook her head slowly and pulled her hand away, horrified that she was pondering whether she found Tom McCormick – Bennett's best friend and her lawyer – attractive. She stood up and turned away from him.

"Damn it!" she gasped. "Perhaps I really am the sad, weak, lonely, desperate widow the feds are painting me out to be."

"I don't believe that for a minute, Kat." Tom responded quietly, as he walked toward her. "When you talked about your love of Greg the other day and when you did that stupid thing in his defense despite the potential impact to yourself, I thought, 'my god, this is a strong and formidable woman.'" He reached out and took her chin in his hand, turning her face toward him, so she was forced to look at him. "Your behavior this week has confirmed to me what I have always thought, Kat: you are a remarkable person. Bennett was a lucky man to have you in his life – and so is Greg."

Kat could not muster a word, but she continued to focus on Tom's earnest eyes and to draw strength from him.

"Do you want to talk with Mitch, Kat? Would that help?" Tom gently removed his hand from her chin and placed it on her arm.

Kat pondered the suggestion. She waited a few moments and took a deep breath before she responded. "If Greg wants to talk with me, you're telling me that he can reach out to me? He's free to try to connect with me?"

"Yes, Kat, he is – so long as there's oversight on both ends."

Kat swallowed hard and looked away from Tom. "Then you call Mitch, Tom. Please. You find out what Greg needs – money, medical attention, whatever that may be. With your assistance, I will do whatever is in my power to help him. But as much as it hurts, I won't beg for Greg to speak with me. When he is feeling better, when he is ready to reach out, he will know where to find me."

"Are you sure that's what you want?"

"No. But I'm at least reasonably certain that that is what I need."

Tom and Kat were still meeting when the phone rang. Tom went to the desk and picked it up.

"Tom McCormick. Yes. Well, that is definitely not the news we were hoping for. Yes. I am glad you called. Thank you for letting me know." As he hung up the phone, Tom looked intently at Kat. She felt a chill run down her neck and back. "That was Mitch. A search party has located remains that the authorities believe may belong to Linda LaVec."

Kat gasped. "Where did they find the remains?"

"In a place called Meeman-Shelby Forest State Park. It's apparently about 20 miles outside of Memphis."

Kat nodded sadly. "I know that park well, Tom. It's adjacent to Greg's property. It's where we hiked on that first morning we spent together."

Chapter 47

Kat couldn't sleep. She couldn't eat. For the entire weekend, all she could do was think – think about Greg; about her life; about her children; about Linda. She played her personal reel over and over in her head, as she caressed the worry stone that Drew had given her on her wedding day.

Eve left Kat pretty much alone, but she remained close. She cooked food and left it on the counter. She washed Kat's bedding and turned down the coverlet. She tidied up the house and placed books and other distractions in strategic locations.

On Sunday afternoon, Kat finally succumbed to her emotions, to her exhaustion. When she awoke, it was just after 3:30 in the morning. The house was dark and quiet. Eve had apparently been up to the room. Kat's glasses were folded and sitting on the bed stand, and the blankets had been pulled up around her neck.

At first, Kat did not know where she was, but as her bedroom came into focus around her, so did her thoughts.

> *3:33 a.m. (to Tom): Can I meet with you and Brian later today (Monday)? I want to go through the entire file – everything you know. I want to help. I need to do something.*

Despite the hour, Tom responded immediately.

> *3:33 a.m. (from Tom): Of course, Kat.*

Chapter 48

Kat was more energetic than she had been in days. Brian and Tom had a conference room arranged when she arrived. Stacks of paper and two computer terminals were placed around the conference room table.

"Where do you want to begin?" Brian asked rather eagerly when she entered the room. "I think this could be a great idea, Kat. Tom and I have gone through everything multiple times. You bring a fresh set of eyes and a different perspective to what we've collected."

"Let's start chronologically," Tom suggested, as he entered the conference room carrying three coffees. "Good morning, Kat. Skim latte, no froth, correct?"

"Perfect. Thank you."

It felt so odd to Kat to have Tom and Brian play back and describe to her the entirety of her relationship with Greg – but for the most private details. Kat was thankful that the agent stopped short of asking her about the intimacy. In any event, how could she ever have described what it felt like – what it feels like, she corrected herself – to have Greg's arms wrapped around her, the weight of his muscular body on hers, the way that she physically responded to his touch, and the pure joy that she felt as she collapsed against him?

"Do you need a break, Kat?" Tom asked.

"No," Kat started. "I'm sorry. I drifted for a moment."

"It's okay. I know this is overwhelming."

When they were about two hours in, Kat interrupted them. "As you know, I'm quite terrible about this tech stuff."

"Yes, we've gathered that," Brian smiled.

"So these may be very obvious questions. But, if my work phone is dual purpose, and I also get my personal emails and texts on it, does that mean that whoever hacked into my work account also has access to my personal things?"

"We don't have your device. I suspect that the Government's computer forensics teams are going through it. We can ask."

"And if they did have access to my personal information, does that mean that we should be checking my accounts for fraud as well? As you may be aware, I received a significant life insurance payment following Bennett's death. I haven't received any notices of large withdrawals or charges on any of my accounts, but should I be doing a more thorough review?"

"I suspect that the federal agents have already checked your accounts – at least to determine whether you were making any sizeable deposits," Tom replied. "Let me talk with them, Kat, before you begin to change any of your account information or passwords. We may need you to order new credit cards as well. But wait until you hear back from me on that. First, it's a lot of work and inconvenience. Second, it may not look good to the authorities if you are messing around with your full financial picture right now, at least without some context."

"Do you know how much they allegedly took from the Company, Tom?"

"The last I heard, it was just over two million dollars."

"Is that all?"

Tom looked at her, surprised. "That's a significant amount of money, Kat."

"And it's well above the threshold to qualify as a felony offense," Brian added.

"I understand all of that," Kat said, "but it's not significant as compared to what was available for that product line. That product was generating revenue hand over fist. The profits could not be reinvested quickly enough. The business was consistently cash rich," she continued, "*very* cash rich. If someone was to go to the trouble of hacking into my account and committing a felony offense – and, apparently, doing it well enough that no one has been able to identify him or her, at least so far, why stop at a couple of million? Why not syphon off as much as you could, at least until the breach was discovered?"

"Maybe they took only what they needed?" Tom offered.

"Or maybe they thought if they took a bit at a time, they were less likely to be discovered?" Brian added.

"Perhaps," Kat said, "but that just seems odd to me. Maybe it's not about the money. Maybe the motives weren't financial."

"Or, perhaps, Kat, you simply don't have the mind of a criminal," Brian noted.

Tom's assistant appeared at the door with boxed lunches.

"Let's take a break," Tom suggested. "I'd rather not work while we have our sandwiches."

"And you'd like to ensure that I eat?" Kat asked.

"Perhaps," Tom smiled warmly and winked.

Kat ate most of her sandwich and the entire apple. She made a point of showing Tom how well she had done before dumping the box in the trash.

"Fair enough," Tom said, his face brightening for a moment.

"As we get started again, gentlemen, can you tell me everything you know about Linda LaVec and her relationship with Greg?"

"We don't know a whole lot," Brian began. "Linda LaVec was born Linda Jones in 1971. Her mother was a suspected prostitute. There is no father listed on her birth certificate. She has two siblings on record, both brothers, and both older. She and Greg attended high school at the same time. From what we can tell, Linda lived in Memphis her entire life and was known to the local authorities. There were a few investigations into potential prostitution and promoting prostitution. But nothing stuck."

"Is there anything to indicate that she and Greg ever," Kat paused.

"We have no way to know, Kat," Tom responded. Which reminds me, you may want to go to your clinic and be tested."

"Tested for what?"

Tom looked initially incredulous, but he quickly softened. "For STDs, Kat."

"Oh, god," Kat replied with a gasp. How had she not even thought of that? She had sex with a stranger about whose history she obviously had no clue whatsoever, and she didn't concern herself with disease? What was she thinking?

Tom talked to Agent North. He was able to confirm that Kat's personal email account had also been successfully accessed. Their forensics team had determined that shadow accounts had been created for each – the same email address with different passwords, running dually. The shadow accounts were still live, although there'd been no activity for a little over a week, just before the FBI raids. They had taken no action to shut them down, in the hope that someone may try to access them again and, therefore, provide the authorities with a virtual path back to them.

Tom and Agent North agreed that Kat would compile a list of all of her accounts, credit cards, and 401(k) and other benefits information that she would share with the agents. The agency would conduct the review to ensure that nothing about Kat's personal finances were amiss. Kat made a list of the things she needed to gather that evening. It would be a long night.

Before she left, Tom called her into his office. "Agent North helped me with one other thing, Kat. He's connected us with a software package that will give you a little more freedom, in the event that Greg reaches out to you – or you decide to reach out to him. Take my phone. Your number has been forwarded to it. If you have communications with Greg, push this icon here," he pointed.

"That will ring me, and I'll pick up. I'll listen silently, but do know that I'll be there."

Kat nodded.

"If, for whatever reason, I don't pick up, the call will be automatically recorded."

"I am so grateful, Tom. Thank you."

Chapter 49

Kat spent much of the night gathering account and financial information. Drew came over to help her, and Eve was happy to cook and care for the two of them. It felt good to be busy, to be doing something – something that was hopefully productive.

The next morning, Kat brought a handwritten list of every account she owned to Tom's office. She hadn't typed it up or put it in an Excel spreadsheet. She was taking no chances that someone else could access an electronic list.

Agent North joined them, and they went through the list together. "This is good work, Kat. We will definitely take a look to see if your personal finances have been compromised. In any event, we will be back in touch when the investigation has been completed. We're working with your employer right now to take care of that on the business front."

"Thank you," Kat replied. "Do you have any idea how much longer this might take?" she asked. "I know it's complex, but I guess I'm just anxious to try to restore my life."

"I wish I knew," the agent said thoughtfully. "Indeed, it is complex. The bad guy is rather duplicitous," he smiled, as he turned to leave.

Kat was startled.

"What did you say?" she asked in a voice that resonated in her head as nearly a shout.

Tom stared at her. Agent North turned to face her. "I was just saying that the bad guy is duplicitous. That means . . ."

"I know what it means," Kat responded sharply. "It's just that that word has particular significance to me."

The agent put his hand on Kat's shoulder. "That is the new password that the bad guy created. Have a seat, Kat. I think we may be here a while."

Of course, Kat had mentioned Christian Christopher during the first interview. This time, however, she described how he had behaved toward her; the anger that he had demonstrated toward her; and how he made her feel. She also described her interactions with Brandy Christopher at the gala. She told them about the note that she had written, kiddingly warning Christian that she was "duplicitous" and instructing Brandy on the word's meaning.

"I know you've wracked your brain, Kat," the agent said, "but can you think of any reason whatsoever that would cause Christian Christopher to dislike you so intensely?"

"I can't. I don't think it was simply the adversarial nature of being across the table from each other during negotiations. I think it was something deeper. Sexism, perhaps, but his reaction seemed a little extreme, even for that. Mitch's wife, Susan, told me that Christian was a Research Scientist by training and does not have any people skills." Kat stopped. "That could be it, Tom!" she exclaimed excitedly.

"What are you talking about, Kat?" Tom asked. "Take a breath. You're not making any sense."

"The motivation, Tom! The motivation!"

Kat turned to Agent North. "The formula!" Kat exclaimed, jumping to her feet. "Has anyone checked the formula?"

"Slow down, Kat," Agent North responded. "What are you getting at?"

"I don't know how this all works," she hurried, "but I believe that access to the Company's product formulations requires a two-step approach. I don't know if I have access to them. I've never had reason to access one. But, at my level of the Company, it's possible. If someone were able to use my access, they'd need one more access to get to the product formulations. A million dollars may not get someone to retirement, but a knock-off product utilizing that formula certainly could."

Tom and the agent continued to look at her. Neither said anything.

"Call the Company, Agent North," Kat pleaded. "I may be wrong, but, under the circumstances, I believe it's a theory definitely worth exploring. Don't you?"

"You can use my office, Agent," Tom offered.

Kat waited in a conference room. Tom had given her a book and a cup of coffee and told her to make herself comfortable. She'd settled into a chair, which she had positioned to face the window. She couldn't keep her focus on much, so she trained her eyes on the horizon and watched the clouds slowly form and dissipate in the sky beyond the glass. The artful swirls calmed her.

Tom came into the office. "They've brought Christian Christopher in for questioning," he announced. "Nice job today. Hopefully, the information you were able to share helps bring some additional clarity and closure to this matter."

"The sooner the better, Tom."

"Agent North has instructed that a guard post up at the house tonight."

"Why?" Kat asked, alarmed.

"He didn't say, but he thought it would be better to be safe. I agree," Tom said, demurely.

Kat stood and faced Tom. She threw her arms around him and hugged him. "Thank you, Tom," Kat paused, "for everything. I will never forget what you've done for me."

Tom hugged her tightly. His lips brushed her cheek. "Hey," he said. "This isn't over yet. Until the federal agents tell us that you've been cleared of all suspicions, you will continue to heed my instructions. All of them. Do you hear me?"

Kat smiled. "I do."

Chapter 50

With Tom seated next to her, Kat dialed Greg's number.

"You've reached Greg's cell phone. I'm not available to talk right now. Please leave a message or try calling again at a later time."

Kat sighed deeply and waited for the beep.

"Greg, it's Kat." She paused. "It's funny, but I'm not sure what to say right now." She took a deep, audible breath. "So much has happened in the last week. I have so many questions. Please pick up or call me." She paused again, gathering her thoughts and pondering how much more to say. "I miss you."

"There's not much else to say right now, I guess," Kat remarked, as she clicked off the phone.

"He'll call, Kat," Tom reassured her, as he pushed a stray hair from her cheek and tucked it behind her ear.

Kat poured a glass of wine for herself and one for Eve. They were both in their pajamas, and Eve, once again, was perusing Netflix options. Kat snuggled up next to her and put her head on Eve's shoulder. "Thanks, Mom, for everything you've done over the course of the last week. I know that I haven't always been the best housemate."

"Of course, darling," Eve said, as she massaged Kat's shoulders. "You are fine, Kat. You are strong. And you will get through this. I simply thought you might need a little help at first."

Kat drained her glass and curled up on the couch. Eve stood and placed a blanket over her. Before Eve could key up the first show, Kat was sound asleep.

Kat awoke to the vibration of Tom's phone. She opened her eyes and groped around aimlessly trying to find it. The phone had slipped between the sofa cushions, and Kat was unable to get to it before the call had gone to voice mail. "Damn it," Kat mumbled, as she reached for her glasses. Mitch. The call had been from Mitch. Kat dutifully clicked the app that would alert Tom and waited. When she heard him click onto the line, she pressed the "return call" button on the cell.

"Kat," Mitch said, "we just heard the news about Christian."

"Yes, he was called in for questioning earlier today."

Mitch went silent. "Kat, he was taken into custody. He posted bail." Mitch stopped. "He is dead, Kat."

"What?"

"He appears to have shot himself. Brandy found him in bed, the poor woman. The children were away for the night, thank God. But Brandy is, of course, hysterical. I'm told that her sister is with her and that they are likely to take her to the hospital to sedate her. The authorities are there now. Further tests will be conducted, but it appears that the gun that Christopher used to end his life was the same type of weapon that was used to kill Linda. The authorities believe that it was Linda who found the password in your room. It's unclear at this moment whether she provided it to Christian or whether Christian was with her at the time. There's still a bit of digging to do there, but, of course, both witnesses are no longer with us."

Kat was silent.

"Kat? Kat?"

She cleared her throat. "I'm here, Mitch. I'm just processing."

"I know. It's a lot to take in, particularly given everything else that has happened in the last couple of weeks."

"How is . . . ", Kat began.

"Greg is doing better, I would say," Mitch responded, choosing his words thoughtfully. Kat suspected that Greg was in the room with him. "We've been told that he is no longer a suspect in either crime. He's staying at our house for the time being, at least until he insists on leaving or Susan is comfortable that he is well enough to do so. She's been watching him like a hawk, Kat, and mothering the poor man like she's on some maternal mission. The girls have been great distractions, as you might imagine. They've gotten him to play some board games and video games with them. He rallies a bit when they're around."

"I still don't understand why he won't talk with me, Mitch."

"He's so afraid of hurting you, Kat."

"But he's done nothing wrong!" Kat rebuked. "He's been cleared!"

"Still, everything that has happened during the last couple of weeks ties directly back to him – the connections to Christian, the connections to Linda."

"That's all bullshit, Mitch, and you know it. I met Christian before I met Greg. I was contemplating why Christian was angry with me long before Greg came into the picture. I would have gotten to know Linda regardless. I was the one who went into her bar after all." Kat began to cry.

"Kat?"

"Don't let him do this, Mitch. It makes no sense. Don't let him shut me out. Talk about hurting me? Nothing could hurt me more than this. You tell him that."

"I'm sorry, Kat," Mitch replied. "I will call you again in the morning."

Mitch dropped off the call.

"Tom, are you still there?" Kat asked between sobs.

"I am, Kat. I'm right here. I'm with you. I'll stay on the line for as long as you'd   like."

"Thank you," Kat whispered.

Chapter 51

Agent North met Kat at Tom's office the next morning. "Everything points to Christian Christopher," he said. "You, Kat, are in the clear. I must keep your cell phone as evidence, for now, but as soon as we have everything we need from it and have determined that we won't need it for trial, we'll have it returned to you, and I'll have someone instruct you on how to clear it and reestablish new accounts. I have someone in my office right now working on what you'll need to protect yourself going forward. While Christian Christopher is no longer a threat, it's impossible to say with whom he may have shared your information. We do have another suspect in custody."

"Who is that?"

"It's a guy named Steve Halter. It appears that Steve may have helped Christian access the formula in question."

"You mean Steve Halter, the facility manager at the plant?" Kat asked.

"Yes, that Steve Halter."

"Uff-da."

Agent North smiled. "'Uff-da' is right."

As soon as Agent North left the office, Kat jumped up and hugged both Tom and Brian. "I can never thank you enough, gentlemen!" she exclaimed. Kat remembered that she still had Tom's phone. She reached into her purse and pulled it out.

"Hang on to that for now, Kat," Tom said, as he motioned for her to put the phone back in her purse. "I suspect that you may have some travel in your near future, and I don't want you to be without the ability to connect while you're away. Just bring my phone back when you get yours from the authorities or are able to purchase a new one."

"That is so kind, Tom."

Tom paused, a little awkwardly. "Take care of yourself, Kat, and let me know if you need anything. Anything at all," he repeated.

Eve met her at the door of the house. She was waiting with a big hug and a cup of tea. "I'm planning to be away for a few days," Kat said as Eve released her.

"I figured that would be the case," Eve replied. "I'll stay at the house tonight, and I'll lock up and head home in the morning."

"Thanks, Mom."

Kat immediately called Drew and Anthony to let them know that she was okay and that she planned to be away for a while.

She then packed her bag. Her packing was haphazard. She didn't know how long she'd be gone. But she was wearing one work outfit and would need jeans, underwear, pajamas, and tennis shoes, regardless of where she ended up.

The phone rang.

"Kat Anderson," she answered.

"Hi, Kat. This is Diane Baker. We need to talk. When can you be in Chicago?"

"I can be there tonight, Diane. You, no doubt, heard that I'm free to travel."

"I have, Kat. Congratulations. That is such great news," Diane responded, with about as much enthusiasm as Kat would have expected.

"Yes, it is, Diane. When and where do you want to meet?"

"Why don't we meet you tonight? Say, 8:00 or so? At the Intercontinental?" Diane replied. "Will that work for you?"

"If there is any unforeseen delay, I'll let you know, Diane," Kat responded. "Otherwise, I will see you there at 8:00."

Kat hung up the phone and rushed into Drew's room. She rummaged through his drawers and shelves until she found what she was looking for. She cupped it in the palm of her hand for a moment before slipping it into her pocket.

Kat arrived at the hotel at 7:00. "One night," she told the front desk clerk, handing over her Corporate AmEx card.

"I'm sorry, ma'am, but that card can't be processed," the clerk said, apologetically, after fumbling with the card for several minutes.

"I thought that might be the case," Kat smiled apologetically. "I tell you what," she continued, "a woman will be coming here within the hour. She will pay for my room for the night. In the meantime, if you are not comfortable checking me in, is there a conference room or another place where I might rest before she gets here?"

"I've seen you here before," the clerk responded, sympathetically. "Let me get you a room."

Kat came down at the allotted time. Diane and Karen were waiting for her in the lobby. "You'll need to pay for my room, Diane," Kat said, as they shook hands. "It seems you've discontinued things before we had the opportunity to talk. Since I can't catch a flight out until the morning, I'll need a place to stay tonight, and I promised the front desk clerk that you'd take care of it."

"Of course, Kat," Diane said. "I'll take care of that now."

Karen fidgeted while Diane was away. Kat didn't mind that Karen was uncomfortable. In fact, she rather enjoyed watching Karen squirm.

Karen could stand the silence no longer. "The Board was very unhappy with the publicity," she began. "The whole fact of you marrying a union boss was quite unsettling – not to mention the embezzlement scandal."

"I suspect you've heard that both Greg and I had nothing to do with the embezzlement, Karen."

"Yes, and, of course, I'm very glad about that."

"Of course you are."

"That being said, there is still the matter of you leaving a note with your password in an open space right next to your computer. That was reckless at best, Kat, and an abuse of trust at worst."

Diane returned. "Do you want to go into a conference room?" she asked.

"No. I'm fine here. Just tell me what you've brought me here to say, Diane."

The kindly clerk ducked away into the backroom, where she was out of earshot – or at least appeared to be.

"At our level in the organization," Diane continued, "we can't afford a breach of trust. When trust is lost, it's nearly impossible to regain. Therefore, we think it in your best interest and ours if we mutually separate."

"I'm not so sure that the loss of my income is in my best interest, Diane, given that I'm a mother of two college students and all."

"We've taken that into account in creating a package, Kat, along with your record of service." Diane handed Kat a document. "We're willing to offer you two years of your base salary, in exchange for a release of claims. It's all here."

"Thank you, Diane. I will have my attorney take a look at it. I suspect I can get it to him within the next several days. He's likely tied up for a bit, given how busy he's been working with me during the last couple of weeks."

"I am sure it's been a very difficult experience, Kat."

"You have no idea, Diane." Kat replied. "I assume I have 21 days to review and sign?"

"That's right."

"Not that I'm trying to do your job or anything, but my laptop is still in the custody of the authorities. I'm not sure when they will be done with it, but I suspect you can work with them to get it back. I do have a couple of files at home. None of them is an original, and I'm happy to either send them to you, Diane, within the next three weeks or to destroy them – whichever you prefer."

"Just send them to me."

"As you wish. Is there anything else?"

"No. I think that takes care of it. Good luck, Kat. I really did enjoy working with you, and I wish you only the very best."

"Alright then. Have a good night – both of you. I assume it's fine if I order room service on your tab? I haven't had the chance to eat."

"Of course."

"Either my lawyer or I will be back in touch."

Kat spun around and headed to her room. She ordered a full dinner and a carafe of the best wine on the wine list.

Kat paced around the room, with phone in hand.

"Hello, it's Kelsey."

"'Hi, Kels, it's Kat."

"Kat! I didn't recognize the number," Kelsey began. "How are you? I've been so worried about you! I saw in the newspaper that you've been cleared."

"It's been quite a ride, my friend."

"I am sure it has." There was laughter in the hallway and a door slammed. "Where are you, Kat?"

"I'm in Chicago for the night," Kat replied. "Karen and Diane were just here."

"Well, that can't be good."

"They offered me a package."

"And?"

"And, what? Under the circumstances, of course I'm going to take it."

"Well, that sucks for me, doesn't it?" Kelsey responded.

Kat laughed. "Yes, of course, Kelsey. It's all about you." Kat paused. "I've really missed that."

"I've missed you, too. Let me know where you land. You'll always be in need of a good assistant."

Chapter 52

Two days later, Kat was sitting on the deck drinking coffee when she heard the lock on the front door turn. She saw him before he noticed her.

"I was beginning to wonder when you'd show up," she said.

She startled him, and he jumped. "Kat!"

"I figured that as soon as you were well enough to come here – to your place of respite and renewal – you would. I certainly have found it to be good for my soul during the last couple of days."

Kat did not get up to greet him. She did not throw herself into his arms. She fought to stay seated. She simply continued talking, as she'd rehearsed, over and over again, in her head. "I will not beg. Despite my sophomoric behavior in the weeks leading up to our marriage, I'm too proud to do that. I can't make you let me in, and I can't make you love me. But I am your wife. You've taken an oath to honor and respect me, and I will demand that much."

Greg crossed the room. He stepped out of the house and onto the deck. The sun lighted his face, and he put his hand up to shade his eyes. Kat was struck by his presence and she immediately felt her resolve weaken. *"Damn him and the power he has over me,"* she cursed.

"Sit," she said, pointing to a chair across the table from her.

Greg did not move at first. He just stood, looking at her. When at last he walked by her, the stench of alcohol clung to him and followed him.

"You're drunk," Kat declared, disgustedly.

Greg did not respond.

"In all of the time I've known you, you've never had more than a couple sips of wine," she observed.

Greg smirked. "And you've known me for how long now?" he asked.

Kat bristled. "Long enough to know that this would be the first place you'd come, Greg. Well enough to understand that if I wanted to talk with you, I needed to be here."

"Don't worry, Kat. Alcohol is not my addict's choice of drug. I'll wake up tomorrow with a headache, but no long term consequences of this."

"Good to know. And we'll see whether I wake up here with you," she seethed. "In the meantime, I'm not going to waste my time explaining to you how much I love you or how difficult it has been to be away from you. I am not going to talk about how I have thought about you every minute of every day, even when I was cursing myself for being so weak and actually wondering whether you had taken advantage of me. I'm not going to berate you with how much you've hurt me by your unwillingness to even talk to me during the last couple of weeks."

Greg rested his head in his hands.

"And I'm not going to hear anything like the bullshit that Mitch was trying to sell me about your mere presence hurting me. Your mere presence would have been a hell of a lot better during the last 12 days than your complete absence!" Kat was fuming. She hit the table with her fist.

Greg looked up with a start. She searched his eye, and, for the first time, she felt the intensity of his pain. He didn't need to say a thing. She had never experienced anything so plain or so frightening. It wrapped itself around her. It threatened to suffocate her with its force.

Kat slowly reached her hand out and touched Greg's cheek. She did not break eye contact. She couldn't. So long as he had her fixed in that stare, she was powerless to look away.

"I am so sorry Greg," she began. "I understand now." Her voice suddenly cracked and she was overwrought with emotion. "I didn't before, but I do now," she said softly.

Greg reached up and took the hand that Kat had placed on his cheek. He moved it away from his face but continued to hold it. He stroked her fingers with his thumb, as he turned away from her and gazed out over the horizon.

They sat in silence.

"Are you sober enough to walk?" she asked tentatively.

"I think I can manage."

Kat led Greg down the path and into the park. As soon as they'd navigated through the breach in the fence and were on the trail, she turned to face him. "Want to engage in an experiment?" she asked.

Greg paused for a moment, reflecting. He looked confused. Then, something seemed to register with him and he answered with a faint, but obvious, smile, "As if the last five months have not been experiment enough?"

Kat squeezed his hand and smiled. "It's all part of the adventure. Just go with me here," she said as she gazed into his eyes. "First, we must 'stop before we start.' Take several breaths and simply enjoy your surroundings. Look at the sky and the shape of the clouds. Notice the ground and the colors, shapes, and textures present there. If something catches your attention, study it gently and thoughtfully, taking in everything about it and committing it to memory."

Greg turned away from her and began the exercise. After only a minute or two, Kat could see his shoulders lower ever so slightly. She could feel some of the fear, anger, and confusion beginning to fall away. She broke the silence. "Now, come with me." She held his hand and began to walk, engaging in a continuous and streaming commentary about everything she saw, painting a beautiful picture of words as they moved along the path. She commented about the birds and the noises that they made. She described the color of the leaves (which were now a silver green), the moss, and the grass and the shade cast by the trees in the most poetic language she could conjure. She talked about the lingering, dusty smell of last night's rains and the texture of the bark on the trees. She handed him stones, leaves, and sticks to examine and describe. She was intent on bringing everything he loved to bright and vibrant life for him.

Kat steered them away from the area where she understood that Linda's remains had been found. She'd done her homework and memorized every path in this park. They would not come upon that painful reminder by happenstance.

As they approached the place near the lake where they'd hiked the first morning they'd spent together, Kat turned to face Greg. "Now," she instructed, "Close your eyes and take three deep breaths." Greg did as he had been instructed. As he closed his eyes, he lost a bit of balance. Kat grasped his elbow firmly and steadied him. "As you do that," she continued, "think about the first time we sat in this spot, watching the sun rise over the lake, my back resting against your chest, your cheek on my hair. When you open your eyes, I want you to kiss me."

Greg kept his eyes closed for what seemed to Kat like an eternity. When he opened them, he placed his hands around her waist, drawing her close to him. He leaned in and kissed her, closing his eyes and exploring her mouth with his tongue. Kat put her hands behind his neck and held him there, relishing the kiss and the closeness after such a period of emptiness – of loneliness.

When at last they returned to the house, Kat sat Greg down at the counter and made him a grilled cheese sandwich. Then she went over to the couch and asked him to join her. She sat stretched out on the couch and motioned for him to take a seat between her legs. He smiled, and obliged. As he leaned back against her, Greg sighed. Kat gathered him into her arms and slowly handed quarter pieces of the sandwich over his shoulder.

"I won't make love to you tonight," she whispered in his ear.

"Even if I beg?" he replied.

"Even if you beg," she smiled.

"I love you, Kat."

"I know."

Chapter 53

Greg went to bed early.

Kat climbed into the hot tub to relax her tense muscles. She tipped her head back and rested it against the side of the tub. The moon was nearly full, and it cast a pale glow over the place. She slipped under the water and let the bubbles draw the hair away from her face. As she resurfaced, the phone that she'd placed on the side of the tub lit up with a text. "Call me," it read.

Kat didn't recognize the number, and it appeared to be only 6 digits. But this was Tom's phone, and perhaps someone was in need of reaching him.

Kat opened the text and pushed the voice call icon.

"Hello?" Kat asked.

"Kat, Kat, Kat," screeched the voice on the other end of the line. "You should have had them disconnect the GPS on Greg's phone," it said. "You do know what GPS is, don't you, Kat? What a silly, technologically challenged girl you are. And so reckless."

Although submersed in steaming water, Kat's body shook with a sudden chill. She fumbled with the phone, nearly dropping it.

"Who is this?" Kat demanded. "Why are you calling me?"

"You know who this is, Kat. We were such fast friends, after all. You even helped me with my spelling as I recall, you condescending bitch: d-u-p-l-i-c-i-t-o-u-s. Who's duplicitous now?" she cackled. "That was quite clever, don't you think, Kat? Particularly for a so-called woman-child?"

"Brandy? Is that you, Brandy Christopher?" Kat called out.

"Shhh, Kat. It's dangerous to know too much." Brandy sighed in an exaggerated fashion "Your friend, Linda, she knew too much.

"Linda knew Christian," Brandy continued. "Christian liked to whore around. And that whore was helpful to him – let him into your hotel room and everything. She was a good help, for sure, right up until she realized that you and Greg were together. Then, she didn't want to hurt Greg. Would have blown the whole thing up. That's when she became a liability.

"Oh, Christian thought that he was so smart. Little did he know that I already had access to your emails and texts – at least the personal ones – through Greg's account. Yes, your work emails were a bit more challenging, but the password he found helped, no doubt."

"It was you, Brandy? You took the money? Accessed the formula?" Kat asked breathlessly.

"Well, it certainly wasn't Christian," Brandy laughed. "He was a stupid bastard, Kat. Mean and stupid." She paused. "Of course, the formula was his idea, but he never could have done it himself."

"And what happened to Christian, Brandy? What did you do to Christian?" Kat asked in an unsteady voice that was almost a whimper.

"Christian liked me, Kat. Trusted me. Right up until the end." She paused and the line was silent for several seconds.

"Men like me, Kat," Brandy continued. "Ask Greg. Men like me. Greg liked me. I saw the way he looked at me. He liked me," she insisted. "At least until you came along. Poor, weak Kat – someone for Greg to fix and take care of. Your texts were pathetic. 'I love you, Kat.' 'I know.' I know? What the fuck was that? When someone like Greg Bodin says, 'I love you, Kat,' you don't respond, 'I know'!"

"What about Linda, Brandy?"

"What about her? Did you happen to walk by her today when you were in the park?"

Kat trembled.

"Answer me, Kat!" Brandy demanded in her shrill voice.

"I was not in the park today."

"Oh, you were in the park, Kat. You were in the park." Brandy continued, "How fitting and convenient that you and Greg are there together."

"Where are you, Brandy?" Kat whispered.

"How about a game, Kat? You guess. I'm someplace quiet. All that I hear is the sound of the cicada. The moon is shining bright on the canopy. The stars are flickering in the sky. Can you guess, Kat? You're a smart girl. Can you guess?"

Kat scrambled to her feet and climbed out of the tub. She ran into the house and slammed the sliding glass doors shut behind her.

"You're afraid, Kat," Brandy said in a sing-songy manner. "You are a smart girl after all. Pity, really. I think we could have been friends." The call dropped.

Kat gathered a blanket from the couch around her, as she rushed to the front door to check the lock. "Tom," she whispered. "Are you there, Tom?"

"I am, Kat. The police are on their way. Hold the line. I'll stay with you. You did really well, Kat. Really well."

A shot rang out. Glass shattered all around as a kitchen window exploded into icy shards. Kat screamed. Another shot sounded. Kat turned in the dark, knocking photos off a shelf. She did not see anyone or hear anyone, but suddenly she was caught up in a tight hold, her mouth covered. "Quiet, Kat!" Greg whispered forcefully. "I'm here. I've got you. You're going to be okay. Can you be quiet?"

Kat nodded her head, and Greg removed his hand from her mouth. He pushed her toward the bathroom. "You hide in here. Get in the bathtub and stay low. Do not come out until I tell you to. Do you understand?"

Kat nodded her head again.

As Kat crouched in the bathtub, she heard the front door open. She listened intently but could not tell whether someone had come in or had gone out. She was shaking uncontrollably. Somehow, she had managed to hold onto the phone. It glowed in her palm. She stuffed it inside her swimsuit, facing it toward her body to block the light. She lowered herself down further into the basin of the tub and tried to calm herself.

Another shot. Kat bit her arm and muffled a scream. The taste of her own blood filled her mouth.

The sliding door moved in its track. Kat's heart beat in her ears as she heard steps in the living room, coming closer and closer. She prayed that no one else could hear her heart's rapid rhythm – that the pounding within her would not betray her.

There was a sudden, muted thud – and then silence.

"I'm coming in, Kat. It's me, Greg. You're safe now, Kat. I'm here," Greg said softly and comfortingly, as he entered the bathroom. He knelt beside the bathtub and gathered her in his arms. Kat pressed herself against his chest, her own chest heaving in sobs. "I'm here," Greg repeated, as he stroked her hair. "I'm here. No one's going to hurt you, Kat. I'm here."

"You're really here?" she asked.

"I'm here, my love. It's okay. I'm here."

Within seconds, they heard sirens approaching and the sound of tires on gravel. Kat freed the phone from her suit and raised it to her ear. "Tom?" she managed. "Are you still there, Tom?"

"I'm also here, Kat," Tom replied.

Greg reached up and flipped the bathroom light switch. "We're in the bathroom!" he yelled. "It's in the back!" But he didn't get up. He didn't release her. He kept holding her to his chest and stroking her hair as he talked.

The front door burst open with a loud crack, and Kat heard the rush of boots on the wooden floor. "Someone's down!" a man's voice shouted.

"We're in here!" Greg yelled again. "We're safe! We're in here!"

"Police!" an officer announced, at the bathroom door. "Are you two okay?"

Kat looked up.

"You're bleeding, Kat!" Greg exclaimed, moving her away from his body, so he could look at her.

"Send an ambulance!" the officer shouted.

"I'm okay," Kat responded, breathlessly. Greg and the officer helped Kat out of the tub and sat her on the floor. A paramedic rushed in. He removed pieces of glass from Kat's leg and bandaged her arm, where she'd bitten through the skin. He took her vitals and talked to her gently, encouraging her to respond.

The officer escorted Greg into the other room. Kat tried to follow, but the paramedic held her in place. "At least until the scene has been cleared," he cautioned. The officer came in and asked her some questions. He also spoke with Tom – who was still on the line. Then, the officer helped Kat to her feet and out into the living room.

When Kat saw Greg, she rushed into his waiting arms. He lifted her chin and kissed her hard. When she opened her eyes, he was staring at her. His own eyes were bright.

"You're here? You're fully here?" she asked quietly, with a cry in her voice.

"I am, Kat," he replied, pulling her closer to him.

"We're likely to be at this all night, folks," the officer noted. "Why don't I help you collect a few things, and one of our squads will take you to a hotel until the morning?"

Kat nodded.

Chapter 54

Kat toweled off slowly and gingerly. The little wounds left by the glass had reopened in the hot shower, and the bath towel was peppered with red. The blood no longer surged in her ears. Her body quieted, she made her way to the bed where Greg was waiting. He was lying on his back with his eyes closed, as Kat nestled in next to him and placed her head against his shoulder.

"Is she dead?" Kat asked.

"Is who dead?" Greg replied.

"Is Brandy Christopher dead?" Kat persisted.

Greg paused. "I suspect so, Kat. I am quite sure I broke her neck."

Kat shuddered. The thought of Greg harming anyone, let alone killing them, left her ice cold. She couldn't help but think about how noiselessly and suddenly he had grabbed her in the darkness earlier in the evening.

The silence was intolerable.

"She was standing outside the bathroom door with a gun. She had already killed at least two people. She left me no choice, Kat. I couldn't let her hurt you."

Kat's stomach lurched. "What's going to happen next?"

"Well, I guess the police will complete their investigation. I am sure we'll be talking with them again tomorrow. They have a guard posted outside our door."

"Tom has talked with them and shared the tape of my conversation with Brandy. I have to hope that that will put to rest any questions about how dangerous she was. Tom will be in Memphis in the morning, in case we need him."

"He loves you, you know," Greg noted thoughtfully.

"Don't be ridiculous, Greg," Kat responded sharply.

Greg stared at her and shook his head slightly. "I'm glad, actually. He has been a complete rock for you the last couple of weeks, and I couldn't be more thankful for that."

"Tom is a very kind man, Greg – and a tremendous lawyer. He was Bennett's best friend, and he feels a keen loyalty to me and to the boys as a result. That's all."

"Okay, Kat. Let me just say this: he was there when I couldn't be, and he helped pull you through a devastating time. I am so sorry that I wasn't the man you needed during the last two weeks – the man you needed when it counted."

Kat braced herself on her elbows above him, her damp hair resting against his cheek, as she stared into his eyes. "You listen to me, Greg Bodin," she urged, her voice trembling with emotion. "You are the man I need. You are the man I love. You are the man I thought of every moment while we were apart. And you were the man who was there for me tonight, when it *really* counted.

"I admit that I was angry at you – so angry – for not taking my calls, for not being present with me through that treacherous investigation. But when I looked into your eyes yesterday – your beautiful, amazing, thoughtful, insightful eyes – I understood. They were muted, disquieted, distant. They were the eyes of someone I didn't know, didn't recognize. The pain in those eyes wrapped itself around me, and I could feel how completely debilitating it must have been for you."

Her tears splashed on his face as she continued, "Don't you ever apologize to me for being ill, Greg. I won't hear it. You couldn't be with me for the last while. It's not that you didn't want to be. It's that you couldn't be. And I will never blame you for that. I will never think less of you for that.

"You talk about Tom, Greg. I told Tom that I have never in my life felt the way that I do when I'm with you – not even with Bennett, who was my husband of nearly 25 years and the father of my children. You have an effect on me that I cannot begin to describe. Your mere presence fills my soul with joy.

"I thank God, Greg, for the day I met you and for every precious day since. And I could not be more grateful for the fact that, despite everything that has happened to us, we are here, together. I am overcome by the ability to lose myself and to find myself in you. I want to spend the rest of my life trying to articulate how very deeply I care about you."

She kissed him like she had never kissed him before, and all of the fear and emotion of the night and the two weeks of nights before this one surged through her body, releasing itself as passion.

After, as the lay breathlessly intertwined, Greg kissed her forehead. "What is that saying of yours?" he asked. "The one about not striving to be normal, lest you miss how amazing things can be?" Greg paused. "Well, this, my dear one, *all of it*," he emphasized, "is a far cry from ordinary."

Epilogue

Kat and Greg spent the next several days in Memphis, submitting to police interviews, completing paperwork, and collecting their thoughts.

Anthony and Drew flew in as soon as they heard the news. Martha and Rick arrived the next day, as did Mitch and Susan. Lilly and Scott drove in from Nashville to join the growing assembly, and Tom – who caught the first available flight to Memphis following the harrowing phone call of earlier in the week – extended his stay through the weekend.

They all gathered at the house on Saturday morning. Kat could not help but think about the fact that when she had been there last, a body lay on the floor and her own blood congealed on her skin. The atmosphere was surreal, as everyone set about, in a hushed and distracted way, trying to restore some semblance of the peace that had once been present.

Martha and Drew cooked, as Anthony helped Mitch and Greg replace broken windows. Rick and Tom filled several holes in the exterior logs and chinked where the mortar had been dislodged. Lilly and Kat spackled the drywall in the kitchen and coated the wall with primer.

Slowly, a certain levity and chatter replaced the somber mood, as they settled into their tasks and all physical signs of violence and disruption were artfully erased.

As evening neared, Mitch gathered kindling and built a fire. Martha and Drew began to set the dining room table. Greg uncorked a couple of bottles of wine and poured everyone a glass.

Greg handed a glass to Kat and wrapped his arm around her shoulders. He looked around the room, taking in the scene.

"I'd like to make a toast," Kat announced. "To family," she declared and raised her glass above her head. "Each of you is a member of our family, and we could not be more grateful for you."

"Cheers," Greg agreed, raising his glass as well. "Thank you all for helping us restore not only our home but our *sense* of home," he added. "When we left here earlier this week, I wasn't sure we could ever be comfortable returning."

Kat interrupted him. "But as I reflect on this day and look at everyone in this room," she paused, "I am more sure than ever that this is where we belong."

Greg squeezed her shoulder and winked.

Kat continued, "This is our home, and we want to continue to share it with all of you for years to come."

A resounding chorus of "Cheers!" and glasses clinking echoed around the room.

Dinner was a joyous affair, as everyone gathered around the large wooden table near the hearth. Stories and laughter filled the air as dishes were passed and wine was poured. Greg and Kat happily immersed themselves in the lively and restorative din of the conversation.

Later that evening after everyone had gone, Kat sat by the crackling blaze as Greg returned the last of the clean dishes to the cupboard. The house was quiet after everyone had gone. *"Serenely quiet,"* Kat reflected. Moonlight entered the room through the new windows and reflected off the freshly painted walls. She yawned.

"You're tired," Greg observed, as he sat and wrapped his arms around her.

"I'm content," she responded, resting her head against his shoulder.

Greg kissed her cheek softly. "Might you indulge me one more request before this night ends?"

"Of course."

Greg walked to the far side of the room. Kat watched as he carefully gathered a tattered paperback, a sketchpad, and the photo of Annie from the shelf. He motioned toward the sliding door.

"Join me in the clearing by the reserve?" has asked, as he extended his free hand. Kat intertwined her fingers with his and followed him out onto the deck, down the steps, and through the moonlit yard. Fireflies flickered in the brush, as if dancing to the cicadas' song.

Greg stopped alongside two small holes that had been dug beside a large oak tree at the edge of the expansive state park.

"I thought it would be fitting to have a brief celebration of life for Linda and for Annie," Greg offered. "A sort of final act of forgiveness and remembrance. I'd like each to have a place here, as well as in our hearts."

Greg looked at Kat. She nodded in approval. He handed her the sketchpad and the photograph.

Greg knelt beside the first hole. He held the paperback against his chest and closed his eyes. "Linda was like a sister to me. This was her favorite book. It is dog-eared and worn and the most perfect symbol of Linda that I could imagine." He laid the book in the hole. "May her curious spirit and love of words always have a place on this land and in this home, and may those who come here know the joy of reading, writing, and good conversation."

Greg returned the small pile of dirt to the hole, covering the book. He patted the mound with his hands and lingered there for a moment before he stood.

Kat's eyes filled with tears as she handed him the sketches and photo.

"May this also be a place where Annie could have been happy," Greg said thoughtfully. "A place where trees, flowers, and creatures grow and thrive." He paused. "And may all who come to this place find peace of mind, love, health, and self-forgiveness."

Greg knelt and lowered the sketchpad and photograph into the second hole, which he, in turn, filled with dirt. When he finished, he kissed his finger and pressed it atop the cool soil.

As Greg rose, Kat fell into his outstretched arms. He rested his earth-covered hands on the small of her back and drew her close. They stood quietly like that for several moments.

Greg loosened his embrace and looked at Kat.

"That was beautiful," she sighed, as she met his gaze and gently stroked his dampened cheek.

The cool night breeze pressed Kat's hair against her cheek and she shivered a bit.

"Let's get you inside," Greg prompted, as he took her hand and turned toward the house.

Kat placed her lips against his back – against the shirt that covered his demon tattoo.

"I love you, Greg Bodin," she whispered.

"I know," he smiled – a smile that filled his face and spilled into the clearing around them.

Thank You!

Thank you for spending time with Kat and Greg and for sharing a part of your life with them. Please share your thoughts and feedback on my Facebook Page (A Write of Passage), and provide a review on Amazon. If you liked this story, please join my mailing list by sending a note to ek@awriteofpassage.com. Another story is in the works and should be out by late 2021.

I also want to extend a special thanks to the following people who were important to this particular journey:

- My husband Nate, for his love, support – and extreme tolerance of and appreciation for my writing;
- Carter, Isaac, and Callan for listening patiently and humoring me;
- Isaac and Robin for their technical assistance;
- Robin, Linda, and Debbie for their enthusiastic early reader status and amazing feedback;
- Amanda for her editing skills - and persistent suggestions that my next protagonist be an attractive employee benefits attorney; and
- Shannon for the wonderful cover design.

It's been a fun adventure.

About the Author

Ella Kennedy is a mother, wife, and lawyer who currently works and lives in Singapore with her husband and Morkipoo.

Ella is intrigued by people – their interactions, conversations, motivations, and the impact they have on one another. An eternal optimist, she believes in the boundless power of caring and the healing power of compassion. Ella has always been an avid reader. She loves words. While much of her professional writing has consisted of legal briefs and memoranda, she writes poetry and keeps a journal as ways to remain present in the moment and to capture the beauty, wonders, and inequities she experiences and observes in the world.

In 2019, Ella challenged herself to follow the NaNoWriMo (National Writing Month) approach to novel writing, and with nothing more than two characters, a meeting, and a wedding in mind, she sat down to write. Over the course of the next thirty days (and countless edits and iterations thereafter), she allowed the characters to do the rest. This is Ella's first novel. A second, Concentric Circles, is expected in late 2021.

Made in the USA
Las Vegas, NV
01 February 2021